BESIEGED

BY KEVIN HEARNE

THE IRON DRUID CHRONICLES
Hounded
Hexed
Hammered
Tricked
Trapped
Hunted
Shattered
Staked
Besieged

THE IRON DRUID CHRONICLES NOVELLAS
Two Ravens and One Crow
Grimoire of the Lamb
A Prelude to War

A Plague of Giants: Book One of The Seven Kennings

BESIEGED

STORIES FROM THE IRON DRUID CHRONICLES

kevin Hearne

DEL REY • NEW YORK

Besieged is a work of fiction. Names, characters, places and incidents either are products of the author's imagination or are used fictitiously. Any resemblance to actual persons, living or dead, events, or locales is entirely coincidental.

2018 Del Rey Mass Market Edition

Copyright © 2017 by Kevin Hearne
Excerpt from *Scourged* by Kevin Hearne copyright © 2018 by Kevin Hearne

All rights reserved.

Published in the United States by Del Rey, an imprint of Random House, a division of Penguin Random House LLC, New York.

Del Rey and the House colophon are registered trademarks of Penguin Random House LLC.

Originally published in hardcover in the United States by Del Rey, an imprint of Random House, a division of Penguin Random House LLC, in 2017.

The following stories were previously published in different form: "The Demon Barker of Wheat Street" in *Carniepunk* (New York: Gallery Books, 2013) and "Goddess at the Crossroads" in *A Fantasy Medley 3* (Burton, MI: Subterranean Press, 2015).

This book contains an excerpt from the forthcoming book *Scourged* by Kevin Hearne. This excerpt has been set for this edition only and may not reflect the final content of the forthcoming edition.

ISBN 978-0-399-18175-7
Ebook ISBN 978-0-399-18174-0

Printed in the United States of America

randomhousebooks.com

9 8 7 6 5 4 3 2

Del Rey mass market edition: April 2018

for Levi and Roscoe:
i do believe you'll go far.

contents

BESIEGED

the eye of horus

Atticus shares this story early on during Granuaile's training period, in between Tricked and the novella Two Ravens and One Crow.

i am often reminded how a small fire underneath a vast sky can bind people together like nothing else. For all that we are social creatures, we are too often shoved into solitary confinement by circumstance. The color of our skin isn't like everyone else's, or our language is different, or our religion isn't the one that gets us invited to dinner by the neighbors. That last one has kept me alone for a long, long time. There are no more Druids walking the earth, unless you count the various neo-pagan versions, who are all operating on nineteenth-century reconstructions.

And despite the fact that I have an apprentice, I suspect she won't be the same sort of Druid that I am—I mean believing in the old Irish gods as I do, paying them respect and offering them prayers, observing the holidays and the rites as the Irish used to do in the days before the invasion of the

Christians. Gaia doesn't require belief in any deity to be bound to her: She merely requires a highly trained mind and unswerving devotion to her protection. With Granuaile I think there is a willingness to see the divine, to acknowledge and appreciate both its wonder and terror, but a stubborn resistance to worshipping it.

But she liked staring into campfires well enough. Fires were warm cups of non-thinking serenity after the daily rigors of training. I had been exhausting her mentally with languages and headspace exercises and then physically with the martial arts. By the time the sun sank behind the baked sandstone cliffs of the Navajo Nation each day, she was ready to lose herself in the yellow and orange flickers of flame. And quiz me about my past.

"Ugh," she said, flopping on the ground by our fire pit and popping open a bottle of beer with a hiss and clink as the top fell to the ground. "What a day. Wish I could just upload kung fu like Neo instead of learning it the slow way." She leaned back against a rock padded with a bedroll and took a swig, winced at some ache or soreness in her muscles, then said, "Tell me about the old days, Atticus, when you were wee and had to walk both ways uphill in feces because no one had toilets."

"You seriously want to hear about that?"

"Well, I'd like to hear about some old shit, but it doesn't need to include actual shit, if that helps. I'm tired, damn it. Just tell me a story."

<Hey, I know what you should tell us,> Oberon said through our mental link. He was stretched out by the fire, lying across my feet, belly up for easy rubbing. Granuaile couldn't hear him, but she could follow along because I spoke my part of the conversation aloud.

"What's that, Oberon?"

<Remember that time we were chased through Cairo by all of the cats ever? Because there was that cat goddess who was mad at you?>

"Oh, you mean Bast. Yes, I remember. Hard to forget something like that."

<Tell us why she was mad at you.>

"You already know why she was mad. She wanted me to return the book of her cult's mysteries that I had stolen long ago."

<Right, but you never told me the details. Where'd you steal it from? Why'd you want to steal a book full of cat people having sex anyway? Was it guarded by mummies? And did they smell bad or ask you to change their bandages?>

"Oh, I see. Heh! Yes, I suppose that would be a good story for the night. Wow, this is going way back to the third century. I was still haunting Europe at the time."

"Wait, Atticus, hold on," Granuaile said. "Is this going to take a while?"

"I'm not sure. Is there some hurry?"

"I don't want to interrupt you in the middle of it. I should answer the call of nature first."

<That's my favorite call! I can always pee.>

"Good call, then. We'll reconvene after a few words from nature."

Some hiding places are better than others. The ones with friendly company are the best, and by friendly I mean people who don't particularly care about your background or what your tattoos mean. They just want a name to call you by, a sense that you'll pull your own weight and contribute to the group's survival, and maybe the occasional joke or roll in the hay. I miss the days of easy anonymity, when I could just make up a name when I got to a village and stay there as long as I could keep from using any magic that would give my position away to the Fae. I met new friends, made myself useful, and disappeared for years at a time.

That didn't mean I was impossible to find. The Morrigan could find me pretty much anytime she wanted. On this particular occasion, she found me hanging out with the Visigoths in what is now the southern tip of modern-day Moldova, since I was doing my best to avoid the Roman Empire. She lighted in a tree as I was collecting deadwood for the night's fire, and her eyes glowed red to demonstrate that she wasn't the average crow. I looked around. It was just me out there.

"Hi, Morrigan. Looks like the coast is clear. You need to tell me something?"

She flew down to the ground and shifted to her human form, the red coals in her eyes dying out. "Hello, Siodhachan. Yes, I am here to deliver a message. Ogma needs to see you rather urgently. You must go now to meet him in Byzantium."

"Byzantium? But that's a mess right now."

The Visigoths I was staying with were a part of that mess, in fact. Byzantium—indeed, most of the Roman Empire—was suffering what historians now call the "Crisis of the Third Century," dealing with various invasions from its borders while internally their currency was taking a gigantic shit on the tiled mosaics of their bathhouse floors, and they had a string of military leaders taking turns at being emperor. The Morrigan came to see me in 269, right before Aurelian came to power and started to piece the empire back together.

"It's going to get worse, especially down in Egypt. I have seen it."

"Seen what, exactly?"

The tiniest of smirks lifted one corner of the Morrigan's mouth. "I have seen you in danger there. So clearly you must go."

"Somehow your words fail to motivate me."

"I'm not supposed to motivate you to go down there. Ogma will do that. I just need you to go see him in Byzantium."

"You *need* me to? Why? What's in this for you?"

"Favors. The finest currency of them all."

That was less than subtle. I owed the Morrigan several favors, if not my life, and saying no to her was not an option. "Where in Byzantium?"

"There is a public house called Caesar's Cup. Ogma will be waiting there."

"It's going to take me a while."

"He is aware. But you had best get started."

"Right. Farewell, Morrigan."

"Until next time, Siodhachan." She shifted back to her crow form and flew off into the dusk. I hauled my wood back to the village, got the evening's communal fire started, then packed my few belongings and slipped into the darkness while everyone was eating their dinner.

Weeks later I strode into Caesar's Cup, all my tattoos hidden to disguise my Druidry, pretending to be just another Roman citizen out for a drink. Ogma was indeed there, seated at the end of a bench table, his head shaven and his tattoos concealed as well, nursing a goblet of what passed for expensive wine at the time and a board of bread and cheese.

He bobbed his head at me and gestured that I should sit down across from him.

"No names in here," he said. "Speak Latin with me. Have a cup?"

"Sure." He called for one and poured me a deep red vintage before continuing.

"Well met. Did she tell you why I needed to see you?"

"Something involving Aegyptus, but no more than that."

"Yes. The Palmyrans will revolt soon and Rome will answer in force. The great library in Alexandria will be in danger."

I snorted. "It's always in danger. Julius Caesar nearly burned it down a couple centuries ago."

"We think this time it will be worse."

"We?"

Ogma's eyes shifted down the table to a couple of men who had drinks but weren't talking to each other. They were most likely listening to us.

"Myself, my sister, and the crow." He meant Brighid and the Morrigan. "Much knowledge will be lost forever. And some of that knowledge should be preserved. I'm interested in a few specific scrolls."

Shrugging, I said, "That's great. Why tell me?"

"I want you to fetch them for me."

I stared at him in silence for perhaps three seconds, then looked down at my drink. "I don't understand. You have all of my skills and more. Surely it must be simple for you to do it yourself?"

Ogma chuckled and I looked up. He was grinning widely. "It's far from simple. It's rather deadly, in fact. These scrolls are well protected."

"It must be fantastic information."

"It is. And right now you are probably wondering why you would ever agree to do this."

"I admit that had crossed my mind."

"You will do it because there is truly wondrous information there. Anything you take beyond what I require, you are free to keep."

I cocked my head to one side. "Can you give me an example of what I might be able to take that's worth risking my life?"

Ogma checked on the men, and they were still making no attempt to converse. He gestured to the rear of the house. "There is a poor excuse for a garden in back. Shall we take in some sun and continue there?"

"Sure."

We rose, cups in hand, and strolled past tables and curious eyes. Being covered from the neck down stood out in the summer, especially in a culture where bare legs below the knee were common. Ogma changed his speech to Old Irish and spoke in low tones as we moved.

"Those men are inept but persistent. They have been following me since shortly after I arrived here. We'll see if they abandon all pretense and come after us or not."

The garden had only a couple of people in it, since it was hot outside and there was limited shade to be had; it was laid out in hedges and flower beds more than trees, and all were starving for water. The scant shelter afforded by the fronds of a lone thirsty palm was already occupied. We strolled to the far side opposite, in full sun but also far away from inquisitive ears. Ogma switched back to Latin and pitched his voice so that only I could hear, even though no one was nearby.

"To answer your question: In the library you will find the mysteries of gods far different from the Tuatha Dé Danann or others you may know. Rituals and spells and secrets long kept locked in the darkness, the kind of thing that might help you one day should Aenghus ever catch up to you. Wards that clumsy wizards can attempt only with great care and sacrifice but that you can adapt and re-craft into elegant bindings."

"That doesn't sound all that great to me."

"Yes, it does. And besides, you are bored. You are, what, more than three hundred years old now? Living with the Visigoths for the last five?"

"They're charming people and impressive open-air cooks. They know how to roast a rabbit on a spit, let me tell you. And they share amusing stories about their sex accidents."

"Pfahh. You yearn for more than this, Siodhachan. You stole Fragarach from Conn of the Hundred Battles. You absorbed the most powerful herblore of Airmid and keep it close to your heart. You cannot tell me you are satisfied to live life as a drear pastoral, that you are content with all you know and will never seek to know more."

"That may all be true. But that does not mean I am anxious to seek my death in Alexandria for your benefit, Ogma, begging your pardon."

"It is for your benefit too, as I said. And if you do this for me, Siodhachan, *I* will owe *you* a favor. That is currency of far more value than any Roman coin."

He spoke Truth with a capital T there. When a god says he'll owe you a solid, unspecified, bona fide favor, you need to take time to consider whether you might not be passing up the opportunity of a lifetime. Or indeed something that might preserve your life later on: Some favors, called in at the right time, might equal a Get Out of Death Free card. Though it was clear that Ogma would not be around to get me out of any problems in Alexandria. Whatever he considered to be so deadly there would be doubly so for me.

"I'm not agreeing yet," I told him, "but you have my attention at least. Tell me more. What am I after, where do I find it, and what's in my way?"

Ogma smiled as victors do, drank deeply, and refilled both our cups before answering.

"There is a sealed room of treasures beneath the library, similar to the burial chambers of pharaohs in their pyramids. Inside there are some scrolls and even a few bound books. There may be some scepters and the like, remarkable for their power more than their beauty. I want a bundle of four scrolls sealed in a lacquered box marked with the eye of Horus. You are familiar with that symbol?"

"Yes. But it's fairly common, isn't it? There might be many such boxes."

"There are not."

"If the room is sealed, how do you know that?"

"The Tuatha Dé Danann have their own all-seeing eyes."

"Ah. The Morrigan?"

"Indeed."

"What's so special about these scrolls?"

The god of languages shrugged. "I can't be sure until I read them." A transparent evasion that meant he'd rather not tell me.

"Who built the room and sealed it, then?"

"Whoever built it is no doubt dead. But at least part of it is supposed to be the private hoard of the Egyptian goddess Seshat."

"I'm not familiar with her."

"Goddess of writing and preserving knowledge."

"Ah. Preserving knowledge. I imagine in this case she's preserving it from would-be thieves."

"Yes. You may reasonably expect some curses."

"Such as?"

"I have no idea."

I threw up my hands. "This chamber is underground and sealed in dead, quarried stone, right? I'll be cut off from Gaia and essentially powerless. I don't see how it can be done."

Ogma nodded at me, offering a small smirk. He'd anticipated the objection. "I have something that will help with that, at least."

He reached into the folds of his tunic and withdrew a golden torc etched in knotwork. "I worked with Brighid on this."

"Brighid is involved?"

"Yes. She wants to see those scrolls as well." He handed the torc to me. "That has some energy stored inside that you can draw upon."

I traced my finger along some of the knotwork. "Are these wards?"

"They are. Broad-spectrum protection against a few classes of Egyptian curses that we've seen before."

"When?"

"In antiquity. Shortly after the Tuatha Dé Danann were bound to Gaia in response to the death of the Saharan elemental."

"Oh. That makes sense."

"We came to restore what order we could and bind the dispersed free magic back to the Nile, if nothing else. The Egyptian pantheon was . . . less than welcoming. These wards allowed us to escape alive. They won't deflect the curses entirely, but they should reduce their severity."

"What are you not telling me? Did someone die back then?"

"Of course. We could not have devised wards if we had not seen their curses in effect first."

"So even though you have this, you won't go fetch the scrolls yourself. Why?"

Ogma pointed to the torc. "Those wards worked thousands of years ago. But they might have new curses now."

I exhaled audibly and shook my head. "This is going to be a pretty huge favor you're going to owe me. What bewilders me is that it's even something to be risked. Why bother writing down something they don't want anyone else to know? Why not simply keep the secrets in an oral tradition, like we do?"

"Shared knowledge can weigh heavy in the scales of power," he replied, and I have seen the truth of it since. "Controlling what you want shared is always the issue, and writing down nothing is the most extreme method of control. But while this preserves our secrets, it also limits our ability to spread our wisdom, does it not? Think of this new religion being spread from Jerusalem called Christianity. They have written down some stories about this Jesus fellow and are spreading it around much faster than we can spread the tenets of Druidry. Few people can read, but his priests hold up some pages and say, 'Christ will return! It is written,' and people accept it as truth. I fear what will happen when these priests appear in Ireland. There are mysteries in the written word as well as the spoken one. Think on it, Siodhachan."

The two men who'd been listening to us inside emerged from the back door at that point and spotted us huddled together, talking over a ring of solid gold that would command a rich price in the market. That, apparently, was cause enough for them to cease their incompetent spying and switch to open belligerence.

"Begging your pardon," one said, thick-necked and swinging arms like pork haunches, "but are you both Roman citizens?"

Citizens were afforded certain rights and could go where they pleased. Those who were not could be harassed or jailed for little or no cause by the Roman authorities. We weren't citizens and they probably already knew that, so it was obvious that they meant to establish it, then find a thin excuse to confiscate the torc.

"Camouflage," Ogma whispered, and he promptly winked out of sight, binding his pigments to his surroundings. I didn't have my charms back then or his powers, so I had to take off a sandal to draw upon the earth before speaking the binding aloud. While I did that, the two men shouted at Ogma's disappearance and told me not to move. I didn't move, but I did fade from their sight a few seconds later.

They cursed and then looked around, as if I might have just moved really quickly when they blinked. It's a natural reaction people tend to have when they see someone disappear, and I always took advantage. While they had their eyes pointed elsewhere, I took the opportunity to move a bit, as quietly as I could, and no doubt Ogma was doing the same thing. That was necessary because the next natural reaction to sudden disappearance is to poke the air where we had been standing. Sure enough, they stepped forward, hands outstretched in disbelief but needing to confirm that we were really gone. They grabbed nothing but air, even though I had stopped very close by. I could have reached out and slapped the thick-necked fellow on his shoulder. His companion, a lean younger man with whipcord musculature, offered a quiet theory.

"I've heard of this kind of thing happening before. They might be Druids."

"Druids? Here? I thought they were in Gaul."

The lean one nodded. "That's where I've heard of such disappearances. But then the legions still get them, because they don't really leave. They are still here; we just can't see them. But maybe we can bleed them." He reached for his gladius and had it halfway out when the left side of his face mashed in with a sound like wet meat slapped on a butcher's block, and teeth flew out of his mouth in a spray of blood. Ogma had sucker-punched him, and he collapsed. Taking my cue, I laid into Thick Neck from the opposite direction and broke a knuckle on his jaw. Still, he went down, and neither of them would be in shape to pursue us soon.

"Let's continue elsewhere," Ogma said in Old Irish to me. "We'll need to leave the city. Word will spread to look for two Druids."

"Right."

We left the two spies moaning in the dirt, slipped out of the public house, and dropped camouflage on the street. Some people were startled by our appearance but didn't think anything of it except that they had missed us somehow. We walked briskly to the nearest gate and exited before word could reach the guards to be on the lookout for suspicious types like us.

"Well? What say you, Siodhachan?" Ogma asked. "Will you fetch those scrolls, take whatever else you like, and earn a favor? Or will you leave this treasure to be destroyed by the Romans?"

I didn't like his either-or framing of the issue but didn't think it wise to comment. "When must it be done?" I asked instead.

"You do have some time to get there, but the sooner, the better. You don't want to be caught in the city when rebellion arrives and the Romans respond. That's what Brighid has seen."

"There are no groves for me to use to shift down there?"

"Unfortunately not."

"Weeks on horseback, then. But every step will be farther from Aenghus Óg. All right, Ogma. I'll do it."

"Excellent."

I shook my hand once out of town and cast a healing spell to bind the broken knuckle back together, sure that it was only the beginning of what waited ahead.

Outside the great library of Alexandria, my nose inhaled salt and fish and baked stone, sweat and blood and rotting garbage. Inside it was different: dust and musty lambskin, inks and glues settling into papyrus, and the occasional whiff of perfumed unguents desperately trying to distract from the scent of an unwashed pair of armpits.

I stabled my horse prior to entering, double-checked my clothing to be sure my tattoos were hidden, and also stuffed what gamers today might call a mighty bag of holding into my robes, concealing Fragarach there as well. Then it was smiling and nodding and a few quick exchanges in Coptic. Most of the scrolls were not free to be browsed. Rather, one had to request information from a librarian and the relevant material would be fetched. There were, however, some shelves one could browse on the main floor, and I pretended to do that while searching for a set of stairs leading downward. Once I found a doorway into which librarians came and went, I put the golden torc Ogma had given me about my neck and felt the power waiting there. I drew on some of it to cast camouflage and entered the stairwell, arriving in a basement thick with dust and disuse. Shelves rose up the walls and also in rows between support pillars. After a quick circuit informed me that few librarians came down here and they were heard before they were seen, I dispelled camouflage to preserve energy. The pillars, I noticed, were covered in hieroglyphs—somewhat unusual, since hieroglyphs had passed out of usage hundreds of years ago. There were also some passages of Demotic, perhaps intended to function much the way the Rosetta stone did, helping modern readers to decipher the glyphs, but that language was already dying out in favor of Coptic.

Ogma had been unclear about the exact location of the sealed chamber or how I was to find it. Seshat had not only sealed the entrance, she had hidden it. Despite not being able to read the hieroglyphs, I examined the pillars closely, one by one, until I identified the eye of Horus present on three of them but not the others. I returned to each of these and examined them more closely, searching for a pattern or any kind of clue that would point the way to Seshat's chamber. I pressed the eyes. I searched the shelves on either sides of the pillars for any irregularities. I looked for cracks in the pillars that might indicate there was a hidden door and a stairwell inside a hollow column. Nothing. Twice I had to hide from approaching footsteps and wait for the librarian to move on.

It required rethinking. The three pillars marked with the eye of Horus necessarily formed the points of a triangle, but it dawned upon me as I checked their relative positions that the triangle in question was a perfect isosceles, like the pyramids. A bit of experimentation and visualization led me to an aisle with no pillars in it, which represented the approximate center of the triangle. Keeping my eyes on the floor, I soon came across the faint tracing of the eye of Horus etched into the stone. Kneeling down, I saw that there was a fine tracery of lines around the etching that indicated the eye might sink into the ground as a contiguous sigil. It wasn't large enough to be accidentally stepped on and activated, though. A firm press of the thumb might work, but I didn't want to try it without a large dollop of caution. Accessing the power waiting in the torc, I lifted the veil of my mundane vision and took a look at the etching through magical sight.

It *was* a simple button, pushing a lever that appeared to activate a series of stone gears hidden below my feet, though it wouldn't work without a magic release first; it would behave as if stuck. Unsticking it, I surmised, would require doing something underneath the massive shelf to my left, stacked high with scrolls protected in wooden boxes. The red magical bindings circling the button streaked that way until they disappeared.

I doubted I could move the entire shelf by myself or that I should even try. The binding might actually continue beyond into other aisles, and I checked first to make sure. No: The binding terminated underneath the shelf. I returned to the aisle with the eye in the floor and examined the bottom shelf. There was one boxed scroll with the eye of Horus painted on the end in faded blue. That had to be a clue. It didn't appear to be trapped or have any juju surrounding it, so I carefully extracted the box from underneath the others, opened it, and unrolled the scroll inside, returning my vision to the mundane in the process.

It was a map of the chamber below, in which the cartouche repeated a warning in hieroglyphs, Demotic, and Coptic that only high priests may enter without consequence. I was about to ask, "High priests of *what?*" but there were hieroglyphic

representations of several deities below that presumably an-
swered that question. I recognized Horus, Anubis, Osiris,
Isis, Bast, Taweret, and one other I expected thanks to Ogma:
Seshat.

Once I entered, there would be a button to close the opening behind me and then a series of seven rooms off a single
hallway: three on each side and a large one at the end. That
was six more chambers than Ogma had told me to expect,
and none of them was labeled helpfully with THIS ONE HAS
THAT THING OGMA WANTS. In fact, they weren't labeled at
all, and neither were there any instructions on how to open
the chamber in the first place. As Ogma said to me in Byzantium, there are ways to control what gets shared. The arrow
and instructions in Demotic and Coptic on how to close the
chamber once inside were the only available clues to what I
might find down there. But there were seven deities pictured
and seven chambers; perhaps they were proprietary and I
would simply need to find the one with a graven image of
Horus on it—or Seshat, since I'd been told she was in charge
of protecting this knowledge.

There still remained the problem of how to get down
there. Perhaps the shelving warranted more attention.

I cleared away all the scrolls, boxed and unboxed, that covered the space over which the red streak of bindings had
disappeared—that included the boxed scroll with the eye
of Horus on it. What confronted me was a black expanse of
shadow, which lacked promise, except perhaps for the promise of spiders.

Casting night vision allowed me to see that there was a
hole drilled in the bottom of the shelving, about the circum-
ference of a thumb and forefinger held up in an "okay" sign. It
did not allow me to see what was in the hole. Should I stick a

finger in there or not? I decided I could live without a pinkie if I had to, so I went with that first. I snaked it in there, felt around, felt the stone floor beneath it. Nothing bit me.

Feeling more confident, I placed my left thumb inside and pressed down. The stone floor sank beneath it and a dull click echoed in the silence, but nothing else happened. Dissolving night vision and switching to magical sight, I saw that the red binding with the bookshelf had vanished. The button in the middle of the floor should now function like one. I pushed down on it with my right thumb and then scrambled away as the floor rumbled and cracked beneath me. The stone irised open like a manhole, and a ladder made of stone rungs dared me to descend. I took the dare, night vision on, and found the button advertised by the map that would close the door. It also turned on the lights: not electric ones, but green flames in sconces placed halfway up the walls of the hallway, fueled by nothing visible that I could see. The word for it didn't exist back then, but they were fucking eldritch, and it was awesome.

As an experiment I pressed the button again, and the lights went out as the portal opened once more. Escape route established, I closed it again and turned on the eldritch flames.

Before proceeding, I pulled Fragarach and my booty bag from my robes. I slung the bag and the sword over opposite shoulders and drew Fragarach from its sheath. I wanted to be ready for anything.

First door on the left bore the imprimatur of Taweret, the hippo goddess, which was often used as a sigil of protection. I knew better than to mess with her chamber. If there was ever a trap laid for thieves, this was it. On the right was Isis, and I didn't feel especially safe messing with her either. But next on the left was Bast, and I'm not really a cat person.

There was no Demotic or Coptic on the doors to help me figure out what waited inside, only hieroglyphs, but there was a fairly obvious circle of stone to push to the left of the door. It slid open under my hand with a grating noise, lights bloomed inside, and I was treated to a wonder far beyond what Howard Carter found in the tomb of King Tutankhamun. Gold and obsidian figures of Bast, lapis lazuli and alabaster and more: scrolls and books of bound vellum, many of them written in Demotic and Coptic. That's where I found the book of Bast's sex mysteries bound in catskin leather, but I also found the sort of thing that Ogma suggested I might find useful: a scroll detailing protective wards—none of which, I noted, were in force on the chamber itself. The finely carved art, however, viewed in the magical spectrum, was surrounded with wards, which I studied but did not disturb.

Across the hall was the chamber of Osiris, and nothing in there had any protection as far as I could tell. Perhaps his high priests figured that after returning from the dead, his worldly possessions didn't matter all that much. I snaffled a few promising scrolls and books and moved on.

The next two doors belonged to Anubis and Seshat. I didn't want any part of Anubis, and Seshat's door, which was supposedly my target, was warded with layers of protections, truly dizzying stuff that could not have been laid down by some priest. The quantity and quality of the mojo I was seeing had to be the work of the goddess herself, and I am not ashamed to say it caused a nervous gulp. Up to that point I could pretend I was merely tiptoeing through the treasures of men, and men I could usually handle. It's very sobering to realize you are only a step or two away from incurring the wrath of a goddess with no softness in her heart for Irish lads.

It was time to finish the job and get out of there, and I hoped I could finish it without trying to go through that door.

The chamber of Horus was the large one in the back, and like the rooms of Bast and Osiris, it was simple to enter. I decided to pursue it, since my target might logically be inside and it was at least accessible, where Seshat's chamber practically vibrated with bad omens. Unlike the chambers of Bast and Osiris, though, it was not a simple security situation inside.

For one thing, there was the body on the floor just inside the entrance. It wasn't fresh, and it wasn't a mummy either. Scarabs and worms were at him, and maybe you could fix the smell with a wagonload of rose petals, but I doubted it. I covered my nose and breathed through my mouth as I inspected him from the hallway, never crossing the threshold.

He'd been in his thirties or late twenties, judging by his wrinkle-free skin, or what was left of it. No obvious signs of violence like a caved-in skull or a spear lodged in his rib cage. His fingernails, however, were torn and sometimes missing, which provided my main clue to what had happened. He'd entered, the door had shut behind him, and that was it. He was trapped without food or water or a handy way of calling for help, because of course this entire area was a secret chamber underneath a basement where only librarians occasionally trod. He had no doubt screamed to no avail. So he had gone mad with fear over his inevitable death and tried to claw his way out—which told me there wasn't a way to open the door from the inside.

That made me check out the door a bit more closely, because it was different from the others, which were standard rectangular jobs that moved via a system of pulleys and counterweights inside the walls. Horus's door was circular, and its mechanical design allowed it to open and close much faster. Pressing the button on the left side caused part of the floor to sink down, creating a slope that let it roll away and slam to a stop inside. Presumably the floor inside the wall would rise when it was time to close the door, and the slab would roll back into position. I wasn't sure yet how the trap had been sprung on this fellow, but I sure wasn't going to let it happen to me.

Drawing on some more of the torc's energy, I thoroughly bound the stone door to its stone enclosure—especially the floor—making sure it would remain open and never roll back into place, even if I tripped the same trap as the unfortunate thief.

Once satisfied, I stepped over the threshold and the body and inspected the goods. Osiris had protected nothing, and Bast protected only the glorious statuettes of her feline magnificence. Horus, or his priests, had laid down protections on the majority of the items I saw spread out before me, but there was no discernible pattern to it—other than some personally assigned value system, I supposed. I also spied what looked like a magical alarm tripwire running along the floor just in front of where all the goodies rested, a good distance away from the door. That was it: Approach the valuables, trip the magical switch, and the door closed. I stepped on the trip and wiggled around on it. The door remained open.

That, however, was the easy part. Finding Ogma's happy lacquer box o' scrolls was going to be far more difficult, especially if they weren't there at all but in Seshat's chamber. The shelves in the room had once been orderly, but before his demise the dead man had indulged in a tantrum and swept things onto the floor or thrown them about the room.

There were finely carved figurines, as in Bast's chamber. Some books, some boxes, some shattered pieces of things that might have been ceramic vessels at one time, a crook and flail of solid gold, an obsidian ankh, and more.

I examined the scattered boxes first, but none had the eye of Horus emblazoned on them. Their littered contents held no special allure either.

Abandoning them, I stepped over the security line to examine the shelves. I found a lacquered box with the eye of Horus on it, undisturbed, in the very back. Yawning spaces framed either side of it, but the dead man had not seen fit in his mortal terror to throw this box. Perhaps that was because it clearly had protections.

Having located it, I surveyed the rest of the shelves and noted many books and scrolls that looked promising. I put the unprotected ones in my bag first. The protected ones, limned in red and yellow in the magical spectrum, I saved for later. I mapped out a course, a sequence beginning with Ogma's box and then proceeding with the others I wished to take, all leading me ever closer to the door. I opened the bag and kept the flap open with my right hand and ran the gauntlet, expecting some kind of juju to thump me good every time I touched something.

But nothing happened. I snagged and shoved all my prizes into the bag, one by one, and felt nary a magical kick to the kidneys. That was odd. Could Ogma's torc be protecting me that well? Or were the nature of those curses more of the long-term variety?

I closed up the bag, drew Fragarach, stepped across the threshold, and waited for something heinous to happen, but nothing did. Grinning at my success, I secured the bag around my shoulder and back, crosswise from Fragarach's sheath. I kept the sword itself in hand as a precaution, but I was feeling jaunty and edging toward ebullience as I approached that button at the end of the hallway that would open up the portal and let me climb the ladder to the library proper.

The door started to open well before I pressed that button. Someone was coming down. I scrambled back, flattening against Bast's door, and cast camouflage on myself.

The bare-chested figure who came down the ladder rippled with muscles, and I knew right away he wasn't merely a buff librarian, and I knew he wasn't a high priest either. I knew this because the figure lacked a human head. Rather, he had the sleek, twitching head of a falcon, and not some elaborately painted spacey-techno mask from *Stargate* either: It really was a falcon's head, albeit an abnormally large one, with a razor beak that opened and closed and scary black eyes that blinked as he stared down the hallway at the open door to his chamber.

It was Horus in the flesh.

And apparently both eyes worked just fine. He'd lost one in a fight with Set, and after it was magically reconstructed he offered it up to help resurrect Osiris, but I guess he had bonus XXL-falcon eyes hanging out in a jar somewhere, waiting to be plugged in whenever he had a free socket. He was doing that bird thing where the head shifts from side to side to aid with depth perception, and that wouldn't be necessary if both eyes weren't functioning. Which meant, unfortunately, he didn't have a blind side.

What had summoned him here? Surely not opening the door. I doubted it was the triggering of his little trap either, because he'd never come to clear out the body of the last fellow who ran across it or to clean up the mess he made. It must have been laying hands on his magical doodads—maybe even the very one Ogma had sent me to steal. Most likely it was precisely that, because the lacquered box had been untouched by the previous thief. It occurred to me that the juju I'd seen wasn't a curse, per se, but rather an alarm calling Horus to provide his own security. And he responded with alacrity.

He was so focused on the breach and finding out why the door to his chamber remained open that he forgot to close the portal, leaving me an escape route. My exceedingly clever plan was to remain still in camouflage, wait for him to pass me by as he went to check on things, and then scramble up the ladder before he realized he'd been had.

My plans rarely work out the way I want them to.

Horus strode right by the first pair of doors but then stopped directly opposite me, that dead left eye looking at me in profile just like a hieroglyph—though I hoped he wasn't looking at me at all. I should have been functionally invisible, but who knew what extrasensory abilities—or even finely attuned regular senses—he had. He might be able to smell my elbow or hear my toenails growing or something.

His right hand moved at his hip, taking out something like a metal baton. It telescoped in both directions and morphed into two distinct shapes on either end: the sloped head of a bennu bird at the top, a sharp-bladed crescent at the bottom. He had himself a fancy *was* scepter, a symbol of power but also clearly a weapon in this case. His chest rose with a deep breath, and that was my only warning: On the exhale, he tried to take off my head with a wickedly fast strike.

I ducked underneath it, but just barely. It shattered the stone, and a shard of it opened up a furrow on my scalp even as I lashed out with Fragarach during his follow-through and drew a line of red across his belly with the tip. That was both encouraging and very bad news, because it meant that he could bleed, but he'd leapt back to avoid the worst of the blow, which meant that he knew I had a weapon and saw it coming. Or, if he didn't see through my camouflage, he sensed it somehow.

Horus danced backward, blocking my path to escape. I spun to my left, into the center of the hallway, backing up a little bit to give myself time to activate the binding that would increase my natural speed and reflexes. The torc was running low on juice and wouldn't be able to cast much else.

While I was casting that, Horus looked down briefly at his wound and screeched. His voice modulated into some kind of low-frequency chirps after that, either cooking up a heal or a buff or something to snuff me. I didn't want to let him finish.

The neuromuscular boost snapped through my body like a tuning fork and I lunged forward, fully expecting to be parried by the scepter this time, and I was: Horus could definitely sense it somehow, despite my camouflage. But I followed up with a straight kick to the gut and that got through easily, forcing the breath from his lungs and cutting his chant short. He reeled back, stunned, and I pressed my advantage, kicking him right in the beak since his head was lowered. Horus squawked, reared, and nearly fell over backward, and I grinned as I realized what it meant: He could somehow sense my sword but not the rest of me. As long as I kept the sword away from my body, he couldn't see my attacks coming. His first well-aimed strike at my head had been an excellent guess based on how I'd held Fragarach in my right hand.

I took too long to process that, however. Horus recovered and cried out, swinging his scepter in a twirling pattern very similar to the sort of thing that I now teach. I was still about seven centuries away from my martial-arts training in China, however, and I hadn't seen that before. I backed up, thinking of how best to disrupt his flailing offensive and regain the advantage. If I could successfully interrupt him, he'd be vulnerable for a precious half second or more. Maybe. I didn't know what counters he might have, honestly, and I felt outclassed.

But since he was focused on the location of my sword, I feinted right with it and then, as he swerved that way to knock it aside, I kicked from the left side. My foot caught his forearm and did interrupt the twirling, but the scepter slid through his hand to lengthen out at the top, and he whipped it in a vicious backhand swing that I couldn't avoid. It caught me just below the collarbone, and I grunted and staggered back until stone stopped me.

Unfortunately, it wasn't a mere wall: I'd been driven back into the ultra-warded door of Seshat's chamber. I don't know if it was Horus's intention to do that, but it made him look damn clever.

My muscles spasmed and pain lanced through all my nerves as I collapsed to the ground, Seshat's defensive wards lighting me up in spite of the supposed protective bindings woven into my torc. Ogma had said they might be only partially effective, and I screamed the Irish equivalent of "Fuck partiaaaal!" as I rolled away in a sort of fetal position to open up some distance between myself and Horus. I was practically back at his chamber door when I felt I could function again, and I realized that had it not been for the torc's half-assed protection, Seshat's wards might well have killed me instantly.

Horus certainly seemed to have expected it, for when I came to my feet, he was still where I'd last seen him, blinking in confusion. He clearly *had* driven me into those wards on purpose, and perhaps now he was feeling a measure of the uncertainty I was feeling: How in nine hells was I ever going to win this?

My personal calculus determined that it couldn't be won but only escaped. He was a superior martial artist and not dependent on a limited supply of strength. I reminded myself that I only had to get past him, not destroy him.

He had no defensive martial screen in place now, so I charged, right arm held far out so that Fragarach would draw his attention and he'd therefore misjudge my center. He raised his scepter and brought it down in a two-handed swing just to the right of my body as I launched myself at his face, left foot extended for his throat. I withdrew my right arm as he committed, and his blow whiffed past my right side while my heel connected with his throat. He made a short choking noise and fell back, my foot planting on his chest as he fell, and I kept running for the exit.

Not that I got away without injury. He stabbed out blindly over his head with the scepter, and the sharpened steel crescent punched into my lower back just above my left ass cheek. I muttered a binding to keep all my blood inside and leave nothing for Horus to use later: It drew all the blood from his blade back into my body.

If adrenaline can add any speed to limbs already quickened by bindings, then it surely did at that point. I was down the hall and up the ladder before you could hum the triumphant opening bars to *Star Wars*.

But there was a figure waiting for me at the top, between the stacks, every bit as surprised to see me as I was to see her: Seshat, keeper of knowledge, whose wards had nearly snuffed me.

I knew who she was because she matched her hieroglyphic

representation: a sheath of cheetah skin draped over her body and a headdress featuring seven points. Like Horus, she had a clue that I was in front of her, despite my camouflage. She hissed, muttered something in ancient Egyptian that I didn't catch, and thrust a hand at me.

I felt as if I'd been thirsty for years—all the moisture of my throat sucked away and my breath choked off besides— but I spun around clockwise and ran past her to the stairwell that would lead to the ground floor and freedom. I sheathed Fragarach on my back, hoping that the leather might some- how have a cloaking effect on the Egyptian gods' ability to target me. Nothing else hit as I ran, and I was able to reach the ground floor and even make it outside before I realized that I had been severely handicapped.

I breathed, "Thank the Morrigan, Brighid, and all the gods below," once I thought myself safe, except that I heard not a syllable of it.

"What?" I said, except that once again there was no sound.

"Am I deaf? Am I mute?" Nothing.

It couldn't be the former. I heard other noises—people walking, sandals grinding against stone. The torc ran out of energy, which caused my camouflage and increased speed to fizzle away, and then men passing by stared at me, a strange pale fire-haired man in the streets of Alexandria, and bid me peace in Coptic or Greek or Latin. Locusts buzzed in the date palms. Horse hooves clopped on the streets. My hearing functioned just fine.

"I'm mute," I said, but heard neither word, and since I couldn't be heard, I added, "Seshat has cursed me." That was the buffet of throat shenanigans I'd felt, which Ogma's torc had not prevented at all.

It was a perfect curse for someone wishing to protect secrets: Ensure that whoever stole them could never speak of them. And it was also the perfect curse for a Druid, since I couldn't bind or unbind a damn thing without the ability to speak.

My exertions must have torn something, for my stab wound from Horus began to bleed freely and now I had nothing to stop it but manual pressure, since I'd been robbed of my power to bind it closed. But of Horus himself or Seshat, I saw no sign. Perhaps they had decided to track me later and were instead assessing what had been stolen.

I did think of asking an elemental to help with Seshat's curse, but this was the one place in the world that didn't have one, thanks to the wizard who'd consumed the Saharan elemental for his own purposes in the time of the pharaohs. The remnants of that magic formed the Nile elemental, but I would have to travel some distance out of Alexandria to reach its sphere of influence. I retrieved the horse I'd left at a stable and joined the light traffic of people heading to Cairo. As soon as I reached the delta area—it wasn't all that far—I dismounted and reached out to the Nile through my tattoos, which didn't require verbalization.

//Help Druid// I said. //Heal wound / Remove curse//

The healing began immediately, but the curse was a different matter. Nile finally had to ask me for clarification.

//Query: Curse?//

//Unable to speak// I explained. //Binding now impossible / Curse on throat needs removing//

There was a wait and then a disheartening reply: //Cannot remove//

Elementals don't kid around. If the Nile said it couldn't be done, then it couldn't. What I didn't understand was why, so I had to ask.

//Unfamiliar magic / Unbinding must be human craft// Nile said.

I sighed in defeat. I'd have to make it all the way back to Jerusalem and hope Ogma could unbind it.

//Or iron could eat it// Nile said, and my confusion must have been broadcast plainly, because the elemental continued. //Iron elemental can consume magic / Remove curse / Leave tattoos / I will control//

All I managed in reply was an //Okay// because I was a bit lost. My archdruid had never mentioned that anything of the kind was possible. We'd heard that there were lesser elementals running around associated with this or that, but it had never been suggested that we could communicate with them, much less ask them to be useful.

//Remain here / Iron elemental on way//

That was a worrisome time, because it was most of the day before one finally arrived. I spent it being eyed suspiciously by travelers worried that I was some kind of brigand lying in wait for them. And I worried that someone would try to take advantage of me, of course, but worried more that Horus or Seshat or even Bast would find me.

Perhaps they would come for me in the night, when they could pass among humans unnoticed. Or perhaps the reason they hadn't found me was because they truly didn't know where to look.

I considered my mighty bag of holding, which held many treasures now. Only those of Horus were cursed with an alarm or whatever he had on them: What if that curse provided not only an alarm but a location? If that were the case, the bag was the safest place possible for them. As soon as I touched them again, Horus would know where to find me. He was simply waiting for me to finger them.

Or they could probably find me and their lost treasures through divination; I wasn't sure how proficient the Egyptian pantheon was at the art, but I felt sure they'd find me if I remained in one place too long.

The iron elemental arrived as the sun sank burning into the sands.

//Be seated and remain still// Nile said. //Touch left hand to sand//

I did so and black iron filings crawled up my arm like ants, crested my shoulder, and encircled my neck. For a brief time they formed a solid band and constricted, but before I could communicate my panic to Nile it loosened, the filings slid back down my arm, and I could talk again.

"Gah, thank the gods below!" I said. "Except maybe Ogma. Yeah. Let's not thank him right now."

//Gratitude// I told Nile, and then, after a sudden thought, added a request: //Query: Can iron elemental eat magic surrounding items inside bag?//

//Query: Which items? / Cannot see//

The road was clear at that moment, and no one was nearby. I upended the bag of holding over the sand, allowing the lacquered box and everything else to spill out without touching my hands. //These items / Please remove magic outside them but not inside//

I appended that last because the items inside the box might be fantastically powerful, but I didn't particularly want to be carrying around cursed items that would summon Horus as soon as they were touched.

It was done in less than a minute. In the magical spectrum the box looked completely normal, and I placed it back inside the bag with a grin.

//Gratitude / Harmony// I said to Nile, and I rode out of

there, powers restored, to meet Ogma in Jerusalem. Gaia and her elementals are ever our friends and salvation, even as Druids are theirs.

I made it to the Sinai Peninsula before I realized what a terrible error I had made and compounded it with another. Resting at an oasis during the heat of the day and assured of some privacy, I opened the books only, one by one, to evaluate what I'd managed to take for myself.

I began with the books I'd taken from Horus and that the iron elemental had attacked to eat away the curses I'd seen in the magical spectrum. Upon opening them, however, I discovered that they were entirely blank. I had no way of knowing if they had always been blank or if their contents had been erased by the wards on them once they left the room, or even accidentally destroyed by the iron elemental. Regardless, they were worthless, and Horus had lost nothing. I hoped that the scrolls inside the box were still valuable and worried that my entire infiltration had been for naught. I scrambled to check the rest of my haul.

The books of Osiris were still in fine shape, having no scrap of magic about them to begin with, and the knowledge inside regarding wards was priceless and worth the trip by themselves. I sighed in relief and thanked the gods below.

I went through Bast's books last. One of them was the *Grimoire of the Lamb*, the true purpose of which I did not discover until centuries afterward, when someone came looking for it at Third Eye Books & Herbs. Another was full of descriptions of protective wards and, like the books of Osiris, proved quite valuable. The last was the book of Bast's mysteries, which had a horrifying effect once opened and perused—though it quite literally crept up on me.

The text was in Coptic and I was reading through it,

mouth half open in horror and unable to look away, like watching someone embarrass himself or rubbernecking at a traffic accident on the side of the road. And then my peaceful reading time was rent at once by yowling, screeching, and hissing from all directions. I scrambled to my feet and drew Fragarach, thinking I was under attack, but once I had time to assess the threat, I realized that I was surrounded by fucking cats! And by that I mean the cats were all actually, if grudgingly, fucking. They didn't seem to enjoy it much, and maybe that's why they were making such heinous noises. For the record, I didn't enjoy it either, and honestly we should all be grateful that cats usually do this in the dead of night, well out of our sight, and usually as a couple rather than as a massive, writhing chorus of carnality. I dove back to the ground, closed the book, and soon afterward the cats stopped what they were doing and even ceased to be cats: They melted into the sands or the wind and disappeared entirely. And then I laughed, for I realized that Bast had woven an unseen curse into the book: Unless you were one of her high priests or otherwise approved, you couldn't read it without being afflicted by a deafening, shivering, teeth-grinding feline orgy.

I met up with Ogma in Jerusalem some days later and handed over the lacquered box of scrolls. He opened it, briefly unrolled and inspected the scrolls within, and then beamed at me.

"You owe me big for that," I reminded him, wagging a finger at the scroll. "I got stabbed. Lost my voice. Had to listen to the worst cat sex ever. Someday I will send you on an impossible quest."

"Understood," he said, and held out a hand, palm up. "The torc, if you please?"

"That's not a keeper, eh?"

"No."

"Ah, well." I delivered it to him, and he radiated smug contentment as he put it away out of my sight and followed it with the lacquered box. We stood soon afterward, hugged, and made our farewells, he to return to Tír na nÓg, I to some new quiet village out of the Roman Empire.

Unfortunately, all Druids heard shortly thereafter through local elementals that they were no longer welcome in Egypt. But I can tell you that the treasures I saw in those rooms in Alexandria have never been found by modern archaeologists, and I suspect they're still hidden away somewhere, guarded now entirely by Seshat's wards.

"Wait," Granuaile said. "No, that can't be the end! What was in the box Ogma wanted?"

I shrugged. "I don't know, beyond the fact that it was full of scrolls, and I never will. I gave it to him without question. You can think of it as the briefcase Jules and Vincent were after in *Pulp Fiction*: very shiny but forever a mystery."

"You seriously never looked?"

"Wasn't my business. I wanted a future favor more than I wanted whatever was in that box. And besides, I had plenty of other material to keep me company."

<You're not talking about your further adventures with the cat-sex book, I hope.>

"No, Oberon, I'm not talking about Bast's mysteries. I mean all the other things I stole. I learned so much from what I stole. I still use that information today; Third Eye Books & Herbs was partially protected using Egyptian techniques.

And I carefully neglected to tell Ogma about the potential usefulness of iron elementals."

"Oh? Does that mean the Tuatha Dé Danann never summon them?" Granuaile asked.

"That's right. I mean, I've told the Morrigan about them now, but I doubt she'll be making friends with one quickly."

My apprentice's eyes grew wide and she shook her head a couple of times but said nothing.

"It was running that errand for Ogma, and then another one a few centuries later, that put me on the path to becoming the Iron Druid and creating my charms as a method of non-verbal binding. Seshat's curse certainly taught me the need for that."

Granuaile snorted. "Yeah."

"Ogma still owes me—twice!—but I'm not sure I'll ever call those favors in. I wouldn't be here today if it weren't for those errands. Becoming the Iron Druid has kept me alive as much as Immortali-Tea has."

"Are we going to hear about that other errand?" Granuaile asked, stifling a yawn.

"Sure. But let's save it for another night around the fire."[*]

<I hope there will be another belly rub around that fire. And more meat. And maybe a poodle with a poufy tail.>

I'll see what I can do, Oberon.

<So next time I see Ogma, I should blame him for being chased by cats?>

No, you can blame me. I'm the one who angered Bast.

---

[*] That other night around the fire refers to "The Chapel Perilous," in which Atticus must recover the Holy Grail for Ogma in Wales in the year 537. And Oberon's recollection of being chased by all the cats ever occurs in the novella *Grimoire of the Lamb*.

<Aww. I can't blame you for stuff, Atticus! You give me snacks, and that's like diplomatic immunity. Not fair!>

It is true, my friend, that life is not fair. But sometimes there is gravy.

<You are so right, Atticus. Gravy is our comfort and our joy.>

GODDESS AT THE CROSSROADS

This story, narrated by Atticus, takes place during Granuaile's training period, after Tricked *but before the novella*
Two Ravens and One Crow.

There is no industrial hum under the skies of the Navajo Nation, and the stars float bright and naked in them, the urban gauze of pollution far away and veiling someone else's view. And in that clarity all you hear is the song the earth decides to sing—well, that, and whatever noise you make yourself. The crackle and whoosh of wood as it burns under a bubbling stewpot is some of my favorite music, and visually it can be mesmerizing—and evocative.

"*Fire burn and cauldron bubble*," Granuaile intoned, staring into the orange heart of the blaze of our campfire as she quoted the witches from Shakespeare. The words triggered a memory and I shivered involuntarily. My apprentice caught it as she looked up from the fire. "What? Are you spooked by those fictional hags?"

"Not the fictional ones, no," I said, and Granuaile grew

still, staring at me. Oberon, my Irish wolfhound, was curled up outside the stones surrounding the fire pit and sensed that some tension had crept too close to his warm repose. He raised his head and spoke to me through our mental bond.

<Atticus? What's going on?>

Granuaile wasn't bound to the earth yet and she couldn't hear Oberon, but she had learned to pick up some of his cues. "If Oberon's asking you what's up, I'd like to know too. What made you shudder like that?"

I briefly wondered if I should tell her or dodge the question but then remembered she had already seen plenty of things through her association with me that she'd never unsee. The visage of Hel, for example, Norse goddess of the dead, was nightmare fuel enough for any lifetime, and she hadn't cracked yet.

"It's a bit of a story, but I suppose we have the time for it."

"We absolutely do," Granuaile agreed. "We have a fire, honest-to-goodness stew that's been cooking all day, and some beers in the cooler. And no chance of being interrupted." She waggled a finger at me. "That's key."

"Indeed. Well, it's a story from England shortly after the death of Queen Elizabeth, when Shakespeare had a new patron in Scottish Jimmy—"

"Scottish Jimmy?"

"That was what the irreverent called King James back then. That was the politest term, actually."

"We're talking about the namesake of the King James Bible?"

"Precisely."

"Hold on. I know you have all of Shakespeare's works memorized, but did you actually meet him?"

"Not only did I meet him, I saved his life."

Granuaile gaped. She knew that my long life had acquainted me with a few celebrated historical figures, but I could still surprise her. "How have you not told me this before?"

Shrugging, I said, "There was always a chance we'd be interrupted before, and as you said, that's key. And I didn't want to be a name-dropper."

"So is saving Shakespeare a different story from the memory that made you shiver?"

"Nope. It's the same one."

Granuaile clapped her hands together and made a tiny squeaking noise, which made Oberon thump his tail on the ground.

What are you getting excited about? I asked him.

<I don't know, Atticus, but she sounds really happy, so I'm happy for her. Did people in England have poodles back then?>

They might have, but I didn't see any.

<Oh, I'm sorry, Atticus. That must have been rough on you. I know it's been rough on me, out here all alone without any asses to sniff . . . >

I know, buddy, I know; we need to go into town soon so you can have a social life.

<I will dream of it! But after we eat. Which I hope is now.>

Looking across the fire at Granuaile, I said, "Oberon's happy for you. He'd be even happier if we ate before I get into the story."

"Sounds good to me. It should be ready, don't you think?"

I nodded, fetched three bowls, and ladled out the lamb stew for each of us, cautioning Oberon to let it cool a little first so he wouldn't burn his tongue.

"So were you in England the whole time Shakespeare was writing?"

"No, I missed the reign of Queen Elizabeth entirely and arrived from Japan shortly after her death."

"What were you doing in Japan?"

"That's a story for another night, but it was an exciting time. I saw the establishment of the Tokugawa shogunate and witnessed early stages of the construction of Nijo Castle in Kyoto. But Aenghus Óg eventually found me there and I had to move, and I chose to move much closer to home because an English sailor had told me of this Shakespeare character. My interest was piqued."

<Wasn't England composed primarily of fleas at that time?>

"Yes, Oberon. It was mostly fleas and excrement in the streets, and people dying of consumption, and Catholics and Protestants hating each other. Quite different from Japan. But Shakespeare made it all bearable somehow."

"Kind of makes his work even more amazing when you think about it," Granuaile commented. "You don't read *Hamlet* and think, This man could not avoid stepping in shit every day of his life."

"It was also difficult at that time to move around London without passing within hexing distance of a witch."

"They were truly that common back then?"

"Aye. And their existence wasn't even a question; people in those days knew witchcraft to be a fact as surely as they knew their teeth ached. And King James fancied himself quite the witch-hunter, you know. Wrote a book about it."

"I didn't realize that."

"Of course, the kind of witches you might run into—and warlocks too; we shouldn't pretend that only women engaged in such practices—varied widely. For many it was a taste of power that the medieval patriarchy wouldn't otherwise allow them."

"Can't say that I blame them. If you don't give people a conventional path to power, they will seek out their own unconventional path."

"Said the Druid's apprentice," I teased.

"That's right. I'm sticking it to the Man!" Granuaile said, extending a middle finger to the sky.

<Yeah!> Oberon said, and barked once for Granuaile's benefit, adding in a tail wag.

"Well, the witches that almost ended Shakespeare certainly wanted to stick it to him."

"Is this why there's a curse on *Macbeth*? You're not supposed to say its name or bad luck will befall you, right, so actors always call it 'the Scottish play' or something?"

"Almost, yes. The way the legend goes, the witches were upset that Shakespeare wrote down their real spells, and they wanted the play suppressed because of it—hence the curse."

"Those weren't real spells?" Granuaile asked, lifting a spoonful of stew to her mouth.

"No, but Shakespeare thought they were. What angered the witches was his portrayal of Hecate."

My apprentice stopped mid-slurp and actually choked a little, losing a bit of stew. "You and Shakespeare met Hecate?"

"That's a polite way of putting it, but yes. I met her and the three witches, and so did Shakespeare, and that inspired portions of what many now call the Scottish play."

My apprentice grinned and let loose with another squee of excitement. "Okay, okay, I can't wait, but I want to finish this stew first. Because I slurp and Oberon turbo-slurps."

Oberon's laps at the bowl really were loud enough to blot out all other nearby sound.

<She's right. I take a backseat to no one at slurping,> Oberon said.

When we'd all finished, Oberon curled up at my feet, where I could pet him easily, Granuaile and I thumbed open some cold ones, and the crackle of the logs under the stewpot provided occasional exclamation points to my tale.

In 1604 I arrived in London, paid two pennies, and witnessed a performance of *Othello* in the Globe Theatre. It smelled foul—they had no toilets in the facility, you know, so people just dropped a deuce wherever they could find space—but the play was divine. That's when I knew the rumored genius of Shakespeare was an absolute fact. Poetry and pathos and an astounding villain in the form of Iago—I was more than merely impressed. I knew that he was a bard worthy of the ancient Druidic bards of my youth, and I simply had to meet him.

The way to meet almost anyone you wanted in London was to wear expensive clothing and pretend to be French. Clothing equaled money, and money opened all doors, and pretending to be French kept them from checking up on me easily while allowing me to misunderstand questions I didn't want to answer. I dyed my hair black, shaved my beard into something foppish and pointy, and inquired at the Merchant Taylors' Hall on Threadneedle Street where I might find a tailor to dress me properly. They gave me a name and address, and I arrived there with a purse full of coin and a French accent, calling myself Jacques Lefebvre, the Marquis de Crève-coeur in Picardy. That was all it took to establish one's identity in those days. If you had the means to appear wealthy and noble, then everyone accepted that you were. And the bonuses to being one of the nobility were that I could openly wear Fragarach and get away with wearing gloves all the time. The triskele tattoo on the back of my right hand would raise far too many questions otherwise. To the Jacobeans, there was functionally no difference between a Druid and a witch: If it was magic, their solution was to kill it with fire.

It is now well known that Shakespeare rented rooms from a French couple in Cripplegate in 1604, but it took me some time back then to find that out. Though I heard from several sources that he was "around Cripplegate," no one would tell me precisely where he lived. That was no matter: All I had to do was ask about him in several Cripplegate establishments, and eventually he found me. Helpful neighbors, no doubt, who could not for ready money remember where he lived, shot off to inform him straightaway after speaking with me that a Frenchman with a fat purse was asking about him. He found me nursing a cup of wine in a tavern. I was careful to order the quality stuff instead of sack or small beer. Appearances were quite important at the time, and Shakespeare was well aware. He had taken the trouble to groom himself and wash his clothing before bowing at my table and begging my pardon but might I be the Marquis de Crèvecoeur?

He wore a black tunic sewn with vertical lines of silver thread and punctuated with occasional pinpoints of embroidery. His collar was large but not one of those ridiculous poufy ruffs you saw in those later portraits of him. Those portraits—engravings, really—were done after his death, in preparation for the publishing of his plays. In the flesh he looked very similar to the Sanders portrait found in Canada, painted just the year before I met him. His beard and mustache were soft wispy things trimmed short, a sop to fashion but clearly not something he cared about. His hair, brown and fine, formed a slightly frazzled cloud around his skull, and he almost always had a smirk playing about his lips. He was neither handsome nor ugly, but the intelligence that shone behind those brown eyes was impossible to miss.

"*Oui,*" I said, affecting a French accent. It was more south-of-France than genuine Picardy, but I was hoping Englishmen would be unable to tell the difference, the same way that most modern Americans cannot distinguish the regional differences between English accents.

"I'm told you've been looking for me," he said. "I'm Master William Shakespeare of the King's Men."

"Ah! Excellent, monsieur, I have indeed been asking about you! I wish to pay my respects; I just saw *Othello* recently and was astounded by your skill. How like you this establishment?" I said, for it was fair-to-middling shabby, and I had chosen it for its visibility more than its reputation. "May I buy you a bottle of wine here, or do you prefer a more, uh, how do you say, exquisite cellar?"

"I know of an excellent establishment if you would not mind a walk," he replied, and so it was that I settled my bill, allowing my coin-heavy purse to be viewed, and navigated the standing shit of Jacobean London to the White Hart Inn, the courtyard of which had played host to Shakespeare's company under Queen Elizabeth, when his troupe was called the Lord Chamberlain's Men.

The November skies permitted little in the way of warmth, so there was never any suggestion that I remove my gloves. I played the fawning patron of the arts and enjoyed my evening at the White Hart Inn, where Master Shakespeare was well known. He ordered a bottle of good wine and put it on my tab, and it wasn't long before he was talking about his current projects. Since King James himself was his patron, he could hardly set aside projects meant for him and do something specifically for me, but he could certainly discuss his work and perhaps, for a generous donation to the King's Men, work in something that would please my eyes and ears.

"I'm quite near to finishing *King Lear*," he said, "and I have in mind something that might appeal at court, a Scottish skulduggery from a century or so past. A thane called Macbeth aspires to murder his way to the throne. But this exposure of a thane's base ambition is lacking something."

"What? A knavery? A scandalous liaison?"

"Something of the supernatural," he said, lowering his voice as one does when discussing the vaguely spooky. "The king possesses a keen interest for such things, and it behooves me to please the royal audience. But I confess myself unacquainted with sufficient occult knowledge to inform my writing. There's my astrologer, of course, but he knows little of darker matters, and he's a gossip besides."

"Do you need firsthand knowledge to write about it? Can you not glean what inspiration you need from others?"

Shakespeare shook his head, finished his cup of wine, and poured a refill from the bottle on the table. "Ah, M'sieur Lefebvre, what I've read is too fantastical to be believed, and I do not wish to tread on ground so well packed by others. I need something compelling, a spectacle to grab you firmly in the nethers and refuse to let go. Even the fabulous must have been kissed by reality at some point to have the appearance of truth, and without that appearance it will not work in the theatre."

"Have you any idea where to find such a spectacle?"

The bard leaned forward conspiratorially. "I do have an

inkling. It is a new moon tonight, and I have heard tales that on such nights, north of town in Finsbury Fields, black arts are practiced."

I snorted. "Black arts? Who would report such things? If one were truly involved, one would hardly spread word of it and invite a burning at the stake. And if one witnessed such rites up close, it follows that one would hardly survive it."

"No, no, you misunderstand: These accounts speak of strange unholy fires spied in the darkness and the distant cackling of hags."

"Bah. Improbable fiction," I declared, waving it away as folly.

"Most like. But suppose, M'sieur Lefebvre, that it is not? What meat for my art might I find out there?" The innkeeper delivered a board of cheese, bread, and sausage to the table, and Shakespeare speared a gray link that had been boiled a bit too enthusiastically. He held it up between us and eyed it with dismay. "One would hope it would be better fare than this."

"Will you go a-hunting, then?"

Shakespeare pounded the table once with the flat of his left palm and pointed at me, amused at a sudden thought. "We shall go together."

I nearly choked and coughed to clear my throat before spluttering, "What? Are you addlepated?"

"You have a sword. I'll bring a torch. If we find nothing it will still be a pleasant walk in the country."

"But if we find something we could well lose our souls."

"My most excellent Marquis, I have every confidence that you will protect me long enough to make good my escape." His grin was so huge that I could not help but laugh.

"I trust you would give me a hero's death in your next play."

"Aye, you would be immortalized in verse!"

I kept him waiting while I decided: If we actually found a genuine coven cooking up something out there in the fields, it could prove to be a terrible evening—they tended to put everything from asshole cats to cat assholes in their stews, simply horrifying ingredients to construct their bindings and exert their will upon nature, since they weren't already bound to it as I was. But the risk, while real, was rather small.

"Very well, I'll go. But I think it might be wiser to go a-horseback, so that we both might have a chance of outrunning anything foul. Can you ride?"

"I can."

And so it was settled. We ate over-boiled meat and drank more wine and I allowed myself to enjoy the buzz for a while, but when it was time for us to depart, I triggered my healing charm to break down the poison of alcohol in my blood. Some people might be comfortable witch-hunting under the influence, but I was not. I arranged with a stable to borrow some horses and, late at night, under the dark of the moon, went looking for the worst kind of trouble with William Shakespeare.

By the time we set out, his cheeks were flushed and he was a far cry from sober, but neither was he so impaired that he could not stay in the saddle—writers and their livers.

The smoke and fog and sewer stench of London followed us out of the city proper to Finsbury Fields, which are simply suburbs, a park, and St. Luke's church now but were liberally fertilized with all manner of excrescence back then, and some had been gamely sown with attempted crops. Muddy wagon trails divided the fields, and it was Shakespeare's idea that we would find the hags at some crossroads out there, if the rumors of witchcraft were true.

"On the continent, one can still find offerings left at cross-roads on the new moon for Hecate, or Trivia," he said, and I feigned ignorance of the custom.

"Is that so? I have never heard the like."

"Oh, aye. It is always at three roads, however, not four; Hecate has a triple aspect."

"So we are looking for worshippers of Hecate, then?"

"The proceedings being held on the new moon would be consistent with her cult. It is a slightly different devilry from dealing with powers of hell but no less damned."

I suppressed a smile at that. The worship of Hecate had taken many forms throughout the centuries—her conception and manifestation was especially fluid compared with that of most other deities. Even today she is the patron goddess of some Wiccans, who look at her as embodying the maiden-mother-crone tradition, a gentler conception than the some-times fierce and bloodthirsty manifestations she took on in earlier days.

Shakespeare, of course, looked upon all witches, regard-less of type, through the Christian filter—evil by default and allied with hell to destroy Christendom. I looked at them through the Druidic filter: Plenty of witches were fine in my book until they tried to twist nature's powers for their own purposes. If they wanted to curse someone with bad luck or sacrifice a goat with a knife to summon a demon, that was their business and frankly not my fight. I was also grateful for those who tried to heal others or craft wards against malevo-lent spirits. But moon magic could be dangerous, and at-tempts to bind weather or possess people or animals would draw my annoyed attention rather quickly. The elementals would let me know what was up and I would come running.

It was because of this that I tended not to notice the benevolent witches or even meet them very often; they did their thing in secret and harmed no one. All I ever saw were the bad apples, and it probably prejudiced me against witches in general over time.

The dirt tracks cutting swaths through Finsbury Fields were not precisely dry, but neither were they muddy bogs. They'd be dry in another day or so, and the horses left only soft depressions in the mud, chopping up the ruts somewhat and moving quietly at a slow walk. The rustle of our clothes and our conversation made more noise than the horses' hooves.

That noise, however, was enough to attract four figures out of the darkness—that and Shakespeare's torch, no doubt.

"Please, good sir, could you give me directions?" a voice said in the night. We reined in—a terrible decision—and four unshaven and aggressively unwashed men with atrocious dentition approached from either side of our horses, taking reins with one hand and pointing daggers at us with the other. A very smooth and practiced waylay, and they knew it. We could not move without being cut, and they smiled up at us with blackened, ravaged teeth, enjoying our expressions of surprise and dismay.

The leader was on my right and spoke again. "More specifically, can you direct me to your purse? Hand it over now and we'll let you be on your way; there's a good lad."

If it had been only coins in my purse, I would have happily obliged. Coins are easy to come by. But the piece of cold iron resting in the bottom was rare, and I didn't wish to part with it.

Shakespeare, who was not only deep in his cups but thrashing about deeply in them, began hurling insults at the leader, who found them rather amusing and smiled indulgently at the angry sot while never taking his eyes off me.

"You raw and chap-blistered rhinoceros tit!" Shakespeare roared. "You onion-fed pustule of a snarling badger quim! How dare you accost the Marquis de Crèvecoeur!"

The bandit laughed, polluting the air with his halitosis. Drawing on the stored energy in my bear charm to increase my strength and speed, I began to mutter bindings in Old Irish, which they would probably interpret as nervous French. "Visiting from the continent, are we? Well, me chapped tits and snarling quim would welcome some French coin as well as English."

His companions chuckled at his lame riposte, confident that they had the better of us, and the one on my left, with a broken nose and a boil on his cheek, gestured with his dagger. "Let's begin with you getting off that high horse, Marquis."

Shakespeare wouldn't let that pass without loud comment, still directing his remarks at the man on my right. "Cease and begone, villain! You have all the dignity of a flea-poxed cur's crusty pizzle! You dry, pinched anus of a Puritan preacher!"

Their gap-toothed smiles instantly transformed into scowls, and all eyes swung to the bard. "What!" The leader barked. "Did he just call me a bloody Puritan?"

"Not exactly," Cheek Boil said. "I think he called you a Puritan's bunghole."

While keeping his hand on my horse's bridle, the leader swung his dagger away from my thigh to point at Will, behind me. "Listen, you shite, I may be a bunghole," he cried, brown phlegmy spittle flying from his maw, "but I'm a proper God-fearing one, not some frothy Puritan baggage!"

While they were all looking at Will, I triggered my camouflage charm, taking on the pigments of my surroundings and effectively disappearing in the dim torchlight. Using the boosted strength and speed I'd drawn, I slipped my left foot out of the stirrup and kicked Cheek Boil in the chest before falling to the right and landing chops on either end of the leader's collarbones. They broke, he dropped both his knife and my horse's reins, and I gave him a head butt in the face to make sure he fell backward and stayed there.

My attack drew the attention of the men watching the bard, and he was not slow to seize advantage of the opportunity. With the gazes of the two men pulled forward, he dipped the torch in his left hand and shoved it into the face of the man on his left. The man screamed and dropped his weapon, stepping back with both hands clutched to his eyes. That startled Shakespeare's horse and it shied and whinnied, ripping out of the grip of the rogue on Shakespeare's right. He began shouting, "Oi! Hey!" and then, seeing that his companions were all wounded or down and he wasn't either quite yet, he muttered, "To hell with this," and scarpered off whence he came, into the dark wet sludge of Finsbury Fields. The leader was discovering how difficult it was to get up with a couple of broken collarbones and called for help. Cheek Boil, who'd not been seriously hurt, recovered and moved to help him, not seeing me.

Fire Face, meanwhile, had morphed from mean to murderous. Nothing would do for him now but to bury his knife in Shakespeare's guts. Growling, he searched for the knife he'd dropped in the dark. I scrambled in front of Will's horse, dropping my camouflage as I did so, and drew Fragarach, slipping between Will and Fire Face just as he found his knife and reared up in triumph.

"Think carefully, Englishman," I said, doing my best to emphasize that I was very French and not an Irish lad.

Fire Face was not a spectacular thinker. He was a ginger like me, perhaps prone to impetuousness, and he bellowed to intimidate me and charged. Maybe his plan was to wait for me to swing or stab and then try to duck or dodge, get in close, and shove that dagger into my guts. Perhaps it would have worked against someone with normal reflexes. I slashed him across the chest, drawing a red line across his torso, and he dropped to the ground and screamed all out of proportion to the wound, "O! O! I am slain!"

"Oh, shut up," I spat. "You are not. You're just stupid, that's all." Turning to Will, I said, "Ride ahead a short distance, Master Shakespeare. I will be close behind." I slapped the rump of his horse, and it surged forward despite the protests of its rider. I kept Fragarach out and stepped around my horse to check on Cheek Boil and the leader. Cheek Boil was trying to help the leader to his feet but was having trouble without an arm to pull on. The pigeon-livered one who ran away could be neither seen nor heard.

"I'm leaving you alive, monsieurs," I said, as I sheathed my sword and mounted my horse. "A favor that you would not likely have extended to me. Think kinder of the French from now on, yes?"

A torrent of fairly creative profanity and the continued wailing of Fire Face trailed me as I goaded the horse to catch up to Will, but I was glad I didn't have to kill any of them. William Shakespeare would probably exaggerate the encounter as it was, and I didn't need a reputation as a duelist or fighter of any kind.

The bard was jubilant when I caught up to him. "Excellent

fighting, Marquis! You moved so quickly I lost track of you for a moment!"

Ignoring that reference to my brief time in camouflage, I said, "You were quite skilled with the torch."

Shakespeare grinned at it, jiggling it a little in his fist. "And it's still aflame! Finest torch I've ever carried."

"Shall we return to London, then?"

"What, already? Fie! That passing distraction is no matter. We have hags to find."

"I doubt we will find them in these fields. They seem to be populated by villains and pale vegetables, and fortune may not favor us a second time."

"Tush! Think no more on it! You are more than a match for any bandits, M'sieur Lefebvre."

"I may not be a match for one with a bow."

"Anyone skilled with a bow would be patrolling a richer stretch of road than a wagon trail in this mildewed fen, m'sieur."

He had a point, damn him. Using one of my charms—newly completed at that time—I cast night vision as a precaution and didn't look toward the torch anymore. If another set of bandits wished to ambush us, I would see them coming. I was so intent on scanning the area on the right side of the road that Shakespeare startled me after a half mile by saying, "There." He pointed off to his left, and I had to lean forward and crane my neck to see what he was looking at. It was a faint white glow on the horizon, a nimbus of weak light in the darkness near the ground. It flickered as if something passed in front of it and kept moving. "What could that be?" he asked. "'Tis the wrong color of light for a campfire, wouldn't you say?"

I grunted noncommittally but could think of no good reason to ignore it. I followed Shakespeare's horse once we came to a track that appeared to lead directly to the light.

As we drew closer we could hear chanting floating over the fen, and I realized that we might have actually found the witches Shakespeare was hoping to find and I was hoping to not. There would be no telling him to turn back while I investigated on my own—and I *did* need to investigate, in case their ritual proved to be an attempt to usurp some measure of the earth's magic. But I couldn't risk revealing myself as a Druid to him if I was forced to act. I would be every bit as damned in his eyes as the witches if he discovered my pagan origins.

We dismounted to creep forward on foot. I doubted the horses would still be there when we returned, but we couldn't take them with us; even though they were quieter than usual in the soft earth, they weren't stealthy creatures. One impatient snort could give us away.

Keeping my voice low, I said, "Conceal the torch behind my body," and watching him step uncertainly in the mud, still quite drunk, I added, "preferably without setting me aflame. It will allow us to see while hopefully preventing our detection."

"I approve of this plan," he said, enunciating carefully, and we stepped forward into the mud. The macabre sounds of muted chanting pounded nails of dread into our hearts. With every step nearer, I grew more certain that we had, in fact, discovered a small coven of witches. The light was indeed from some kind of fire, but the wood wasn't burning orange and yellow as it should. It was silvery, like moonlight. Perhaps there was phosphorus at work. Or something arcane.

I began to worry about Shakespeare's safety. I had my cold iron amulet tucked underneath my tunic to protect me against magic, but the bard had nothing. I wanted to tell him I had protection but couldn't tell him I had bound the cold iron to my aura. I had to craft a lie that he would accept. "Master Shakespeare, should we be discovered, let me go ahead. I have a blessed talisman that may shield me against their, uh, infernal practices." I wasn't sure where he stood on the Holy Roman Church, so I settled for the generic *blessed* rather than *Pope-licked* or *Cardinal-kissed* or any number of other vaguely holy-sounding phrases. I drew Fragarach from its scabbard. "I also have this, should it be necessary."

Shakespeare's breathing was coming quicker and his eyes had widened. "Your plans continue to be well conceived, Marquis."

We crept closer still, the voices growing louder, and a faint rumble and hiss could be heard, which I imagined to be something boiling in the cauldron. It was a large black iron affair, the sort one uses to feed armies and that's usually transported in a wagon, and I could only imagine how they had lugged it out there and what might be boiling inside it. Perhaps the darkness concealed an ox and cart nearby. The unnatural white flames glowed underneath the cauldron and licked at its sides, consuming what appeared to be normal firewood.

As we grew close enough to distinguish words, I recognized that the chanting was in Greek, which Shakespeare did not understand but I understood very well. I chose to be a classically educated marquis and translated for the bard in whispers when he asked me if I could make sense of their babble.

"It's an invocation to Hecate, pleading for her guidance—no, her *personal* guidance. As in guiding them, in person, right here! They are trying to summon her."

"A summoning! For what purpose?"

"I know not."

We were close enough now that I, with my aided vision, could distinguish shapes in the darkness; I doubted that Shakespeare could see anything, except something that kept moving in front of the firelight.

There were three witches circling the cauldron, naked but smeared with dark streaks—blood or animal fat would be my guess. Their ages were indeterminate; by appearance they were somewhere on the happy side of middle age, but I knew that in reality they could be much older than that. As they circled the fire they also spun around, raising their arms and voices to the sky. I wondered how they kept from getting dizzy.

Their right hands each held a short dagger—no special curved blades or gilded guards, nothing you might call an athame; they were merely sharp, efficient knives.

"Master Shakespeare," I whispered, "they are armed, and I do not doubt they will attack if provoked. We should probably keep our distance."

"How can you see anything, Marquis? I can only see shadows in the dark. My eyes need some assistance and I must see better; this could prove to be a fine provocative sauce for my play."

I could hardly cast night vision on him without revealing my abilities, so I sighed and said, "If we're going to get any closer, I suggest you put out that torch."

I expected a protest but he complied instantly, jamming it into the mud behind me. He dearly wanted to get a closer look; to this point he hadn't seen nearly so much as I had.

We inched forward, ignoring the filthy ground, fascinated by the lights and the ritual playing out before us. I was fairly certain by then that I would have no official role to play as a protector of the earth, but playing protector to Shakespeare could be even more dangerous if we were discovered.

The cauldron, I noticed, squatted in the middle of a cross-roads, but the three-way sort to which Shakespeare had alluded earlier. What possible need the witches could have for Hecate's personal appearance I could not imagine. Their hair was tied and queued behind them, and I perceived that they wore theatre masks straight out of ancient Greece, albeit with visages of bearded men strangely attached to what were plainly female bodies. Masked rites might make them Thracians, but if so their presence in England was especially bewildering.

The only possible motivation I could come up with to conduct such a ritual near London was the upset or even overthrow of King James's reign, but I was surprised that Greek cultists would care about it. Perhaps they didn't care but were doing this on a mercenary basis—I had heard there were plots boiling all over the country, mostly by Catholics opposed to King James's very existence. We were only twelve months away from the Guy Fawkes Gunpowder Plot, after all. But if those witches were Catholic, then I was the son of a goat.

"What token of hell is this?" Shakespeare breathed next to me, his eyes wide and fixed on the spectacle. We were crouched low to the ground on our haunches. "Bearded women cavorting and, and . . ." He fell speechless. Sometimes there simply aren't words, even for him.

"Draw no closer," I warned him, listening to their chant. "Their words have changed. The invocation is set and now they are waiting."

"What are they saying?"

"They are literally saying that they are waiting. *Periménoume* means 'we wait' in Greek, and they're just repeating that, spinning around."

"For what do they wait?"

"My guess would be a sacrifice. Maybe they know we're here and they're waiting for us to get closer, and then they will sacrifice us to their goddess."

Shakespeare did not fall for my scare tactics. "Did they not sacrifice something already? There has to be something in that cauldron."

"Aye, but a chicken or a newt will not summon a goddess to English shores. It will only secure a flicker of her attention. They need something bigger."

"How know you this?"

"I am a witch-hunter of sorts myself," I said, "though I confess I did not expect to find any tonight."

"You doubted me, m'sieur?"

"No, I doubted the stories you heard." But now that I heard the witches were "waiting," I wondered how long they had been coming out here during the new moon to wait. Those stories of lights and croaking hags looked to be true now.

"Why not simply bring the necessary sacrifices with them?" Shakespeare asked.

"It is a matter of power," I said. "If the sacrifices come to the crossroads willingly, it would be better for their purposes."

We heard the neigh of a horse behind us—quite probably one of ours. The witches heard it too. They didn't stop their chanting or their ritualistic circling of the cauldron, but their masked faces pointed in that direction—in our direction, in fact. I didn't have to tell Shakespeare that he shouldn't say another word. We emulated the movement and speech of stone gargoyles in the darkness and kept our eyes on the coven.

Soon the approach of hooves reached our ears, a soft rumbling thump in the mud, and an angry voice shouted, "That has to be them up ahead, or someone who saw where they went!"

It sounded like Fire Face to me. Apparently he had recovered from thinking I had slain him and now he wanted a piece of both of us. Chucking Will on the shoulder, I gestured that we should get off the road, and we rolled in the mud until we were naturally (rather than magically) camouflaged in a sodden field of disconsolate cabbages.

It was Fire Face, all right, riding my horse, and riding double on Will's were Cheek Boil and Pigeon Liver, a surprise guest. The latter must have returned and offered to make up for his earlier cowardice. And Fire Face's spleen must have been full of rage to pursue us so blindly and abandon their leader somewhere behind. Fire Face was the de facto leader now and clearly not expecting to find three naked, masked, and dancing witches at a crossroads in Finsbury Fields. The leader had been left behind with his broken collarbones, and were he there to witness what happened next, he would have counted himself fortunate.

The witches stopped chanting "We wait" and each said in turn, "The time is now," and then, in concert, "Hecate comes!"

The bandits reined in short of the fire, and Cheek Boil exclaimed, "What the bloody hell?" shortly before it all became a bloody hell.

I sat up to yank off my right boot so that the binding tattoo on the sole of my foot could contact the earth and allow me to draw upon its energy. The witches broke their circle and streaked directly at the horses, knives held high and moving much faster than humans should. I would need to speed up just to match them.

"What are these naked wenches?" Fire Face said, and then

one leapt straight over his horse's head to tackle him backward out of the saddle. Cheek Boil and Pigeon Liver were similarly bowled over, and the horses bolted, not bred or trained for war. The strength of the witches became evident in the next few seconds as they stood each bandit up and employed those knives, drawing them across the men's throats with an audible slice of flesh. As their life's blood gouted into the mud, the men tried in vain to stanch the flow with their hands, but the witches dragged them to the crossroads in front of the cauldron, then pushed them into a triangle formed by their shoulder blades, each of them facing a different direction.

"Come to us, Hecate, Queen of the Moon!" they cried. "Your vessels await!"

"Oh, no," I said, and rose to my feet, drawing Fragarach. They really were going to summon her.

Shakespeare would have joined me, no doubt, but was trying to vomit quietly on the cabbage instead. His earlier drinking had soured his stomach, and seeing a murder so starkly committed brought a good measure of it back up.

I couldn't reach the witches in time to stop the summoning and I had Shakespeare to worry about, so I had to watch. We'd be leaving as soon as he finished emptying his guts. The bandits began to twitch, then shudder, then buck violently against the witches' staying hands on their sternums; their eyes rolled up in their heads and their tongues lolled out of their mouths while blood continued to squirt from their carotids. And then it all stopped for a second, the air charged, and the hairs on the back of my neck started like the quills of the fretful porpentine, for Hecate slipped out of whatever netherworld plane she'd been occupying and into the bodies of those three bandits, simultaneously her sacrifices and her new vessels. Their lives were forfeit, their spirits expelled who knows where, and Triple Hecate had new flesh to command far from Thrace.

Except she didn't much like the look or feel of that flesh—it was male, for one thing. So she set about changing it to suit her, and that was when Shakespeare looked up from his retching to see what else could horrify him.

The witches stepped back from the bodies, since Hecate was occupying them now and they stood on their own power. But the skin of the men's faces split and melted as it changed shape, and muted popping noises indicated that their very bones were being broken and re-formed to suit the will of the goddess. The bard did me an enormous favor at that point and fainted into the cabbage patch after a single squeak of abject terror. It meant I wouldn't have to pretend to be a French nobleman anymore or hide my abilities.

His squeak, however, did catch the attention of one of the witches, and she was just able to spy me and hiss a challenge into the night. "Who is there?" she said in accented English.

The other two swiveled their heads at that, and the one who had killed Cheek Boil said in Greek, "I will look. Hecate must not be disturbed in transition."

She darted in my direction, bloody knife out, as I was thinking that perhaps Hecate *should* be disturbed in transition. Any aspect of the goddess summoned in this manner would fail spectacularly on measurements of benevolence and goodwill. Deities that manifest through animal and human sacrifice tend not to engage in acts of philanthropy.

The witch located me and rushed forward, no doubt assuming that I was as slow as the bandits had been. But I was not only as fast as she but better armed and better trained. Her unguarded lunge, meant to dispatch me quickly, got her an arm lopped off at the wrist and a face-first trip into the mud. Her mask crunched and she howled, cradling her shortened arm with her good one. She was far too close to Shakespeare for my comfort, though she hadn't seen him yet. The wisest thing for my own safety would be to cast camouflage and disappear, but they might find and slay William while searching for me, so I kept myself visible and moved purposely away from him to the other side of the road, which looked like a turnip field. The witches all tracked me, and the one I'd wounded pointed with her good hand.

"He's not human!" she shouted in Greek. "He moves like us!"

"I'm a Druid of Gaia," I announced in the same language. If Shakespeare revived and heard any of this, my cover wouldn't be blown. "I mean you no harm if you mean no harm to the earth."

"No harm!" the wounded witch shrieked. "You cut off my hand!"

"You were trying to kill me with it," I pointed out. "And I chose to maim when I could have killed. Considering what you've just done to those men, I think I have the moral high ground." The hot waxen features of the former bandits were slowing, congealing, solidifying into female faces, and their hair was growing long and dark at an alarming rate; their frames shrank somewhat in their clothing as they transformed into feminine figures. "Isn't talking more pleasant? Let's chat. Why are you summoning Hecate here?"

"The Druids died out long ago," one near the fire said, ignoring my question.

"It's funny you say that, because I was going to say there were no Thracian witches in England."

With a final crescendo of chunky bone noises and a slurp

of sucking flesh, Hecate finished transforming the bodies of her vessels into her preferred manifestation, and three women who could have stepped off a Grecian urn—long noses, thin lips, flawless skin, and all kinds of kohl on the eyelids—took deep breaths and exhaled as one. They weren't of differing ages in the mold of maiden-mother-crone: They could be teenaged triplets, which made sense since it was really a single goddess in there, and I regret now that I never asked her if she took pleasure in confounding storytellers with the problem of whether to use singular or plural pronouns. I'll stick with plural for the moment, because after the synchronized sigh that the witches and I all simply watched in awe, their eyes fluttered open and they spoke in creepy unison: "Blood."

That was a pretty dire omen, but it got worse. Triple Hecate's heads swung to look directly at me and smiled. "His will do. Bring me his heart."

Her hands shot in my direction and she spat, "*Pétra ostá!*" which means "stone bones." She wanted me to stand petrified while her witches carved me up, but her hex ran into my cold iron aura and fizzled, resulting in nothing more than a thump of my amulet against my chest. I played along with it, though, freezing up, widening my eyes, and warbling in panic as the two healthy witches raced forward to do Hecate's bidding. Had they been the least bit cautious—a lesson they should have learned after the experience their sister had in coming after me—I might not have been able to handle two at once. But they came in unguarded, unable to fathom the idea that their goddess's powers might have a counter or a limit.

Still, I didn't kill them. They were too undisciplined to be a true threat, but since I couldn't have them ganging up on me either, they each got a slash across the belly to make them sit down and work on healing for a while. If they were half decent at witchcraft—their accomplishments suggested they were—they'd eventually be fine, but it would take them some time. And then the easy part was over.

Triple Hecate, unlike her witches, was very disciplined and knew how to coordinate the attacks of her vessels. And she was able to juice up those bodies even more than I was, though I didn't know at first what fuel she was using for it; if it was blood, then she would need more soon, and Shakespeare was still available. Hissing, she launched herself at me and spread out, two of her vessels flanking me and dodging my first wide swing. She lunged forward in coordinated strikes and danced out of the way of my blade; I got a kick in the kidney, a hammer blow to the ribs that cracked one, and a breath-stealing punt to the diaphragm before I remembered to trigger my camouflage. She had a more difficult time targeting me after that and couldn't track the sword but still got her licks in, because I fell down and she heard it, aiming her kicks low. I was able to get in a few of mine, though. Fragarach was able to cut her a few times—never deeply, but she slowed noticeably after each one. She really did need that blood to fuel her speed and strength; she wasn't feeding on the life energy of the earth but rather on the energy of sacrifices.

The dismembered witch, whom I'd forgotten about, cried out in discovery. "Queen Hecate! There's a man asleep over here! His blood will set you right!"

Triple Hecate backed off and turned away, and I looked as well to see the witch pointing with her good hand toward Shakespeare. There was no way I'd be able to get up and run over there faster than Hecate.

I swung quick and hard with everything I had at the legs of the nearest vessel, taking off a foot and chunking into the other leg, but the other two dashed off to feed on the bard.

While my target fell over and I rose to my knees, gasping for breath, the other two called for a knife to cut Shakespeare's throat.

"I lost mine in the mud," the witch wailed, her voice making it plain that she feared Hecate's displeasure.

"Check your belts," one of the other witches moaned, reminding Hecate that her vessels had been wearing clothes and, yes, weapons. As one, the vessels—including mine—looked down, spied their daggers, and drew them. The mobile vessels were closing on Shakespeare and would end him in seconds. There was no time for subtlety, only a desperate chance at saving him. Scrambling on my hands and knees to the fallen vessel, I thrust upward into her skull from the bottom of her jaw just underneath the chin, shoving through into the brain and scrambling any chance of healing that particular mortal coil. She'd heard my approach, though, and at the same time stabbed into my vulnerable left side with her newfound dagger, sinking it below my armpit into a lung. I collapsed on top of her as she expired, and I heard a cry in stereo: The other two vessels stopped, shook as if gripped by a seizure, and then exploded in a shower of chunky meat and bone.

It had worked—though on a significantly more gory level than I expected: Triple Hecate could not occupy only two vessels. Kill one and you killed them all.

Or you hit the reset button anyway. I was under no illusion that Hecate had really been slain; she'd merely been banished to whatever Olympian ether she'd come from, and she could be summoned again, though I imagined it would be difficult.

A hush born of shock settled about the field for a few seconds, and then the weird sisters shrieked—and not over their various wounds. They'd toiled and waited a long time for their moment, for whatever reason, and most likely thought Hecate invincible. To see all of that crushed in the space of minutes caused them more than a little emotional distress.

Wincing, I yanked out the knife in my side and triggered my healing charm, drawing plenty of power through the earth to fuel it. It would take a while to heal, but I felt sure I'd survive; I still had doubts about Shakespeare. The first witch was standing over him and might kill him out of spite. Lurching to my feet was impossible to do quietly, and the witches all turned at the sound. They couldn't make me out but knew I was there.

"We will curse you for this, Druid," one of them promised. She was clutching her guts together in the mud.

"You can try, but it would be a waste of your time," I said. "If Hecate's curse didn't work on me, why would yours?"

They didn't have a ready answer for that, so they took turns suggesting various sex acts I could perform with animals, and I let them. The longer their attention was focused on me, the closer I staggered to Shakespeare. I goaded them a couple of times to keep them going, and then, when I was close enough, I poked the first witch with the tip of Fragarach, just a nick, which caused her to yelp and leap away from him. She cradled her stump, which I noticed she had managed to stop bleeding. I stepped forward, placing myself between her and the bard's prone form, and dropped my camouflage.

"Hi. Back away, join your sisters, and you can live. You might even summon Hecate again someday. Or I can kill you now. What'll it be?"

She said nothing but retreated, always keeping her eyes on me, and I watched her go, keeping my guard up.

With a little bit of help from the elemental communicating through the earth, I located the horses—they hadn't run far—and convinced them that they'd be safe if they returned to give us a ride back to town; when we got to the stables they'd get oats and apples.

While I waited for them, I knelt and checked on Shakespeare. He was unharmed except for his drunken oblivion; he'd likely have a monstrous hangover. But while he was out of immediate physical danger, he still needed magical protection. The witches might not be able to curse me, but they could curse him, and it would occur to them to try before I left the field. But the piece of cold iron in my purse that I'd been anxious to hold on to earlier would do me yeoman service now. I fished it out and, having no string or chain on me, bound it to his skin at the hollow of his throat and made it a talisman against direct hexes. It wouldn't save him from more carefully crafted curses using his blood or hair, but I'd address that next.

The witches huddled together and eyed me through their bearded masks as I hefted Shakespeare over his horse's back, a task made more difficult by my wound. I did what I could to hide his face from their view and was particularly careful about leaving anything behind for them to use against us later. I located Shakespeare's vomit and my blood and, with the elemental's aid, made sure that everything got turned into the earth and buried deep.

I snuffed out the fire too, binding dirt to the wood to smother the unnatural flames, and that not only left the crossroads really dark but prevented the witches from doing much else that night. They complained loudly that they needed it to heal.

"Don't try to summon Hecate in England again," I called over their cursing, giving the horses a mental nudge to walk on. "England and Ireland are under my protection. I won't be so merciful a second time."

A tap on my cold iron amulet warned me that one or more of them had just tried to hex me. Since Shakespeare didn't immediately burst into flames or otherwise die a gruesome death, I assumed his talisman protected him as well.

"Good night, now," I called cheerfully, just to let them know they'd failed, and we left them there to contemplate the profound disadvantages of summoning rituals. The risks are almost always greater than the reward.

Once we were well out of their sight and hearing, I paused to recover my cold iron talisman and place it back in my purse. Shakespeare helpfully remained unconscious until we returned to the stables and his feet touched ground. He was bleary-eyed and vomited again, much to the disgust of the stable boy, but rose gradually to lucidity as his synapses fired and memories returned.

"Marquis! You live! I live!" he said as I led him away to the White Hart, where I would gladly fall into bed in my room. His eyes dropped, and he raised his hands and wiggled his fingers the way people do when they want to make sure that everything still works. "What happened?"

I remembered just in time that I was supposed to have a French accent. "What's the last thing you remember?"

"The witches—"

"Shh—keep your voice down!"

More quietly, he said, "The witches—they killed those men."

"Yes, they did. Is that all?"

His eyes drifted up for a moment, trying to access more details, but then dropped back down to me and he nodded. "That's the last thing I remember."

Fantastic! That was my cue to fabricate something. "Well,

they threw the men in the cauldron, of course, while I threw you over my shoulder to sneak out of there."

"What? But what happened? Did they eat the men?"

"No, no, it was all divination, the blackest divination possible, powered by blood. They were asking Hecate to reveal the future for them."

"Zounds, God has surely preserved me from damnation. And you! Thank you, sir, for my life. But what did they say?"

"I beg your pardon?"

"What matters did the hags seek to learn? The future of England?"

"I heard nothing beyond a general request to let the veil of time be withdrawn, that sort of thing. They were out of earshot before they got to specifics."

"But the chanting, before—you heard all of that; you translated some of it for me. What were their words, exactly—I need a quill and some ink!" He staggered into the White Hart Inn to find some, time of day be damned.

And that put me in the uncomfortable position of creating something that sounded like a spell but wasn't. I couldn't very well provide Shakespeare with the words one needed to summon Triple Hecate, knowing that he would immortalize them in ink.

So once he found his writing materials and demanded that I recount everything I could recall, providing a literal translation of the witches' chanting, I spun him some doggerel and he wrote it down: *Double, double toil and trouble . . .*

"And now you know why I shivered, Granuaile, when you said, '*Fire burn and cauldron bubble.*'"

Granuaile cried, "*You* wrote the witches' lines? No way!"

Shrugging and allowing myself a half grin, I said, "You're right. Shakespeare didn't write what I said into *Macbeth* verbatim. He played around with it a bit and made it fit his meter. Much better than what I said, to be sure. And the mystery of Hecate's summoning remained a mystery."

"The words alone wouldn't have been sufficient to do the deed, would they?"

"Not initially; I was worried about the cumulative effect. With such frequent invocation, the goddess might have grown stronger and chosen to manifest at any time, with or without a sacrifice, and you don't want that version of Hecate to appear in a packed theatre."

Granuaile shook her head. "No, you don't. Why did they curse the play, then?"

"Shakespeare never saw Hecate summoned but knew that the witches looked to her somehow, so she got written into *Macbeth*. The Hecate in his play is a single character and not particularly fearsome or strong. They thought his portrayal was demeaning, and *that* inspired the curse."

"So they remained in England?"

"Long enough to see the play, yes. I don't think they realized that they had met the playwright in the past; they simply took grave offense and foolishly cursed it in concert within the hearing of others. They were caught and burned soon afterward."

<I'm kind of glad I didn't live in that time, Atticus,> Oberon said. <Over-boiled sausages are so disappointing. Dry and flavorless like kibble.>

That was your takeaway? Bad sausage at the White Hart Inn?

<Wasn't that the climax to your tragedy? Or was it the

end where you and Shakespeare never even took a spoonful of what they were cooking in that cauldron?>

It wasn't a tragedy, Oberon. Nobody died except for those three guys, and that was only because they were too stupid to leave us alone.

<Nobody ate anything delicious either, so it sounded like a tragedy to me. I mean, you had witches smeared with blood and fat, so there had to be some meat cooking in there.>

It truly was a rough time. Luckily, your circumstances are different. You got to eat what we cooked over the fire.

Oberon rolled over, presenting his belly, and stretched. <Yeah, I guess I have it pretty good. But shouldn't you be getting to work, Atticus? This belly isn't going to rub itself, you know.>

I obliged my hound and asked Granuaile if she felt like round two. She nodded and tossed me another beer from the cooler, grabbing one for herself. The pop and hiss of the cans sounded loud in the darkness, but after that it was only the occasional snap of the comfortably orange fire and the song that Gaia decided to sing to us under the unveiled stars.

the demon barker of wheat street

This story, narrated by Atticus, takes place six years after Tricked, Book 4 of The Iron Druid Chronicles, and two weeks after the events of the novella Two Ravens and One Crow. It was originally published in the Carniepunk anthology and has since been slightly revised and expanded from that version.

i fear Kansas. It's not a toe-curling type of fear, where shoulders tense with an incipient cringe; it's more of a vague apprehension, an expectation that something will go pear-shaped and cause me great inconvenience. It's like the dread you feel when going to meet a girl's father: Though it's probably going to be just fine, you're aware that no matter how broadly he smiles, part of him wants you to be a eunuch, and he wouldn't mind performing the operation himself. Kansas is like that for me. But I hear lots of nice things about it from other people. My anxiety stems from impolitic thinking a long time ago. I am usually quite careful to shield my thoughts and think strictly business in my Latin headspace, because that's the one I use to talk with the elementals who grant me my powers as a Druid. But once—and all it takes is once—I let slip the opinion that I thought the American central plains were a bit boring. The elemental—whom I've thought of as "Amber" since the early twentieth century, thanks to the "amber waves of grain" thing—heard me, and I've been paying for it ever since. The magic doesn't flow as well for me there anymore. Sometimes my bindings fizzle for no apparent reason, and I know it's just Amber messing with me. As a result, I look uncomfortable whenever I visit, and people wonder if I'm suffering from dyspepsia. Or maybe they stare because I don't look like a local. I'd fit right in on a beach in California with my surfer dude façade, but at the Kansas Wheat Festival, not so much.

Said Wheat Festival was in Wellington, Kansas, the hometown of my apprentice, Granuaile MacTiernan. We were visiting in disguise because she wanted to check up on her mother. We'd faked Granuaile's death a few years ago—for very good reasons—but now she was worried about how her mom was coping. For the past few years she'd been satisfied by updates from private investigators willing to do some long-distance stalking, but an overwhelming urge to lay eyes on her mother in person had overtaken her. I hadn't been able to fully persuade her that it was a bad idea to visit people who thought you were dead, so I tagged along in case she managed to get into trouble. Granuaile said I could look at it as a vacation from the rigors of training her, and since I'd recently escaped death in Oslo by the breadth of a whisker, I hadn't needed much convincing to take a break for my mental health. We brought my Irish wolfhound, Oberon, along with us and promised him that we'd go hunting.

<Set me loose on a colony of prairie dogs, Atticus. I'll show them what a real dog is,> he told me. <Or point me at some antelope. Can we go after antelope?>

Sure, buddy, I replied through our mental link. *But that's*

*going to be quite a run. Hard to sneak up on anything in a land
like this.*

<You can hum the theme music from *Chariots of Fire*
once we hit full stride. It will make the antelope run in slow
motion like the movie, and then it will be easy.>

I'm not sure it works like that.

Red hair dyed black and shoved underneath a Colorado
Rockies cap pulled low, Granuaile had already taken care of
her most distinguishable feature in one go. She had on a pair
of those ridiculously oversize sunglasses too, which hid her
green eyes and the freckles high up on her cheeks. A shirt
from Dry Dock Brewing in Aurora, a pair of khaki shorts,
and sandals suggested that she was a crunchy hippie type
from the Denver area. I was dressed similarly, but I wore my
Rockies cap backward because Granuaile said it made me
look clueless, and that's precisely what I wanted. If I was a
clueless crunchy guy, then I couldn't be a Druid more than
two thousand years old who was also supposed to have died
in the Arizona desert six years before.

Everybody in Wellington knew Granuaile's mom, because
everyone knew her stepfather. Beau Thatcher was something
of an oil baron and employed a large percentage of those
locals who weren't wheat farmers. A few inquiries here and
there with the right gossips—we posed as friends of her late
daughter—and small-town nosiness did most of the work for
us. According to reports, her mother was properly mournful
without having locked herself in her house with pills and
booze. She was taking it all about as well as could be expected,
and once we expressed an entirely fake interest in dropping
by to pay her a visit, we were ruefully informed by one of her
"best friends" that she was off on a Caribbean cruise right
now or else she'd be at the festival.

I hoped my relief didn't show too plainly. Though I'd wrung a promise from Granuaile that we wouldn't visit her house, there had still been a chance of an unfortunate meeting somewhere in town. Now I could relax a bit and bask in the success of our passive spying in the vein of Polonius: *And thus do we of wisdom and of reach, / With windlasses and with assays of bias, / By indirections find directions out . . .*

Having satisfied Granuaile's need to know that her mother was adjusting well, if not her need to see her in person, we enjoyed the festivities, which included chucking cow patties at a target for fabulous prizes. Oberon didn't understand the attraction.

<I don't get it. You guys look down on chimps for flinging their own poo, but you think it's fine to fling other kinds of poo around? I mean, you get opposable thumbs and this is what you do with them?>

The town had invited an old-fashioned carnival to set up alongside the more bland wheat-related events. It had some rides that looked capable of triggering a rush of adrenaline, so once the sun had set, we passed through the rented fencing to see if we could be entertained. Since sunglasses weren't practical at night, Granuaile just kept her hat pulled low.

Though health codes didn't seem all that important to this particular operation, I cast camouflage on Oberon so that we wouldn't get barred from the venue. The spell bound Oberon's pigments to the ones of his surroundings, which rendered him invisible when motionless and as good as invisible at night, even when on the move.

It's odd how a dog roaming around is a health code violation but serving fried death on a stick isn't. The food vendors didn't seem to rank using wholesome wheaty-wheat in their foodstuffs high in their priorities, despite the name of the festival to which they were catering. Salt and grease and sugar were the main offerings, tied together here and there with animal bits or highly processed starches.

Bright lights and garish painted colors on the rides and game booths did their best to distract patrons from the layer of grime coating everything. The metal parts on the rides groaned and squealed; they'd taken punishment for years and had been disassembled and assembled again with a minimum of care—and a minimum of lubricant.

The carnies working the game booths were universally afflicted with rotting teeth and gingivitis, a dire warning of what would happen if one ate the carnival food and failed to find a toothbrush afterward. They made no effort to be charming; sneers and leers were all they could manage for the people they had been trained to see as marks instead of humans. Granuaile wanted to chuck softballs at steel milk bottles.

"You go ahead. I can't," I said.

"Why not?"

"Because the carnie will mock me for not winning his rigged game, and then I'll be tempted to cheat and unbind the bottles a bit so that they all fall over, which would mean I'd receive something enormous and fluffy."

"If the game's rigged, then you're not cheating. You're leveling the playing field. And if you decided to reward your apprentice with something enormous and fluffy for all of her hard work, then there's really no downside."

<Hey, Atticus, I'm enormous! And if you adopted a poodle bitch, then she would be fluffy. You could make us *both* happy with a poodle, see?>

"The downside is I'm not on good terms with the elemental here. Using the earth's magic for something trivial like that would hardly improve matters. Camouflaging Oberon so he can walk around with us is bad enough."

<I'd be happy to walk around in plain sight, Atticus.>

You might scare the children.

<What? But I'm cuddly! "Single Irish wolfhound likes long walks on the beach and belly rubs.">

Granuaile went a few rounds with the milk bottles, and the carnie tried to chivy me into "rescuing" her. My apprentice nearly assaulted him for that but showed admirable restraint.

"Whatsa matter, can't hit the ground if you fell out of a plane?" he called to me.

"Whatsa matter, employers don't provide a dental plan?" I responded.

He didn't want to open his mouth after that, and Granuaile finished her game play scowling.

"It's funny," she said as we walked away. "People come here to be happy, but I bet they wind up in a fouler mood than when they walked in. Kids want plushies and rides and sugar, and parents want to hang on to their money and their kids. And everybody wants to go away without digestive problems, but *that's* not gonna happen."

"I can't argue with that."

"So why do people come here?"

I shrugged. "Because we pursue happiness even when it runs away from us."

We passed several booths, ignored the pitches of more carnies with alarming hygiene issues, and examined the faces of people walking by. There were no smiles, only stress and anger and frustration.

"See, there's no happiness here," Granuaile pointed out.

Distant screams of terror reached us from the rides. "Maybe you would find it amusing to experience the joys of centrifugal force." I waved toward the flashing lights of the carnival's midway. "Allow the machinery to jostle the fluid in your inner ear."

"Oh." She grinned at me. "Well, if you put it like *that*, it sounds irresistible."

"Step right here!" a voice cut into our conversation. "Priceless entertainment for only three dollars! Gape at the Impossibly Whiskered Woman! Thrill at the Three-Armed Man and watch those hands! Chunder with the force of thunder at the Conjoined Quintuplets! Guaranteed to harrow your soul for only three dollars!"

The barker hawking hyperbole was a dwarf on stilts. Dark pinstriped pants and oversize clown shoes masked his wooden limbs and remained very still while his torso gesticulated and waved wee, chubby, white-sleeved arms at potential spectators. A red paisley waistcoat flashed and caught lights from the midway, giving his torso the appearance of flickering flames. His eyes were shadowed by a bowler hat, but his mouth never stopped moving, and it was effective. A line of people queued outside a yellow pavilion tent, drawn there as much by the barker as by curiosity over the stunned people coming out the other side.

"Amazin'," one mumbled as he staggered past me. His eyes were unfocused and his mouth hung slack in disturbing fashion. He didn't seem to be addressing anyone in particular. "Incredible. Whadda trip. Sirsley. I mean rilly. Nothin' like it."

My first, somewhat cynical thought was that he was a plant by the management. But then I noticed that more and more people kept coming out of the tent with their minds clearly boggled, too many to be in on the shill. The barker kept fishing with his verbal bait and was hooking plenty of people.

"It's not a House of Horror! It's a Tent of Terror! Add thrills and add chills and you get *adventure!* Only three bucks to reap what you sow!"

The last line struck me as a non sequitur, and I looked around to see if anyone else had been bothered by it. It was an odd pitch to make for a carnival amusement, but people were forking over their cash to a muscle-bound hulk at the entrance and walking inside as the barker continued to weave together rhymes and alliterative phrases in a tapestry of bombast.

"Two tumescent tumors on either side of her nose! Face cancer ain't for the faint of heart! We have the freaks but you can't get freaky—all you get is a peekie! See the sights that can't be unseen for only three dollars!"

"Huh," Granuaile said. "That sounds interesting. What do you think they have in there? A woman who let someone draw on her face with a Sharpie?"

"Only one way to find out."

<Can I go in too?>

Sure, if you can keep close and sneak past the bouncer.

We joined the queue and observed a profound lack of excitement in our fellow entrants. The mood was one of passive resignation to the coming rip-off, albeit garnished with a wedge of hope, sort of like stinky beer graced with a slice of orange.

Oberon easily slipped through into the tent with us once we paid the mountain of beef manning the door. We were immediately confronted with a slab of painted plywood serving as a wall and a lurid sign that shouted at us: LAST CHANCE: CHOOSE HEAVEN (left) OR HELL (right).

"Is it the same either way?" Granuaile wondered aloud.

"No idea," I said. There was a bit of a backup going to the hell side, so I suggested we go left.

"Well, in case it's different, I'd like to see what's going on in hell," she said. "Let's split up and compare notes outside."

I shrugged. "Okay. See you soon." Then I asked Oberon, *Which way do you want to go, buddy?*

<I think I'll go with Granuaile. Curiosity killed the cat but never hurt a hound, you know.>

All right, keep talking to me and let me know what you see.

<I see a poodle in my future.>

I'm sure you do, I replied, as I turned left and followed a couple of switchbacks.

<She is a black standard poodle and her name is Noche. That's Spanish for "night.">

Yeah, I know.

<We chase squirrels in the morning and then we lie down on a bed of sausages.>

I wasn't soliciting your fantasies, Oberon. I was rather hoping you'd tell me what you see in the present.

<I don't see any poodles at present. No sausages either.>

I sighed and dropped my eyes to the bare ground over which the tent had been erected. What grass remained was well trampled and forlorn, perhaps wondering why it, of all grass, had to suffer a herd of bipeds crushing it into the earth. Rounding another plywood barrier, I was confronted with a large woman wearing a costume beard, Grizzly Adams–style. The elastic band keeping it in place was plainly visible over her ears. Next to her stood a man with a cheap old-fashioned prosthetic arm attached to his chest via a clever arrangement of suspenders and bungee cords. He grabbed the forearm with his left hand and raised it a bit, then wiggled it to make the plastic hand flap at me. I shook my head in disgust and moved on, hoping something more inventive would be around the next sheet of plywood.

<Hey, Atticus, is it normal for there to be stairs in a tent?>

What? No.

<We're going down a staircase. Looks like they slapped wood planks on top of solid earth. We've been walking on wood the whole time, actually.>

I spun around and searched for trapdoors or anything else that might indicate a trip down below on my side. Nothing. No wood flooring either. The idiot three-armed man flapped his prosthetic hand again, figuring I wanted additional proof of his dexterity.

Have you seen anything stupid posing as a thrill?

<No, we turned a corner and *boom*, stairs headed down.>

That's weird. It's completely different on this side. Seems more elaborate than all their costuming.

Maybe it was a thematic thing. Their side was supposed to be hell, after all. If my side was heaven, though, where was the stairway to it? I hurried around the next corner and saw the woman with two "tumors"—they were red gumdrops attached to her cheeks with adhesive. And the conjoined quintuplets were there too: "They" were one guy with two shrunken plastic heads resting on either shoulder.

How could anyone walk out of here and praise this farce? It made no sense, especially since the few other people who'd chosen this side with me were obviously annoyed by the extent of the swindle. I didn't know what to expect around the next wall—most likely the exit—so I was surprised by a little blond girl, maybe eight years old, in a pretty pink dress and shiny black shoes. She would have been adorable had her eyes not been glowing orange. The smile she smiled was decidedly un-girlish—more like inhuman—and her voice was one of those low basso frequencies that shiver your bones.

"You came alone and it was the most amazing thing you've ever seen," she rumbled, and a wave of her power—or perhaps I should say *its* power—did its best to slap me upside the head. Since my aura was bound to the cold iron of my amulet, the mojo fizzled and delivered a small thump to my chest, as if someone had poked me right on the amulet. She was standing on a square of plywood. I blinked as I realized that the deception going on here was much grander than a three-dollar fraud.

I kicked off my sandals and stopped hiding from Amber the elemental. I'd been powering Oberon's camouflage with magic stored in my bear charm, but it was running low and the orange-eyed girl demanded more resources, seeing as how she was casually slinging around hoodoo and speaking as if she had a giant pair of balls that dropped two feet after puberty. I drew energy through the tattoos that bound me to the earth and watched as the girl repeated the ensorcelling phrase for the person behind me. It was a young man in a white cowboy hat, and he rocked back visibly under the little girl's greeting before his expression assumed a thousand-mile stare and he became a mouth breather.

<Atticus, something isn't right.>

No kidding. I activated the charm on my necklace that allowed me to see in the magical spectrum and discovered that wee miss was an imp crammed into a human shell. That shell was the same thing as a hostage: If I attacked it and it couldn't bamboozle people anymore, those same people would think I was assaulting a child.

<We just went through this weird door made of this jelly stuff. More like an orifice, really . . . We sort of squirted through

the middle and it was gross. It smells bad down here. Blood and bad meat and that poo you like to fling around. It's coming from someplace ahead.>

I frowned. *Stop. Don't go any farther. I'm coming to join you. In fact, go back.*

<But Granuaile is going forward.>

She couldn't hear Oberon's thoughts yet, since she was still about six years away from getting bound to the earth. *Grab her by the shirt or something. Pull her back. Don't let her go.*

I spent a few seconds trying to think of how to beat the imp without a kerfuffle, until I realized it wasn't trying to prevent my escape. All I had to do was act dumb and walk out. Picking up my sandals, I did precisely that, vowing to return later. Once safely outside, I sprinted around to the front of the tent to have another shot.

<She's getting mad at me, Atticus. She's telling me to stop and let her go. And there are people cramming in behind us.>

Don't let her go! It's important, Oberon. I'm on my way.

<I'll try, but she's really determined.>

The line at the front of the tent was just as long as when we'd entered—perhaps longer. The barker, I saw through magical sight, was actually a full-fledged demon. The huge man at the door taking money was an imp, so the barker was the boss. His words came back to me: "Guaranteed to harrow your soul." "Reap what you sow." And then, in writing, an offer to choose hell. I couldn't afford to wait in line again.

<Um, Atticus, we've moved down the hall a bit. There's another weird door ahead, like a full-body turnstile, and I think these things are one-way. Great big bears! The smell is awful now, and people on the other side of it are screaming and trying to get back to where we are, but they can't. And the people on this side—Granuaile included—can't wait to walk

through to where the screaming is. This isn't any fun, and I think you should get your money back.>

Can't you stop her?

<I tried! She *hit* me, Atticus! On the nose!>

That didn't sound like Granuaile at all. She loved Oberon every bit as much as I did. Only one thing could explain her behavior.

Oberon, she's under a spell. These are demons at work. You have to stop her. Knock her down and sit on her if you have to.

Oberon weighed more than she did. He could keep her pinned.

<Demons? Why don't I smell them?>

Normally demons smell so bad that it takes a herculean effort to keep your lunch down. I shot another look at the demon barker but saw no one violently ill in his vicinity. Neither the man at the entrance nor the girl at the exit had set my nose twitching.

They've sewn themselves up tight in human bodies. Have you got her?

<Not yet. She's not the average human. You've been training her for six years.>

I'm going to dissolve your camouflage and hope the sight of you helps. You have to stop her, Oberon.

I dissolved his spell and then triggered camouflage for myself, which would allow me to slip past the imp at the door.

However, nothing happened.

"Oh, no, not now, Amber," I said, and then reached through my tattoos to speak directly to the elemental of the central Great Plains. *Speaking* was a relative term; elementals don't speak any human language but rather communicate via emotions and images. My recollections of such conversations are always approximations.

//Demons on earth / Druid requires aid//

Amber replied immediately, not even pretending that she didn't know I was around. //Query: Demon location? / None sensed//

//Demons here// I replied. //My location / Demons using wood to mask presence//

The bloody barker hadn't been insecure about his height; he needed the stilts to make sure the earth never twigged to his presence.

Demons on the loose were usually the responsibility of their angelic opposites, but I've run into them more often than I would care to. The problem with them from a Druidic perspective was that they kept trying to hijack the earth's power to open and maintain portals to hell, draining life in the process and endangering the elementals. Aenghus Óg's giant suckhole to the fifth circle, for example, had destroyed fifty square miles in Arizona. If there was a gateway underground here, Amber should have felt it.

//Query: Power drain in this area?// I asked.

//Yes / Intermittent//

//Demons responsible// I said.

Amber's judgment and sentence took no time at all. Her anger boiled through me as she said, //Slay them / Full power restored//

//Gratitude / Harmony//

//Harmony// Had I the time, I might have shed a tear at that—or celebrated with a shot of whiskey. It had been far too long since I'd shared a sense of harmony with Amber—because these were feelings, after all, not mere translated words, and it was impossible for either Amber or me to lie about feeling harmony. But I had an apprentice and a hound in danger of going through a mysterious unholy orifice, as well as another mystery to solve: Since the demons obviously had some kind of portal down there, how were they hiding it?

<Okay, Atticus, she's down, but she's hitting me and yelling, and that hurts.>

You're a good hound. We are totally getting you some gourmet sausages for this. Keep her down. She'll apologize later.

I cast camouflage successfully this time and melted from view. It didn't make me completely invisible when I moved, but it was good enough; no one would be able to see me in time to react well.

Except perhaps the demon barker.

"You, sir! What do you think you're doing?" He was staring right at me, even though I was camouflaged and still. Damn it. I didn't have a weapon either. Since stealth didn't seem to be an option, my only hope lay in speed and some martial arts. I bolted for the entrance and the barker shouted, "Gobnob—I mean George! Stop that man!"

The imp's name was Gobnob?

"What man?" the hulk said as I whisked past him. Apparently only the demon could pierce my camouflage. Advantage: Druid.

Indiscreet shoving was necessary to get past the line of people and down the stairs. I heard lots of "heys" and "what the (bleep)s" as I endangered ankles and hips.

"Sorry," I called. "It's an emergency."

<Aughh! Atticus, she got away from me! She's heading for the second thingie!>

Grab her pants leg in your teeth and pull back hard. Don't let her get traction!

<Fail! She's through!>

Go after her and protect her!

The first bizarre "orifice" was ahead. An imp in a human

suit was stationed there and charming people much the way the little girl imp was at the exit on the heaven side, except that this fellow was telling people, "You can't wait to get through the next doorway after this one." That's why Granuaile and the rest of them kept going even when they heard and smelled something awful ahead.

It was time to put a stick in their spokes.

There wasn't any need to think about it: Amber had ordered me to slay the demons, so I was going to do it. These weren't living bodies the demons had possessed but rather fresh corpses they were inhabiting, like hermit crabs squeezed into shells. But while dwelling in human form, the imps were subject to at least some human limitations. Before I passed through the gross doorway, I placed one hand on top of the imp's head and the other underneath his chin and jerked it violently to the side, snapping his neck. He might get out of his shell soon, but he wouldn't be charming anyone else until he did.

As he crumpled I yelled, "Go back! They're killing people in here!" The "what the (bleep)s" multiplied, and I hoped that their sense of self-preservation would win out over curiosity. The carnival goers were quite confused, because they hadn't precisely seen me kill the imp, but they did know that something had gone horribly wrong and someone had been severely injured. Some of them pulled out cell phones and dialed 911, and at least a couple expressed a loud desire to get out of there and headed back up the stairs.

The orifice was wet and smelled fishy and I had to sort of slither through it, since it was a slit cut into a quivering wall of protoplasm; I felt as if I'd been squeezed out through a pastry chef's frosting gun. Dubbing it the Anchovy Gate due to its odor, I decided, for my own sanity, not to dwell on whether its substance had been secreted or shat or otherwise spawned from unsavory origins. It was a kind of gelatinous, semi-translucent slab of dead lavender sludge that filled the space completely from floor to ceiling, a tight sphincter sealing one environment off from another. Its function was clear: Without the protections it provided against smells and sound, nobody would want to continue onward, for the stench on the other side of it made me gag and the howls of people dying ahead filled me with fear for Granuaile and Oberon.

What's happening? I asked my hound.

<Atticus, I don't think we're in Kansas anymore.>

Nonsense. I can still hear you.

<They are killing people in here. Granuaile kind of woke up and figured out we're in trouble. But so did everybody else.>

Almost there.

<Hurry!>

Everyone ahead of me had been charmed. Their need to get through that next gate was the call of a siren. If the first one had been the Anchovy Gate, this was the Needle Gate, I suppose. It was designed like those tire-shredding devices: You were fine to go through it one way, but try to back up and you'd be punctured with slivers of steel.

Still, whatever was happening on the other side, people were opting for the needles and trying to push backward through them, getting cut up in the process. Pelting through the charmed victims until I reached the gateway, I drew on the earth's power for enhanced speed and strength.

The Needle Gate was a mass of hinged, bloody steel spikes, doubtless constructed in chunks and then assembled here, like the tent and the rides and everything else. The metal didn't burn my skin—in fact, it was quite cool, as one might expect metal underground to be. The fabled temperature of hell wasn't in play here; the horror of it was.

I pressed through the clacking hiss of needles and came through low onto a killing floor, rolling out of the way of a desperate middle-aged man whose face was streaked with snot and tears and spattered with blood. He tried to stick his arm into the gap in the gate I'd just vacated and wound up puncturing it on all sides. The needles must have had wee barbs on the outer sides so that as one passed through the gate they wouldn't snag; but once you tried to back up, you'd be not only stabbed but hooked. There were at least a dozen other people crowding the gate, trying to get out as I was trying to get in, and some of them had caught their hands and arms on needles in their desperate attempts to escape. Now they could either tear free or remain stuck, but either way they had pain to deal with on top of their terror. Two people—a man and a woman—had been pushed into the needles by accident or design and were now wailing in agony, unable to win free. It looked as if others, in the frenzy of their fear, might be more than willing to tear them loose forcibly or even use their bodies to wedge the gate open if it meant escape. Thankfully, Granuaile wasn't one of those crowding around the gate.

Oberon? I'm through the door.

<Go to the right and help us with this thing!>

I squeezed through a couple of more rows of panicked citizens and emerged into an abattoir. The floor was cheap, splintery wood laid over the earth. The ceiling was surprisingly high—we had descended deeper than I thought. The reason for the height lay at the far end of the room, which was about the length of a high school cafeteria: Ghouls had stacked bodies nearly to the top and were adding more rows of fresh kills, presumably for later consumption. A demon with a scythe was supplying the freshness, and right then he was after Granuaile.

He wasn't the actual grim reaper but a demon that had assumed the likeness; enough people associated a robed skeletal figure with hell that it made sense for a demon to take that form. It was certainly working on the psychological front.

The reaper had on the iconic long black robe but had pulled back the cowl, exposing the rictus of a merciless white skull. Tiny fires blazed in his eye sockets, and he appeared competent with the scythe, whirling it around by the little handle halfway down the shaft. Granuaile was leaping over or ducking under his swings and was losing steam, but she would have been dispatched long ago if she hadn't trained the last six years with me in tumbling and martial arts.

Oberon had quite rightly concluded he couldn't be a dog in this fight; he was barking and trying to distract the demon but otherwise staying out of range of the scythe.

Like many long weapons, scythes are fearsome if you're right at the arc of their swing. But they're slow and cumbersome to wield, and if you can get inside that arc, you have a decent chance to deal a debilitating blow to an ill-guarded opponent.

Back me up, buddy.

I charged the demon and went for a slide tackle that would have made Manchester United proud. I dissolved my camouflage as I moved so that Oberon could see me, but unfortunately the demon also caught this in his peripheral vision. If he was anything like the barker, he probably could have seen through it anyway, but my abrupt pop into view triggered a reflex action. He leapt over my slide and landed astride me, raising the scythe high above his head to harvest my dumb ass. With his eye sockets cast down at me, he didn't see Oberon coming.

My hound—a buck-fifty and all muscle—hit the demon square in the chest, bowling him over. Oberon's momentum caused him to trample the demon and keep going, which was just as well, because the reaper rolled and regained his feet with a backward somersault, still holding on to his weapon and facing me.

Well done, Oberon. Stay behind him but don't charge. He knows you're back there. Growl and keep him nervous.

The reaper advanced on me, swinging his weapon in a weaving pattern that forced me to backpedal. But once I had the timing of it down, I lunged inside the blade following a backswing and turned my right forearm to block the shaft, continuing to spin around to the left so that I could ram my left elbow into his teeth. Seeing that stagger him, I followed up, shoving the heel of my right palm as hard as I could underneath the reaper's jaw. The skull, bereft of convenient muscles and tendons to anchor it firmly to the neck and shoulders, popped clean off, and the flames died in the sockets.

<Attaboy, Atticus! Don't fear the reaper!>

This isn't done.

I checked on Granuaile. She was breathing heavily and looked exhausted but not wounded.

"You okay?" I asked. She nodded in the affirmative right as a chorus of roars erupted from the far side of the abattoir. The ghouls had just realized I'd killed the reaper, and their rage was answered by a new wave of screams from the carnival goers. A few stragglers had poured in during the fight, and the nightmare set before their suddenly cleared minds was of the brick-shitting sort.

Ghouls are unclean, since they feast on the dead or on bits of the dead and get exposed to all sorts of filth and disease. Conveniently, they're immune to infection and poison, but wild ones like these weren't terribly worried about spreading such things around. Their fingernails—which should probably be classified as claws—are coated with all sorts of virulent shit. One scratch would probably spell a death sentence without a source of high-powered antibiotics nearby. Of course, if a ghoul is trying to open you up with its claws, the likelihood of you living long enough to die by disease is small.

Back in Arizona, there was a small group—or I should say a shroud—of ghouls that had learned how to blend in well with the population. They were incredibly handy lads to have around, because they made bodies disappear and cleaned up scenes that would be difficult to explain to local authorities. Most paranormal communities rely upon such shrouds, for obvious reasons—they're key to keeping humans oblivious and believing that the only predators out there are other humans. Antoine and his boys drove around in a refrigerated truck and were able to pass for human, as long as they didn't get too hungry and kept their claws trimmed. They were also quite scrupulous about waiting for people to die on their own before eating their bodies.

These ghouls weren't in Antoine's class, however. If Antoine's shroud went to Harvard, this shroud was illiterate. Savage, gray-skinned, black-toothed, and covered in viscera, they looked only too willing to kill their food if the reaper couldn't do it for them.

"Take the scythe," I told Granuaile. "I will throw them to you off-balance. Finish them or else get out of the way."

"Ready," she puffed, and nodded at me. She looked ready to hurl; the smell of death and sulfur was inescapable. But she could handle the scythe; I'd been training her primarily in the quarterstaff, and she could adapt some of those moves.

I approached the shroud, wagering that since dead bodies rarely fought back, they'd be rather unskilled fighters that depended largely on their strength and claws to win the day. There were eight of them, though, and I doubted they would politely wait their turns to take me on one at a time. The wood flooring that concealed the demons from Amber also cut me off from drawing any more power; I had to fuel everything on what I had left in my bear charm. Perhaps a gambit was in order.

The laws of Druidry tend to frown on binding animated creatures, and it's impossible to bind synthetics and difficult to mess with iron. But apart from that, anything goes. The flooring wasn't nailed down—it was simply plywood sheets atop the dirt. I created a binding between the middle of one sheet and the denim jeans of a body halfway up the stack on the far wall. Normally this would make both the jeans and the plywood fly to meet each other, but since the body wearing the jeans was crushed underneath so many others and couldn't budge, only the plywood was free to move. Once I energized the binding, the plywood flew up and back to the wall and, functioning like a giant bookend, mowed down a couple of ghouls on the way, though without doing them much harm. More important, it left some exposed earth, where I could access more energy.

I stepped into the space, felt the earth replenish me, and

set myself in an aikido stance. The shroud of ghouls saw the challenge and charged me.

Not for the first time, I wished ghouls were truly undead, like vampires. If that were the case, I could simply unbind them back to their component elements. But ghouls were living creatures, a human variant now mutated into a dead end, har de har har. Back when I was a much younger man—in the second century or so—an idiot wizard somewhere in Arabia had created the first *ghul* by summoning a demon to possess a poor young man. The demon had a taste for necrotic flesh and grew stronger by it, forcing the host to gorge on bodies that the wizard provided. Eventually the wizard realized he'd made a horrible mistake—perhaps because he was getting tired of procuring bodies—and exorcised the demon. He didn't realize that the man was forever changed, despite the exorcism. When the wizard went to kill the man—for dead men tell no tales—he presumed him as weak as any human, only to discover that the man was quite strong indeed. Said man instead killed the wizard and escaped. Continuing to hunger for dead flesh, the man noticed that his skin was turning gray. He soon realized that if he fed that hunger on a steady basis—defiled graves and feasted on what he found—he could maintain a normal appearance and even enjoy strength beyond that of ordinary humans. His abilities—and his curse—got passed down once he married and had children. His kids were perfectly normal until they hit puberty, when they began wasting away and turning gray. At that point Daddy took them to a cemetery and said, "Here, kids—what you need is a nice corpse snack. Clotted blood! Om nom nom!"

All ghouls were descended from that common ancestor, but this particular branch of the family had clearly decided to throw in their lot with the demons that created them. They weren't making any effort to appear human—or to charge me with a modicum of respect, considering that I'd just taken out a reaper. Their tactics seemed confined to run, leap at my throat, and roar at me.

Aikido is a discipline ideally suited to redirecting energy and using the opponent's momentum in your favor, and it includes a training set called taninzudori, in which one practices against multiple attackers. I'd found it a refreshing twentieth-century adaptation of older styles. The ghouls, therefore, found themselves thrown or spun awkwardly behind me, where Granuaile was waiting with the scythe. Though the weapon is somewhat unwieldy, it tends to deliver mortal blows, which Granuaile distributed quickly. The last three, seeing what had happened to the rest of the shroud, reconsidered their charge and slowed down. They began to spread out in a half circle.

Meanwhile, behind me, the unbridled panic of the other carnival goers was subsiding just enough for them to start shouting questions, since they had seen us kill some bad guys and assumed we must have all the answers.

"What's going on? Can you get us out of here? What are those things? Don't you have a gun?"

I didn't know how any of this would be explained to the survivors—somehow I doubted they'd believe it was a pocket of swamp gas—but first I had to ensure that there would *be* survivors. And I also needed to find the portal that the demons had used to get here. So far I hadn't spotted it, but I hadn't had the luxury of time to look around either.

I didn't want to go on the attack, because it would leave my back open and they were set now, so I hawked up something juicy and spit at the one on my right. It landed right on his forehead, and he promptly lost his ghoulish composure. It wasn't that he was grossed out; ghouls find far fouler substances than sputum to be quite tasty. He simply knew an insult when it smacked wetly on his face. Enraged, he lunged at me, and I tossed him at the one on the left, sending them both tumbling. That left the ghoul in the center all alone for a few seconds with no backup. I charged him and shoved my fingers into his eyes. He scratched me deeply on either side of my rib cage, burning cuts I'd have to work hard to heal, but he backed off and would never see the coup de grâce coming. I grabbed one of his arms and whipped him around so that my back was to the wall of bodies, then kicked him in the chest so that he was staggering backward, where Granuaile could easily finish him. I backpedaled at the approach of the other two, who had disentangled and were coming now.

Peripherally, I saw that Granuaile had dispatched the blinded ghoul and was also advancing, coming up behind the others as Oberon bounded forward to take advantage. He nipped at the heels of the one on my left, which sent him sprawling and allowed Granuaile to catch up and end him. The last one leapt at me and I dropped onto my back and tucked my knees against my chest, catching him on my feet and then kicking him up and over my head. It threw him into the pile of bodies against the wall. He made a wet impact noise and then crunched down headfirst onto the blood-soaked floorboards. Not a kill shot, but it dazed him to the point where Granuaile could hustle over and eviscerate him. Then she dropped the scythe, exhausted.

Ragged cheers and cries of relief rose up from the Needle Gate. There were perhaps twenty people crying and clasping hands while thanking their gods and me for deliverance. I smiled and waved at them once before they all died: The

Needle Gate exploded and perforated them in at least a hundred different places. Many of the needles passed completely through the people who had been stuck on the barbs of the gate and went on to sink into the flesh of people in the next rank. None of the needles reached us on the far end of the room; they'd shot off to either side or punctured the body of some hapless victim. We flinched and gasped and only then saw the cause of the explosion.

It was the demon barker, now free of his stilts and stalking toward us dramatically to imbue his wee stature with menace. He still wore his bowler hat, but it was pushed back enough to see that his eyes were glowing orange. "You two stay back here," I murmured. "He's going to have hellfire." Oberon and Granuaile agreed, and I ran forward to close the distance between us and get to that bare patch of earth. There was no time to create bindings to remove any more boards, and I needed to engage him a safe distance away from my vulnerable companions.

He saw what I intended and rushed to prevent it, acting on the premise that you deny your opponents what they want. With a roar, he shed his human skin. The red waistcoat, the bowler hat, the entire wee man, turned to bloody mist as the demon's preferred form burst out. What we then had was a tall, pale, skinny monstrosity with bony thorns all over it. But the lack of muscle tone did not correlate to a lack of strength or an inability to throw a punch. I ducked under the first one, thinking I'd scramble on my hands and knees if necessary, but a sharp thorn from its wrist shot over my back and gashed a deep groove there. It seared my flesh, and when I reared back in agony, the demon connected with a left, the spikes on its knuckles tearing holes in my cheek, sending me spinning.

Hellfire bloomed and shot forth from the barker's hands and he laughed, thinking he had already won. But his punches had been more effective. My cold iron aura shrugged off hellfire, but I screamed and rolled anyway, right toward the open patch of earth. He let me do so but followed close, just as I had hoped. Once I felt the earth underneath me and saw that he touched the earth too, I pointed my right hand at him and said, "*Dhófaidh!*"—Irish for "Burn!"

Had I been standing, I would have collapsed, because that's what casting Cold Fire does to a guy. It kills demons 100 percent of the time, but the trade-off is that it takes some time to work and weakens the caster, no matter how much magic is flowing through the earth. Brighid of the Tuatha Dé Danann—a fire goddess, among other things—had given it to me some years ago to aid my fight against her brother, Aenghus Óg, who had allied himself with hell. For the next few hours, I'd have trouble fighting off a hamster, much less a greater demon.

"So what's all this, then?" I asked, twitching a hand to indicate the room. "Upward mobility for you?"

Scowling because I had not obligingly burned to a crisp, the demon bent and wrapped long, sticklike fingers with too many joints entirely around my neck. He began to crush my windpipe, and all I could manage by way of defense was a feeble Muppet flail. I hoped the Cold Fire spell would take hold sooner rather than later. Its delay could well kill me. The demon grinned at my weakness.

"Yesss. Months have I prepared. Small harvests in small towns."

I couldn't breathe, and my vision was going black at the edges as his fingers continued to constrict my throat. Why wouldn't he die already?

"But now I provide a bounty for hell. I will harvest more souls than—" He broke off and his eyes widened. He released me and I sucked in a desperate breath of foul air. He clutched at his chest and said, "What—" before he convulsed, coughed blue flames, then sizzled to a sort of frosty ash and crumbled on top of me, burned from within by Cold Fire.

Seeing that there were no more immediate threats to her person, Granuaile vomited. I felt close to the edge of doing the same. I was taking deep breaths to recover from choking, and the smell really was overwhelming.

Oberon trotted over and licked the side of my head. <Atticus, you're still bleeding.>

Yeah, so a wet willy was exactly what I needed, thanks.

<You're welcome. Can we go now?>

The way was clear through the Needle Gate. I didn't know if the Anchovy Gate was one-way or not. I had to believe that police would be arriving soon; there had to be some response from all the spectators who had fled after I'd killed the imp in the hallway. While I might have welcomed their help earlier in getting people to safety, now there was no one left to save. All they would do was get in the way of the work I still had to do.

Not yet, Oberon.

I sent a message to Amber through my bond to the earth: //Demons slain below / Two imps remain above / Search for portal beginning//

//Harmony// was the only reply.

//Query: Collapse tunnel between this chamber and surface if it is clear of people?//

Amber's answer was to cave in the hallway. That would buy us some time.

"We need to find the portal to hell," I said. "There has to be one around here somewhere. I don't care how dodgy carnivals are; reapers don't travel with them."

<I don't see anything on the walls.>

Granuaile, looking up, said, "It's not on the ceiling. It's probably underneath one of these boards."

I didn't have the energy to lift them all up, and I wanted this over as soon as possible, so I bound each sheet to one of the side walls and sent them flying. We found the portal close to the Needle Gate, near the spot where Granuaile had played dodge-the-scythe with the reaper.

Hellish arcane symbols traced in salt formed a circle a bit bigger than a standard manhole. Inside this circle was nested an iron disc, which was itself etched with symbols similar to those on the ground, but it covered up the inner halves of the salt symbols, neatly bisecting them.

"Clever," I said, leaning on Granuaile a bit for support as I inspected the setup. "It's still active but dormant while the iron shorts out the spell. Remove the iron cover and the portal flares open. Drop it back down and the mojo fades. They can get their people in and out in seconds, and Amber doesn't think it's worrisome enough to call me. No wonder they were able to keep this on the down low."

"Keep what, exactly?" Granuaile asked. "What was this all about?"

"Souls. The demon barker wanted to move up in the underworld, and this was his scheme. Make people willingly choose hell and then kill them."

"But how could they possibly get away with it? I mean, look at all those poor people. Nobody noticed?"

"This was likely the first time they tried it on a large scale. On the heaven side of the tent, they have an imp slapping a memory charm on people as they walk out. Keeps them from searching for their friends when they don't come out, and when they finally realize they've lost their friends, their memories will tell them they couldn't possibly have lost them here. By the time missing-persons reports actually get filed, the carnival is on its way out of town. The ghouls would have stayed in this chamber and eaten until all the evidence was gone, and you know how it goes—no body, no crime. The mass disappearance would get explained as an alien abduction before somebody suspected a mass murder underground."

"Well, we're not just going to leave them all here, are we?"

I surveyed the ruin and shook my head. "No. Their families deserve closure. The elemental can move their bodies to the surface for us when the coast is clear."

"Okay." Granuaile returned her attention to the portal. "So if you lifted that cover right now, we could jump into hell?"

"Or something could jump out, yes. And it would drain a lot of power from the earth while it was open. We can destroy it pretty easily, though."

Binding like to like using the energy of the earth, I fused all the salt crystals so that they lifted from the ground and met above the iron cover, forming a ball. I let it go and it dropped onto the cover. The salt had rested in shallow troughs traced by a finger, so I erased those as well by smoothing out the ground. I checked the circle in the magical spectrum to make sure it was safe before moving the cover. There was no telltale glow of magic anywhere around it, and the cover could be broken down and reabsorbed into the earth.

"Kick the cover a bit for me?" I asked. I doubted I could make it budge in my condition. Binding spells, by comparison, were simple, since they used Amber's energy, not my own. Granuaile pushed the iron disc a few inches with her foot, and the ground underneath remained satisfyingly solid. The ball of bound salt on top rolled off. Satisfied that the situation couldn't get any worse, I informed Amber that the portal was destroyed and asked her to create a path to the surface for us. As we watched, the earth itself created a stairway leading up from the base of the nearest wall.

I cast camouflage on all three of us, since appearing dressed in blood in the midst of a carnival might incite some comment. We emerged behind a row of gaming booths, and the stairway closed behind us. We took a moment to reacquaint ourselves with what fresh air smelled like. The voice of the carnie running the milk-bottle booth was taunting new marks.

"Be right back," I said, and left Granuaile and Oberon to check on the tent, though I couldn't muster much of a pace. Still, I saw that the hulk at the entrance was gone and that someone had called the police. The exit was manned by officers too, and there was no trace of the little imp girl or the people inside who'd served as the bearded lady, the three-armed man, and so on. The police clearly hadn't found any bodies yet or they would have been doing more than simply closing the exhibit. Any report the police received would have been for the imp whose neck I'd snapped—a mundane affair as far as they knew. No one who had seen the supernatural had survived except for us. The imps who'd escaped would have to be hunted down as a matter of principle, but they didn't have the power to reopen a portal by themselves. We could afford time to recuperate and think of how best to proceed.

I returned to Granuaile and Oberon behind the game booths and dissolved our camouflage, since we were alone, and if someone spied us, they wouldn't see the blood right away in the dark. Granuaile was squatting down and staring at the ground, arms resting on her thighs and hands clasped between her knees. All around us, oblivious carnival goers continued to seek entertainment. The lights and sounds of the midway, bright and alluring before, now grated on my nerves. We couldn't be amused by those rides anymore. I squatted next to her in the same position.

"I told you once what choosing this life could mean for you personally, but those were just words," I said. "Now you know."

Granuaile nodded jerkily. "Yes, I do." She was trembling all over, coming down from the adrenaline and perhaps entering shock now that the enormity of what had happened was settling in.

"But you did well in there," I said. "Thanks for the assist."

"Same to you." Granuaile's lip shook and a tear leaked out of her eye. "I didn't have time to think. My mom could have been in that room."

"Yes. I'm relieved she wasn't. Great time to go on a cruise."

She wiped at her cheek and sniffed. "But somebody's mom is in there. Probably some people I know too."

"That's most likely true. But we couldn't have saved any more than we did. You do realize that we definitely saved some people tonight by shutting that down? Probably hundreds, or even thousands, if they planned to keep doing this in other places."

"Yeah. But I can't feel good about that now. I'm thinking of all those we didn't save."

"Understood." Oberon moved closer to Granuaile, dipped his head under her hand, and flipped it up, inviting her to pet him. She hugged him around the neck and cried on him a little bit, and he bore it in silence—or at least silence as far as my apprentice was concerned.

<She doesn't remember hitting me down there, does she?>

I don't think so. Probably best not to bring it up. You can see that she loves you. And so do I.

<That so?>

You know it is. But to erase any doubts, I'm going to see if we can arrange a liaison. An amorous rendezvous.

Oberon's tail began to wag. <Are you talking about a black-coated poodle?>

We will call her Noche. There will be sausage and occasion to frolic.

Oberon got so excited about this news that he barked, startling Granuaile. She reared back and he turned his head, licking her face.

"What! Oberon!" She toppled backward and hit her head on the back of the gaming booth. "Ow!" Then she laughed as Oberon swooped in and slobbered on her some more. The laughing, however, proved a gateway to sobs as some of the shock wore off, and the restrained tears she had shed earlier gave way to a more cathartic release.

<Extreme sadness alert, Atticus! We need an emergency snuggle, stat!> Oberon folded his legs and laid his giant head in Granuaile's lap. She petted him with her left hand and bent her head down over him, dropping tears into his fur as I sat back from my squat to rest against the booth wall beside her, taking her right hand. She gripped it tightly.

"I'm sorry," she said between sobs. "There were just so many of them."

"No, it's fine. It really is. I understand. And I would understand if you'd rather rethink this and do something else."

"No," she said quickly, and looked up at me, shaking her head. "No. This is what I want to do. I want to save people and save the earth too. More than ever."

"Okay."

She nodded at me. "Okay." She let go of my hand and returned to petting and crying on Oberon, and we both waited patiently for that storm to run its course, knowing that there would be calm and recovery soon enough and, with it, burgeoning growth.

One way or another, dogs make everything better.

Except my fear of Kansas. I still have that.

gold dust druid

***

This story, narrated by Atticus, takes place during Granuaile's training period, after the events of "The Demon Barker of Wheat Street."

anyone who's had more than one child—or more than one pet, for that matter—knows all about the grief and stress that comes with having multiple demands on their time. Imagine being the only Druid that the world's elementals can call on for the better part of two millennia. There would, admittedly, be long stretches where everything was just fine, followed by intense periods where everything happened at once. Training a new Druid in secret was like that—long stretches of peaceful routine interrupted by days of time-consuming errands. When our normal errands were compounded by requests from elementals in New Zealand and Zimbabwe and a sly, half-drawled demand from Coyote—all on the same day—Granuaile overheard me mutter that it was as bad as the Gold Rush and asked me about it later, when we had returned to our routine of mental and physical training followed by relaxed evenings in front of the fire pit.

"What happened during the Gold Rush, Atticus?" she asked, as the logs popped and sent orange sparks into brief arcs of glory. We were having barbecue, smoked brisket and baked beans washed down with some cold beers. I told Oberon to stay away from the beans, to save my nose later.

"A bunch of idiots were into summoning demons at the time, and I had to pop around the world to deal with them when I was supposed to be hiding."

"You mean like covens summoning hordes of hellions, or what?"

"No, individuals in different places. And if they're summoning them, trading their souls or whatever for a favor, and then banishing them, that's usually fine and none of my business. Elementals inform me that something's being pulled through the planes just in case it gets out of hand, and sometimes it does."

"Out of hand how?"

"Well, you remember what happened in Kansas not so long ago?"

"I could hardly forget those ghouls and all those poor people. The smell of it still haunts me."

Oberon, my Irish wolfhound, with whom I have a mental bond, paused briefly from devouring his barbecue to chime in. <Yeah! Ghouls and demons smell really bad! Like, way worse than mustard.>

"The danger to the earth wasn't so much the ghouls— I mean, they were certainly a danger to the people they were killing, but not a danger to Gaia. The danger was the demon who'd opened that portal to hell and was draining the earth to keep it open. When the demons get loose, they almost always want to bring as many of their buddies along as they can to party with them, and that is without exception at Gaia's expense."

"So demons got loose in the mid-nineteenth century?"

"Just one. But a really old and powerful one."

<Was it worse than Gozer the Gozerian, who took the form of the Stay Puft Marshmallow Man?>

"Yes, Oberon, much worse than Gozer the Gozerian."

"Excellent. Do we get a story for dessert, then?" Granuaile asked. "It sounds like this will be most instructive."

"All right. After we do the dishes and wrap up the left-overs."

<I like how you assume there will be leftovers, Atticus. It's so optimistic of you. I'm ready for my third plate of brisket. Or you could just plop the rest on my plate and I'll gnaw on it at my leisure.>

The trouble began in Palermo, Sicily, in the middle of January 1848, when a Qabbalist summoned a demon to aid him in fomenting revolution against the Bourbon king of the Two Sicilies—

<Wait, Atticus, is the Bourbon king of the Two Sicilies like the Sausage King of Chicago?>

"No, Oberon. It means he was just one of several different kings from the House of Bourbon that ruled some European countries at the time. Monarchies were dying out and facing plenty of opposition in 1848—lots of people wanted consti-tutions and an end to feudal systems—but they weren't en-tirely gone."

<So his name is just Bourbon? He doesn't have anything to do with manipulating the bourbon market, thumbing his nose at common decency, or destroying the livers of an entire nation?>

"Bourbon was his name, not his game."

<Huh. Well, that's a missed storytelling opportunity, Atticus. I'm not impressed. One star.>

"What? You didn't even let me finish my first sentence!"

<That's more than most books get these days. Lots of people post reviews before a book is even written.>

"What if there are poodles in this story, Oberon? You will have given one star to frolicsome, poufy poodles from another age."

<You mean . . . *vintage* poodles? There are vintage Italian poodles in this story?>

"Let me continue without interruption and you'll find out."

As I was saying, the Sicilian rebellion had a bit of help from a demon summoning that allowed Sicily to remain free until May of 1849, when Ferdinand II—the Bourbon king in question—reconquered it. I never bothered to go there, because the demon had been dismissed successfully and I didn't travel through Tír na nÓg unless I absolutely had to. But I traced the trouble back there later on, to a Qabbalist named Stefano Pastore, who fled Sicily in May and came to California, having heard about the discovery of gold in the Sierra Nevada. Like so many others, he thought he'd find his fortune there, picking up gold nuggets off the ground as the first few prospectors in the area were able to do.

But by the time he got there in the fall of 1849, the easy

grab-'n'-go gold was all gone. You had to dig a shaft or pan for it, and there was plenty of competition. Stefano Pastore didn't have the patience for such labor. Once the snow fell in the Sierra Nevada, he spent the winter in San Francisco, watching the miners who struck it rich burn away their fortunes in gambling or grow them by investing in large chunks of real estate or business ventures. He didn't think them particularly brilliant or deserving of their fortunes: They'd just been lucky enough to get there first. That thought festered and convinced him that working hard for his fortune was a sucker's game. So when spring arrived in 1850 and the miners headed for the hills again with picks and pans, he stayed behind to make his own luck, with the help of a pet demon. He probably thought, What the hell, my last summoning gave Sicilians sixteen months of freedom under the rule of Ruggero Settimo, and I could use sixteen months or more of being ridiculously rich.

So he got his candles and salt and all the other paraphernalia he needed for a major summoning and carefully inscribed his circles and wards on the floor and waited for the proper phase of the moon to spin around on April 26. He completed the summoning just fine—I was chilling out at the southern tip of South America on that date and got the report from Sequoia, the elemental for that stretch of California coast from the Bay Area up to the Klamath Mountains.

But it wasn't long before the report stating the simple fact of the summoning became an outright request for aid. Sequoia woke me in the dead of night, in fact. //Druid required now// the call came, shuddering up my body and filtering into my consciousness. //Large demon free//

I'd been staying out of North America as much as possible

once the Old World discovered the New World, because it quite frankly depressed me. Gripped by the unshakable conviction that they were perfectly justified in doing so—that, in fact, it was all their god's plan somehow and he'd be pleased by their behavior—Europeans were busy wiping out Native Americans and enslaving Africans and doing whatever they could to exclude all nonwhite people from sharing in the riches to be gained by exploiting the continent's abundant natural resources. I would have been in a constant rage if I had to deal with that level of stupid cruelty on a daily basis—and there was nothing I could do about it if I didn't want Aenghus Óg to find me and deprive the earth of its only protector or get myself killed some other way while trying to protect humanity from itself—so my best option for much of the eighteenth and nineteenth centuries was to chill out where other people were not.

Sequoia's call forced me to shift into the redwoods near San Francisco and witness the great American Gold Rush. Once I got into town, I noticed immediately that I wasn't dressed properly, and so did everyone else: It was the rare individual who wore a sword instead of a six-shooter. But I'd worry about blending in later.

I made my way to the boardinghouse where Stefano Pastore had taken a room. Sequoia directed me to where the portal in the planes had been opened. She could tell me the equivalent spot on the earth where the drain on her resources had occurred, but I discovered that it was a three-story building and had to search the rooms on each level until I found the gory aftermath on the third floor.

Stefano Pastore's body lay sprawled in a pool of his own blood, his throat crushed and his blue swollen tongue hanging out of his mouth, eyes staring at the ceiling. The blood originated from a bonus and unnecessary disembowelment, considering his crushed airway. It had congealed and darkened now, the oxygen all gone, and stained the ring of salt he lay in. There was another, smaller ring nearby, into which he had summoned the demon. This was the setup diagrammed in *The Greater Key of Solomon*, albeit with some minor changes. He was supposed to be protected in one ring of salt while the demon was supposed to be contained in the other, but both rings had been deliberately broken by the toe of someone's boot. That spurred plenty of questions. Had it been Pastore's own boot? If so, he'd win an award for one of the most elaborate ritual suicides in history. But if it hadn't been Pastore, who had broken the rings and gotten away with it? There weren't any other bodies in the room. So the demon either purposely let the person live or he possessed the person. I was betting on the latter, because so-called "large demons" are rarely up for buddy capers with a random human. Tying up victims with their own intestines is much more their idea of a good time. And besides, demons can't walk around without people noticing the smell. The only way they can pass undetected is to do what we saw them do in Kansas: possess a human, or animate a person's corpse, and let the human façade disguise the demon's true nature. And as long as that possessed human wore boots or walked on a floor separated from the earth, Sequoia wouldn't be able to pinpoint the demon's location for me.

I needed more information, but there wasn't a convenient journal lying around in Pastore's hand to tell me which demon he'd summoned. Which meant I'd have to wait for the demon to start whipping up some chaos and try to catch up.

There were two problems with that plan: One, San Fran-

cisco was already pretty chaotic without demonic help—
there were sixty thousand men and two thousand women at
the time—and, two, none of those people would automatically report anything strange to me. Nobody knew who I was.
But they would report to Sheriff Jack Coffee Hays, San Francisco's first official sheriff, who had just been elected three and
a half weeks earlier, a barkeep told me.

The barkeep was quick to add, as he poured me a shot of
rye, that Jack Coffee Hays had seen some shit. He'd been a
Texas Ranger and then a colonel in the Mexican-American
War and had somehow survived more than his fair share of
fights. He wasn't easily impressed.

Approaching him for help in this matter would take some
finesse. If I walked up to him as I was—barefoot, in home-
spun clothes I had made myself—he'd dismiss me immediately. To be taken seriously I'd need a new outfit, something
that said I had plenty of money and therefore deserved respect. Nothing made one so respectable as the appearance of
wealth, and in almost any country, in any century, clothes
were the easiest way to achieve that appearance. Except finding such clothing in San Francisco at that moment would be
problematic. I didn't have time to wait for something be-
spoke. I needed something much sooner, and since I wanted
someone else to find Pastore's body and report it to the sheriff before I met him, I took the opportunity to return to the
redwoods and shift planes into Central Park in New York
City. New York had a ready-made clothing industry by then,
and hundreds if not thousands of tailors were doing alterations in the city. Many of them were Irish immigrants, in fact,
because the potato famine was in progress, and many of them
were working out of their homes for next to nothing. Once I
had my basics from a men's shop and stopped at a barber's to

make myself presentable, I spent a lovely couple of hours with the Flanagan family while Mrs. Flanagan worked on my alterations. I paid her nine times the going rate to set aside her other work, and I brought in a week's worth of groceries besides and a bottle of the Irish for when they needed some fortitude down the road. I traded stories and laughs with Mr. Flanagan and his wee boys, and every one of us was happier and richer for the experience when I bid them farewell.

"Time-out," Granuaile said. "Wasn't there something you could have done about the potato famine?"

"That was the first I'd heard of it, honestly, five years in progress by that time. It wasn't something an elemental would have shared with me. The Irish had grown dependent on a monoculture of potatoes, a mold arrived to feast on that monoculture, and that's why we should always grow a wide variety of cultivars. But of course Americans are ignoring that lesson now and growing a single potato for all of its French fries. French Frymageddon is coming, I promise you. It would have come already except for the tons of pesticides they're using to keep the crop viable."

<I've always appreciated that you feed me a wide variety of meats, Atticus,> Oberon said. <But now I understand that eating the same thing is not only boring, it's dangerous. I'd better not have any more of this brisket tonight.>

"You're full, aren't you?"

<Yeah, that too.>

The first thing I did when I returned to San Francisco was visit the impressive bookstore of Mr. Still on Portsmouth

Square to look up something, and then I took a room at the American Hotel for an indefinite stay. Fragarach was stowed in the manager's tall floor safe, which contained quite a few rifles in addition to the expected collections of wealth. I was careful to wear my new pair of uncomfortable shoes to prevent any of the Fae from tracking me via the effervescent joys of happy plant life—normally not a consideration, but my plane shifts in and out and in again to San Francisco had probably alerted Aenghus Óg that I was interested in something near there. All he had to do was inquire of Sequoia if something was wrong and she'd tell him about the escaped demon. Either he or one of his minions could very well show up at Stefano Pastore's murder scene and begin the hunt for me even as I hunted for this demon—which meant the quicker I resolved this, the better. But horrors loosed out of hell never behave in such a way as to make my life easier.

I arrived in gloves to hide my tattoos; a burgundy satin waistcoat with a gold pocket watch ticking away inside; a ridiculous tie with a sunburst pin; all covered by charcoal-gray pinstripe coat and pants and topped with a bowler. My hair was straightened and greased and combed into a reddish oil slick, and I made sure to wax my mustache and coo approvingly at my bristling sideburns. In lieu of my sword I carried a cane, which would do as a short stave if it came to fighting but which gave the appearance that I was nursing an old injury like a trick knee.

That's what I looked like when I stepped into Pastore's murder scene for the second time, but there were two men standing over the body, muttering about how damn strange it was. I froze in the doorway and gasped to draw their attention, but added, "Oh, bollocks," to signal immediately that I wasn't American. "I'm too late."

The two men rounded on me, one of them dropping his hand to his gun. He relaxed when he saw one hand on my cane, the other clutched in a fist over my heart, as if I was shocked by the scene.

"Who are you?"

I dropped my left hand on top of my right over the handle of the cane and gave a name befitting my disguise as an English toff, voice stiff as if I'd been laundered with the queen's own starch: "Algernon Percy, Fourth Duke of Northumberland, expert on the occult and much too late to stop Mr. Pastore there from doing something terminally stupid." Algernon Percy really was the name of the Duke of Northumberland at the time, though I doubt he looked much like me beyond the fact that we were both rather pale, and he certainly was no expert on the occult. But should the sheriff take the trouble to verify the name of the current duke, at least he wouldn't catch me that way. I'd lifted the name straight out of a recent history of England's military exploits that I found in Mr. Still's establishment, working on the theory that officers were often noblemen, and, sure enough, the good duke was an admiral or some such.

"You know this man?"

"I do. And who might you be, good sir?"

"Sheriff Jack Hays," the man with a star on his coat said, his voice carrying a bit of a Texas drawl. He had a broad forehead and eyes like coal, which glittered with a hint of diamond in them. His hat was in his hand, and I noted a thick wave of dark hair sweeping about his ears and a square jaw to hang his beard on. He kept his neck shaven, though at this point he had a day or two's growth on it and it looked as if it would fight with a square of sandpaper to see who was rougher. He nodded over to the other man, a clean-shaven, sunburned lad with straw-colored hair, who wore a star on his coat as well. "This here's my deputy, Kasey Princell."

"It's my very good fortune to meet you both. I do hope I can be of some service to you, since I've traveled around the earth chasing after this fellow."

"What can you tell us about him?" Deputy Princell asked. He wasn't from Texas; the vowels and inflection were different, had more of a lilt than a drawl to them, and that was the beginning of my education in American Southern accents. I found out later that he was from eastern Kentucky, in the Appalachians.

"He's an Italian occultist, and I don't mind telling you I've had a devil of a time finding him—if you'll excuse the pun."

The lawmen squinted at me, which I supposed meant they hadn't caught the pun at all. "I'm not exactly sure what you mean by that," Hays said. "I've seen my share of dead men, y'understand, but I ain't never seen nothin' like this." He looked down at the body. "Choked to death an' then his guts pulled out. Or maybe it was t'other way around. Overkill either way. And then there's all these things on the floor. Salt and candles and whatnot. Looks like some kinda magical fixin's if I had to guess. I dunno. Would you know anythin' about that?"

"I would. I would indeed. May I come in?"

"Sure. Just don't step in any o' this mess."

"I wouldn't dream of it." I moved forward and surveyed the scene, pretending to take it all in for the first time. "Hmm. Yes. A bit diabolical, eh?"

"I dunno. Who do y'think mighta had it in for Mr. Pastore?"

"Well, we are clearly looking for whoever broke the circles

of binding and protection and gave the demon a free shot at the deceased."

"What now?" Hays said.

"Did you just say 'demon' or—Jack, what the hell is going on?" Deputy Princell said.

"Hell is precisely what is going on here, Deputy," I replied. "You see the evidence of it before your eyes."

"Maybe you better explain what you're seein' that we're not," Hays said.

"These circles you see here, the Hebrew and the Greek, the black candles, the silver dagger—what you called 'magical fixin's'—all of it was used to summon a demon. And it was a successful summoning."

"Are you bein' serious right now?" Deputy Princell said. "An honest-to-God demon?"

"Typically, demons are neither honest nor of God, but, yes, Deputy, I am deadly serious. Mr. Pastore's body can attest to how deadly serious this sort of magic is. And I would point out that I would hardly journey all the way from England at great expense for the thrill of playing a small joke on a pair of complete strangers. I am telling you the absolute truth as I know it, gentlemen. This man summoned a demon, which escaped when someone broke the circles there and there, allowing the demon to do precisely what you see before you."

"Well," Hays said, "if we assume that's all true—which is a damn big chaw to fit in my mouth, Mr. Percy, I don't mind tellin' ya—then that leaves us with some questions."

Deputy Princell snorted. "Yeah, questions like 'Are you shitting me?' and 'Why would anyone think summoning a demon was a good idea?'"

A flicker of a smile passed across the sheriff's face at the deputy's comment, a brief meteor of amusement streaking across the sky. But then he focused on me, glittering dark eyes promising a reckoning if I couldn't answer to his satisfaction.

"Who besides you would have known this guy was summoning demons, Mr. Percy? And where is that person now? And, more important, where is the damn demon you say we have runnin' around?"

I liked what I saw in Jack Hays. Give him a problem and he wanted to solve it, not worry about whether it was impossible. He was going to try first to see if it really was impossible. Of course, his first question had an edge to it. I was already a suspect.

"I assure you I have no idea who was responsible. But the demon in question has probably possessed him, since you see only one body here and not two. That possessed person will, I guarantee, be sowing chaos in your city. And when you find him and confront him, the demon may fight, or it may leave that host and possess someone else, leaving his victim bewildered at why the sheriff wants to arrest him."

Deputy Princell shook his head. "Psssh. Sheriff, I've heard some bullshit in my day, but this is the biggest pile I ever heard."

The sheriff's eyes slid sideways to his deputy for a moment, then back to me. "Maybe it is and maybe it ain't. Look, Mr. Percy, I appreciate you comin' by. We gotta clean this all up. Is there a place I can find you if I need you later?"

"Certainly. I'm staying at the American Hotel. If you arrest someone who can't remember the recent past, please do let me know. By tracing their paths we may be able to figure out where the demon is heading next."

"Right. Thank you." He'd dismissed me at that point as a wealthy eccentric, a crackpot with nothing better to do than tilt at windmills; he was swayed not only by his deputy but by a general disbelief in the fantastic. That was fine. When the bodies started piling up, he'd come find me and point me in the right direction. That's all I wanted. I lowered my head slightly and put my fingertips to the brim of my bowler.

"Good day, sir." I returned to the hotel, ordered tea in the lobby like a proper Victorian subject of the queen, and opened up a copy of *The Pickwick Papers*, which I'd purchased from Mr. Still's shop. Dickens' turgid prose is often painful to read, but I was just beginning to be amused by the appearance of a cockney character in chapter ten when Deputy Princell came to fetch me, apparently against his will.

"The sheriff would like to see you, Mr. Percy," he said, his face communicating that he thought the sheriff was making a mistake. I put Dickens down and grabbed my cane.

"I'm at your service."

The deputy, grinding his jaw the whole way and deferring all my questions to the sheriff, led me a couple of blocks north to a saloon and gambling house, which proved to be the dominant business model in the city. Exactly the sort of place a demon would find delightful. I smelled the carnage before I saw it: that sickly coppery smell of spilled blood with a top note of sulfurous fumes. I wrinkled my nose and the deputy saw it.

"I know. Smells like somebody ripped the biggest ol' fart this side of the Mississippi and it's just gonna live there from now on like your nasty in-laws."

It occurred to me that the deputy might have some domestic issues. "I know you're a skeptic, Deputy Princell, but that is the smell of a demon."

He didn't reply, just shook his head and invited me to precede him into the saloon.

Overturned tables. Shattered mirror behind the bar and

the bottoms of broken bottles of booze, their tops shot off. Five bodies sprawled on the floor, but only shot this time, not choked or disemboweled.

A bearded man, perhaps the proprietor, stood behind the bar, in a stained white shirt with black bands around his biceps. With a bleak expression he stared at one of the bodies, as will a young person who realizes at some point that his childhood has run away and if he ever sees it again it'll only be from a distance. Sheriff Jack Hays stood on the other side of the bar and had just finished asking him a question when I stepped in, but he was getting no response. He called the man's name and snapped his fingers at him to focus his attention: "Stafford? Stafford. Hey, Bill." My arrival turned the sheriff's head.

"Ah! Mr. Percy. Maybe you can tell me if this situation here has anything to do with, uh . . . with what we discussed earlier."

"Perhaps." I joined him at the bar, ignoring the bodies, and pointed at Bill Stafford. "Can he tell us what happened?"

"I was just trying to get him to go through it again. Stafford!"

The man startled and rounded on the sheriff. "Hmm? Yes?"

Using a small amount of power stored in my bear charm, I switched my vision to the magical spectrum and saw that Stafford's aura was still entirely human. But the demon had been here, in the open; the smell attested to that.

"Tell us one more time what happened."

"Oh. Sure." He had a Texas drawl like the sheriff's, helping me get the cadence down for later use. "Well, that feller over there—the one that smells real bad—he came in a little while ago and started winnin' big on the faro table. So big, in fact, he'd drawn himself a crowd, and there were side bets goin' on and all manner of stuff. All I knew was that he was cleanin' me out and we were gonna go bust if he kept goin' on. Had my man Collins go over and say all nice 'n' polite that he oughtta take that amazing luck of his somewhere else because we couldn't afford him no more. An' that's when things got violent. He pushed Collins and told him to go spit, Collins pushed back, and then that man just picked Collins up and threw him across the room like he was a rag doll. Collins crashed into a poker game, and those men all got up to tell the guy who threw him a thing or two. Then there were guns out, and the lucky man wasn't a smart man. It was four against one, and he shoots one dead and the others unload on him. But even though he had three bullets in him and got some more besides, he kept firing, one shot in the heart to each poker player, and only then did he fall down and die."

"I see. And the other people in the bar?" I asked.

"They all ran out when the shooting started. I notice they took a bunch of money with them."

"When did it start to smell in here?"

Stafford frowned. "I think it was when the faro player died."

"And who was the last to leave?"

"Collins."

The sheriff spoke up. "Your man who got thrown across the room and crashed into a table?"

"Yeah. Thought he was unconscious or maybe even dead, but he kinda jerked awake and staggered out, laughing like it was all funny. Didn't say a word to me. I guess he quit. Wouldn't blame him for wanting a new job after that."

"That's him, Sheriff," I said, and he raised an eyebrow at me. "We need to find this Collins. That's who we want."

"He didn't do nothin' except what I told him to," Bill Stafford said.

"What does Collins look like, Bill?" the sheriff asked. "We just want to ask him some questions."

"Tall. Six foot. Green waistcoat, brown hair, blue eyes, and one o' them funny Irish caps, you know the kind I mean? The ones that are flat on top."

"Does he have a gun?"

"Naw. He'd move in close if he had to throw somebody out, then punch him out cold before he could draw."

"Did he go right or left out of the door?"

"Left, I think."

"All right." The sheriff turned to Kasey Princell. "Deputy, I'd appreciate it if you could round up some help and get these people sorted so Mr. Stafford can get his business going again as soon as possible. I'm going to look for Mr. Collins with Mr. Percy here."

We found Mr. Collins in an alley not one block away, moaning and vomiting in a sulfurous miasma.

"Ah, Lord a'mighty," he said, his Irish accent plain as he dragged himself to a sitting position. "I feel terrible. What's that fecking smell?"

I checked his aura: no demonic presence, just that lingering smell. He'd jumped into someone else already.

"What's the last thing you remember?" I asked him, squatting by his side.

"Sailing across the saloon when some cheeky bastard threw me. He didn't look that strong. Ugh, me back feels like shite. D'ye know where I am and how I got here?"

"A block away from the saloon," I told him, deciding it best not to tell him he'd been briefly possessed. "I don't suppose you remember seeing anyone after you got thrown?"

"No, I don't."

"All right," Sheriff Hays said, "let's get you back to the saloon." We helped Collins up and walked him back, which took some effort because he really wasn't in good shape. He'd need some rest and maybe a doctor, though doctors at that time were often more harm than help. I let the sheriff do most of the talking and wondered if the demon had abandoned Collins because of his injuries or if he was really smart enough to switch hosts while no one was looking. If he was, then Pastore hadn't summoned some low-level imp anxious for destruction but something truly dangerous. Which fit perfectly with Sequoia's alarm, but it still gave me pause.

Once we had a moment to speak freely outside, I told the sheriff, "We will most likely suffer through a few more of these imbroglios before we catch up with the beast."

He squinted at me. "Are you talkin' 'bout fights and usin' a five-dollar word?"

"Apologies. Yes. Dead people accompanied by the smell of sulfur nearby."

"Huh." Hays grimaced and spat into the street. "Somethin's been botherin' me, Mr. Percy. Still not sure I believe in all this, but just in case: Say we catch up to this demon. Then whadda we do? 'Specially if it can give a man super strength and jump from person to person?"

"We bind it and exorcise it."

"Exorcise, not exercise? You mean like with a priest?"

"No, there are other methods I'll employ."

"Am I gonna get to use these methods?"

"Unfortunately not."

"Shootin' it won't do anything?"

"As the testimony of Mr. Stafford revealed, it will do

plenty to the person it's possessed, but the demon will simply choose a new host like Mr. Collins."

"Well, how are you gonna do anything to it?"

"I'll use the utmost caution to protect others, Sheriff, but will otherwise need to keep the process a secret."

"Figured you'd say that. Mystery and unknowable crap. It's like goin' to church."

"Ha! Yes, I see what you mean. Except I won't ask you for a donation, Sheriff."

"Yeah, you'd better not. What are you going to do next?"

"I'm going to take in the city, I think. Search for the beast in some other saloons. Now that he's caused the death of five souls, he'll be hungry for more."

"I'll let you get to it, then. Let me know if you find anything."

He ducked back into the saloon to help Bill and his deputy with the crime scene, and I spun on my heel to look for new saloons. My plan was to stroll the streets and poke my head into each saloon to survey the auras of the crowd, in hopes of finding something unusual. It wasn't much of a drain on my reserves and at least I'd get to know the town that way.

Unfortunately, I found something unusual in the very first place I visited, which was so packed that I had to step inside to do a thorough job: Across the room, a faery wearing the glamour of a surly, dusty miner glowered at the other patrons, doing the same thing as I was: Searching for someone. Searching for me.

The face underneath the glamour was a familiar one. He was one of Aenghus Óg's boys, and, remarkably, he had a gun and wore gloves so that he could handle the iron. I exited with alacrity and prayed to the Morrigan that he hadn't seen me. Then I prayed there weren't any more faeries in town, or, if there were, they'd take care of the demon for me and I could simply leave.

In the meantime, I needed to hide and not do anything to draw attention. I retreated to my room with *The Pickwick Papers*, after first retrieving Fragarach from the hotel safe, and told myself it was a perfectly logical course of action to lay low for a small while. This demon was clearly a threat to humans but not, at the moment, a threat to Gaia, and I could afford to wait out the Fae and let them believe I wasn't in San Francisco. Give them a day or two or five and they'd move on.

The demon didn't move on, however. Sheriff Hays banged on my door in the middle of the night to report a new massacre in another saloon, which followed the same pattern: An incredibly lucky gambler drew plenty of attention until, suddenly, violence erupted and people died. That was food for thought, but I doubted I'd learn anything more by visiting in person, and I didn't want to leave my room yet.

"I can't help unless you know precisely where the demon is this instant, Sheriff," I told him, which earned me a clenched jaw and a glare.

Once he left, I thought about the similarity of the incidents. The greater demons found it amusing to hunt via the seven deadly sins, and this demon appeared to have a pattern: He began by appealing to greed. The anger and violence necessary to harvest the souls was a necessary end but not the means by which he led them into temptation.

I remember sitting in my room on a rather uncomfortable chair at that point and saying out loud, "Oh, shit," and putting Dickens aside. "What if it's Mammon? What if Pastore was crazy enough to summon the biblical manifestation of greed?"

And once I framed my thinking that way, I knew what I

had to do. Get out of town for a few days to throw off the Fae, sure, but I also needed to beat Mammon at his own game. I inquired at the front desk where I might be able to purchase a horse, and by dawn I was negotiating the sale of a recently captured mustang named Sally, about a hundred years before the song or the sports car came along. After breakfast I was outfitted and galloping south to round the San Francisco Bay. Once I got there on Sally's own power, I dismounted, took off my shoe, and had a brief conversation with Sequoia, letting her know what I was up to and asking her to give Sally energy. With the elemental's agreement and help, I remounted Sally and we headed west faster than Gandalf on Shadowfax, completely hidden from the awareness of Aenghus Óg and the Fae.

<Wait, Atticus, wait. I'm trying to picture this. You were wearing some kind of special hat as you rode Mustang Sally, right? Please tell me it was pointy.>

"It was a bowler hat, Oberon, which has a rounded top. Not a pointy wizard hat."

<Yet again you fail your audience! The embellishment was there, waiting to be plucked like a Thanksgiving turkey, and you passed it by. And I haven't heard about any vintage poodles either! One star.>

Leaving a demon behind me didn't come without a good measure of guilt. In all likelihood I was dooming who knew how many men to die as a result of their own greed. But if I stayed in town, I may well have spent the days I'd be traveling trying to catch up to the demon anyway and they still would have died. And if the demon truly started to drain Gaia, Sequoia would tell me and I could shift back. In the meantime, it was important for me to ditch the Fae and fetch some demon bait.

We rode for a couple of days until we got to the foothills of the Sierra Nevada in Calaveras County, a good while before Mark Twain wrote about its celebrated jumping frog. By that time, Sequoia had communicated to the Sierra elemental what I needed, and it was waiting for me in a crevice of a granite cliff face that expanded into a small cave. It was an impressive pile of pure gold nuggets, the sort that dust-covered miners dreamed about, coaxed from the volcanic geology and collected for me in a shallow basin, ready to be stowed in my saddlebags. Just a small fraction of what would eventually be pulled out of those mountains, but it represented a fortune and the key to solving the problem of Mammon.

There was a mountain snake guarding the hoard like a miniature dragon, though he wasn't particularly motivated. He gave me a desultory flick of his tongue but otherwise ignored me.

"Hold on," Granuaile said. "You had Colorado move all that gold here so that Coyote could use it. Why didn't you do the same thing back then?"

"Well, Coyote wasn't there to force me to do it, I guess. And I had to get out of town anyway. Plus, this was my first experience of any kind with mining. I'd never bothered with it before, preferring to let the earth keep her treasures."

• • •

I got back to San Francisco near the close of business on the third of May, confident that the Fae would have given up and moved elsewhere by then. South of town, I dismounted from Mustang Sally and removed my right shoe so that I could draw upon the earth's energy. I took the tiniest sip, just enough to unbind a gold nugget into gold dust and then re-bind it to my coat and hat and even my pants, with a few flecks on my face and in my mustache for good measure. I was no longer a drab English nobleman: I was a shiny rich young man, quite literally covered in wealth.

It was not a plan without risk, but at that time in San Francisco, the only way to inspire more greed than winning big at gambling was to walk in with a huge haul of gold. Every new strike was cause for feverish excitement, and word got around fast when miners came in with their ore. My load of nearly pure nuggets and the gold dust on my clothes would cause instant excitement, and it did. I made it to the bank of Henry M. Naglee on Portsmouth Square just before close of business, and I had a significant crowd following me by that time, walking alongside Sally, eyeing the saddlebags, and licking their lips with thoughts of what must be in there. Their auras all churned with the angry orange tones of avarice, but none was a demon walking around in a meat suit. I didn't give the name of Algernon Percy to the man who asked, "What's your name, mister?"

"Silas Makepeace," I told him in a drawl I hoped sounded like the sheriff's, making the name up on the spot, because you could still do that back then. Nobody in the crowd knew me as Algernon Percy, the Duke of Northumberland, so there was no reason to wear that mask.

"You're probably wearing a hundred dollars of gold dust on your coat. That must be some claim you have."

"I'd say it is," I allowed, giving him a grin, even though I wasn't too sure what he meant.

"Where's your claim?" someone else asked.

"Same place as everyone else's. In the Sierra Nevada."

"Yeah, but is it your claim or someone else's?"

"Mine, of course."

"So where is it?"

"That's my business."

"You gotta have it filed with the county anyway. Might as well tell us."

That was alarming news. I had not filed any claim or even known that was something I was supposed to do. That's the danger of living away from the world: You're going to have to come back to it sometime, and customs and laws seem to always change to your disadvantage. I'd expected and prepared for someone to try to take my gold by force, but the idea that someone could use a legal maneuver to take it had never occurred to me. But it sounded as if I had at least a delaying tactic at my disposal. "You might as well go look up the file, because I ain't tellin'."

The man grumbled at that, but others laughed at him and said I was under no obligation to do anything but file my claim within thirty days of staking it out.

Once the bank was in sight, I reached out to Sally and told her to run for it, leaving the crowd behind. If I let them walk with me all the way there, it wouldn't end well. One or more of them would offer to help me carry all that gold in. And when I refused, they'd find a way to escalate. There'd be a fight, and my gold would be stolen by one or more of them. So this was my chance to leave them behind, and they had no warning of it since I'd given no audible command to Sally. A couple of them were knocked down, having drawn far too close.

They shouted and chased after me, and in truth I had only fifty yards on them once I reached the hitching post, but it was enough to dismount and sling the saddlebags over my left shoulder, slip inside the bank, and close the door in some angry faces, shooting home a sliding bolt. Their shouts of dismay and fists hammering the door made me smile.

"Hey now," a querulous voice said. "You can't just bar the door like that. This is a business, and these are business hours."

I turned my head and beheld a man with epic swaths of dark mustache sweeping down to billowy muttonchops on either side of his face. His chin was shorn clean, but his mouth would have been invisible under that mustache except that it was currently frowning at me, giving me a peek at a drawn lower lip. Predatory eyes glared at me over a long, straight nose, giving him the appearance of a hairy eagle. That was Henry Naglee, who eventually got out of the banking business and went on to be a vintner and a Union Army general in the Civil War.

"I've got a whole lot of gold here, mister," I hollered over the pounding on the door, shrugging my shoulder once to indicate the heavy saddlebags, "and these gentlemen were fixin' to take it off me. If I could sell it to you first, I'd sure feel a lot better about opening the door."

Despite his insistence that the door remain open for business, there weren't any customers besides me. He rose from his chair, which was situated behind a counter with a locked entrance, and emerged moments later with the jangling of a key, calling to someone unseen to come forward and help. Two men shortly appeared from the back, both impressively armed and bearded and ready to defend the riches inside the building. The three of them loomed behind me and shouted at the men outside to cut it out, the bank was closed. My pursuers gave up eventually but promised they'd see me later. That's precisely what I wanted, so I taunted them and said through the door, "You do that."

Word would get around now: Some punk named Silas Makepeace brought in one hell of a haul, and they were going to find out where he got it. They'd be loud about it, and their collective greed would draw the attention of the demon for sure. One way or another, we'd run into each other. There was no chance he'd go anywhere else when so much greed was concentrated in this city.

Satisfied that no one would be busting into the bank now, Henry Naglee pointed to my saddlebags. "May I?"

"Sure." I flipped open one of them and watched his eyes as he peered inside at the nuggets. They widened, but only a bit, before he confined himself to a short nod.

"Very well, I see we have business to conduct, Mr. . . ."

"Makepeace."

"Welcome, sir." He asked one of the armed men to remain at the door and told the other to watch the back door. "If you'll meet me at that window, Mr. Makepeace, we can begin to assay your find."

It was a lot of waiting around after that as Henry Naglee weighed my nuggets on his scales, but I had thirty pounds of solid stuff there and then another few ounces of gold dust on my clothes, which we laboriously brushed off once I surreptitiously unbound it from the material.

"Where you from, Mr. Makepeace?" Naglee asked me as he worked. "Sounds like you might be from the South."

"Middle of nowhere, Texas." I hoped my accent sounded

convincing. Mr. Naglee, being from the North, might not be able to tell the difference between Southern accents very well, and I only needed the identity to hold up a little while longer. "Got tired of cows and decided to come west and see what all the fuss is about."

"Looks like you've found the fuss."

"I sure did. Don't know much about this claim business, though."

The banker paused and looked up at me. "You didn't mine this from your own claim?"

"Well, what if I didn't?"

"Then you must first prove that it wasn't from someone else's claim, and if it's from unclaimed land, then you can file claim to it to prevent others from mining on it."

"Oh. And how do I claim land?"

"First you must mark the boundaries of your claim with stakes—"

<Whoa, Atticus, wait. *Steaks?* You would just claim land by leaving delicious steaks around to rot?>

"No, Oberon, *stakes*, as in a wooden stake you drive into the ground. It's a homophone."

<Oh, good. I was going to say I'd never claim any land if I have to give up steaks to do it. And also? English is stupid. And I'm still waiting on a vintage poodle.>

"And you've been so patient too."

Naglee continued, "And once you've finished staking your claim, you have thirty days to file the boundaries with the county and pay associated fees and so on. I assume you're an American citizen?"

"Yeah," I said, though of course I wasn't. He didn't question me, though, since I didn't sound like I was from Europe.

"That's very good. The city passed a foreign miners' tax a couple weeks ago that comes to twenty dollars a month."

I made no comment but learned later that that law was the first measure of many designed to discriminate against the Chinese, though of course it also would have affected men like Stefano Pastore. That might have been what pushed him to summon a demon rather than try to make a living at mining. Twenty dollars back then was like five hundred now.

Once I'd satisfied him that I hadn't jumped someone else's claim, Naglee eventually named a figure, and I didn't argue but just took what he gave me. It was plenty for my purposes, which was to draw greedy eyes in my direction. A certain pair in particular. And I'd thought of how to use the claim laws in my favor.

When I emerged from the bank, clothes all clean of dust, saddlebags empty, but flush with disposable wealth, some of the unwashed men who'd followed me were waiting nearby. The sun was setting and I saw them silhouetted against the sky.

"There he is," one said, and another said, "Let's go." I was still a target. The wealth had changed from gold to various coins and bills, but I was a newcomer who didn't have any friends or even a gun. And they had come to California thinking they'd get rich quick but didn't, which meant I was the best opportunity they would have for a while. All they had to do was roll me. But I still had my sword, and once I threw the saddlebags over Sally's back, I drew it. That slowed them down. They weren't all wearing guns: Only two of the five approaching me had them.

"If y'all wanna talk, talk from a distance, or I'll open you up."

"Sure," one of them said. "That's all we wanna do. Talk." Their body language said different, but I pretended he was being sincere.

"Fine. I don't know about you, but I'm thirsty. First round's on me, gentlemen. Where's can a body get somethin' good to drink in this town?"

"The U.S. Exchange is pretty good," one of the figures said. "They only water down their whiskey a little bit."

"Sounds good. Maybe they'll have a bottle hidden somewhere that isn't watered down at all. Lead the way."

It was only a couple of blocks or so to the U.S. Exchange, which sounded like a bank or a financial institution but was really a gambling hall that served liquor. Like everyplace else in San Francisco at the time, it had been hastily constructed out of wood, because when a boomtown is booming, you don't want to miss a night of profit by building to last—the booms only last so long, and then the wooden structures are easily abandoned when the money dries up.

It was at least making pretentions of being fancy: They had a piano player, and I could only imagine where they'd shipped that piano in from. Surely not over land.

They had a couple of blackjack tables, faro tables, a roulette wheel, and plenty of other tables for poker or other card games. There were three women pouring whiskey and flirting with the miners. One of them came around to our table with a tray of glasses, and I bought one round to shoot and then another to sip.

I'd describe these men for you, except that I don't remember their names. I was simply using them as a source of focused greed, hoping it would draw the demon to this particular building.

I slung them a fabricated story about my claim's location, how I'd stumbled across it by accident, how there was so much more gold just lying around, no tunnels to be dug or anything, and I was sure it was the same all through that stretch of mountains, and they ate it up. They kept drinking. They were practically unconscious after an hour, but I was fine, because I kept breaking down the alcohol internally to prevent getting drunk. I didn't have to fight them, and I gradually got the attention of everyone in the place, because word quickly spread throughout the hall, courtesy of the whiskey server, that I had found quite the strike somewhere and was rolling in it. Buying a round for everyone also got me some attention.

Leaving my would-be assailants behind in a drunken stupor, barely able to sit up, I performed what might be called an amateur mosey toward the roulette table. I took some time to understand the game and to chat, then I began placing bets. And cheating.

Not for any personal gain, of course: It was merely to attract my target. I would lose some but win a bit more so that, over time, I was amassing more and more money and others were riding along, placing their side bets.

"Time-out," Granuaile said. "How did you cheat?"

"Whenever I wanted a sure win, I bound the surface of the roulette ball to the number I'd chosen, just long enough for it to stay in its little slot."

"They never caught on?"

"I'd lose enough that they didn't suspect. And I kept buying drinks and giving wads of money away to others, who would promptly lose it. The house was doing fine. I was winning enough to basically stay even with what I'd brought in. In the meantime, the atmosphere of greed kept rising."

<Yeah, but what was the food like?> my hound asked.

"I was just getting to that, Oberon," I said.

I took a break for dinner; the U.S. Exchange provided some sliced beef in a sugary barbecue sauce, pinto beans in the same glaze, and a mountain of cornbread. It allowed me time to tell some jokes and ingratiate myself with the staff. I couldn't finish my meal—the portion was huge—so I asked if they might have a hound who'd enjoy it.

"We surely do," said the bartender, who gave his name as Perkins and informed me that he was also the proprietor. He had curled his mustache with wax on the tips and had a cleft chin jutting out beneath it.

"What breed?"

"Standard poodle. The tall ones, you know, not the miniature kind."

"Name?"

"Felicity, because our meeting was felicitous. Found her out on the Oregon Trail; she was near starved to death. She'd lost her people, and I'd lost mine, and we kept each other going."

"Sorry to hear about your troubles," I said. "I don't suppose I could say hi to Felicity? I haven't seen a dog for a long time. Maybe she'll bring me enough luck to maintain a winning streak."

He grinned at me. "Sure, why not. I'll have Lucy take you back."

Lucy was one of the women serving whiskey, and at Perkins' request she took me back into the kitchen past the cook, where the poodle was bedded down. Felicity had a fine curly white coat and looked well fed. Her tail thumped the bed a couple of times and then she rose to say hello. She got some scritches and beef from me, and I learned from her that she thought Perkins was much nicer than most humans she'd met. That was good to know.

<Did she pee on the ones who weren't nice to her?>

"What? Oberon, no."

<Did you ask her?>

"It's not something I would think to ask."

<Well, I'll give you one extra star for finally including a poodle and feeding her but then subtract it for pandering to me. So you're still at one star.>

"It's not pandering! Felicity still has a part to play in this. I said at the start there would be vintage poodles. Would you just let me finish?"

Granuaile did a poor job of stifling a laugh when she heard me protest the pandering charge.

<All right, go on,> Oberon said, all high and mighty as if he were doing me a favor.

When I returned to the saloon, I hoped that the mood would have noticeably shifted and my quarry would have appeared. A scan of the hall's auras revealed nothing unusual, so it was back to work. I gambled and caroused and laughed. I got asked about my sword a lot and why I wore gloves. They were lucky, I said, and left it at that.

Gambling halls back then didn't have closing times as long as there was money to be made. And since there was quite a bit of money changing hands—I was making sure of it— Perkins didn't go to bed at a sensible hour. He had someone come in to take over but he stayed on, keeping an eye on things. There were several fights that broke out at the poker tables, but I kept everything cooking along nicely at the roulette table. Like the king in Hamlet, I took my rouse and kept wassail. But even with breaking down the alcohol and taking breaks every so often, I was getting tired and thinking about giving up. It was long past midnight—three A.M., if I'm not mistaken—before something shifted in the air.

A man with a slight beer gut strode into the hall then, wide-brimmed hat pulled low, his full dark beard kept trimmed, and a slim cigar smoldering at one corner of his mouth. Two guns hung low at his hips, and he had pointy steel-toed boots that were meant to be seen as much as worn; he wasn't a working cowboy or a miner. He was something else.

Checking him out in the magical spectrum, I saw the black roiling stain in his aura that meant he was possessed. A demon was riding this man around like a meat limousine.

I finished up my roll at the roulette table, hoping to lose that round, and I did. I excused myself for a break and opted for a saunter instead of a mosey, beckoning to Perkins.

"Yes, sir, Mr. Makepeace, what can I get for you?" he said. I crooked a finger at him so that he would come closer and no one would overhear me.

"I'm not really Silas Makepeace," I said, letting the Texas drawl go and returning to my English accent. "My name's Algernon Percy and I'm working undercover for the sheriff.

A man we've been looking for just walked in the door. Could you send someone to fetch Sheriff Hays here immediately? Tell him Percy's found our man."

"Okay. Is there going to be trouble?"

"Quite likely, but I hope we'll be able to take care of it without anyone getting hurt. The faster the sheriff gets here, the less likely it is you'll suffer any damages."

"Which man?"

"Slim cigar, wide hat, fancy boots, string tie around his neck." I bobbed my head in the general direction of the front door.

Perkins' eyes shifted, stopped, and narrowed. "Never seen him before. But that doesn't mean anything. All right, I'm on it."

The piano player from earlier in the evening had gone home, and the new one was playing so ecstatically he might have been floating in a haze of laudanum, which is a hell of a drug.

The possessed man's eyes fixed on the roulette table, where the largest concentration of greed was centered. If he followed the pattern he'd established elsewhere, he'd start betting there and keep winning until Perkins asked him to quit. Then things would get violent. And he would take as many people down as he could before slipping out of this body and finding a new host.

While Perkins sent his extra barkeep out to find the sheriff, I turned around and focused on those holsters. I used some energy in my bear charm to bind the iron to the leather so he'd never be able to draw. The iron resistance, both on my end and on the part of the gun itself, meant it took more energy than I would have liked. For good measure I fused the hammers down so he wouldn't be able to shoot through the holster. It didn't leave me with a whole lot of magic to draw on, but I hoped I wouldn't need much more. Drawing power now would bring the wrong kind of attention.

The demon took his time scoping out the hall before moving to the roulette table, and I left the bar before his eyes got to me. I circled to the far side of the table and hid myself behind a couple of hangers-on. It wasn't a long wait before he appeared at the table and started to manipulate things. Cheating, in other words, as I did. I watched in the magical spectrum. He made sure the main bettor lost while his side bet won. He would become the main bettor soon, and that would put us all on a dangerous path. I needed to get him away from the others before he seduced them with greed and killed them, claiming their souls for himself.

Upgrading to a brisk walk and carrying Fragarach in its scabbard in my left hand, I flanked the demon and tapped him on the shoulder before he could place his next bet.

"Say, partner, don't I recognize you? What's your name again?" I smiled at him as he turned to face me. He deliberately puffed a toxic cloud of cigar smoke my way before answering.

"Stephen Blackmoore."

"Naw, that's not your name. You're Mammon, aren't you?"

I did not expect the fist that plowed into my gut at that point, nor did I expect its speed or power. I thought I'd get a squint and a raspy Clint Eastwood challenge along the lines of "What'd you call me, punk?" before we got into trading fisticuffs, but, nope, I got a pile driver into my diaphragm. Doubling over was instinctive and I couldn't help that, but I staggered back so he couldn't follow up easily. He clipped me anyway on the shoulder, and the force of it caught me off-balance and drove me to the floor. I rolled, gasping for air, to avoid the stomp or kick I was sure would follow. He took a couple of pointy kicks at my head and missed; my tumbling took out a fun-sized man, who wasn't aware that a fight had broken out and fell over me, cursing. That slowed down the demon long enough for me to regain my feet.

I was just in time to see another fist coming at me, and considering the power of his other punches, if I let it land I'd have my nose driven into my brain. I swept my left forearm in front of my face, knocking his fist to the left, and struck a couple of stiff fingers into his throat a split second later. The demon might not care about air or much else, but the meat wagon he was riding had reflexes. He reeled back and the cigar fell from his lips. I caught it, flipped the lit end toward him, and shoved it right down that gasping mouth. That gave him something more to think about. He might even be thinking about leaving the body of Stephen Blackmoore a bit early, since demons aren't that great at healing.

Given enough space and time to breathe, I drew Fragarach from its scabbard and pointed it at him. "Freagroidh tu," I said, activating the enchantment worked into the blade, and that bound him in place as well as any ward or ring of salt could. I let him spit out the cigar, but then I followed up in Old Irish: "You may neither move nor speak without my permission." It didn't matter if he understood me: Fragarach did. He froze up, glaring at me, and then I was faced with the old proverb about what to do when you catch a tiger by the tail. You'd better not let go.

The problem was that I had just done this in front of a whole bunch of witnesses. They might not have understood right then that they were witnessing a Druid squaring off against a demon from hell, but they knew something was weird, because a man with two guns wasn't even trying to face down a guy with a sword, and the guy with the sword talked funny.

"Sorry, everybody," I said in my uncertain Texas drawl. "We'll take this elsewhere and let you carry on with your evenin'." To the demon I said, "Let's move over by the door and talk, real nice."

By moving the tip of Fragarach, I could give him a bit of a nudge in the right direction but not really force him to move. The enchantment was designed to prevent movement more than to push or pull people around. And the demon inside Stephen Blackmoore really did not want to cooperate.

His hands dropped to his guns and he attempted to pull them out, only to find that he couldn't. He shook and trembled all over, trying to break free of the enchantment, perhaps even to escape his host and possess someone else, but he was well contained. His eyes turned the color of boiled lobsters as his frustration and rage grew; his mouth dropped open, and the sound that erupted from it wasn't the sort of thing a healthy person ever makes: It was pitched low, as if he ate a bad burrito an hour ago, but it was unmistakably a battle cry filled with a berserker's promise of doom.

The saloon fell silent as everyone turned to stare. The piano player even stopped his mad tinkling of the keys.

"This man ain't well," I said. "Don't touch him, please, just give us some space. He knows he needs to do what I say, but he doesn't want to. Sorry, y'all. We'll get out of your way as soon as we can."

Stephen Blackmoore kept trying to shuck his guns free. "They're not coming loose. I made sure of it. So let's go talk, all right? It's the only way to be rid of me."

That was as much for the crowd as for the demon. Satisfied that there wouldn't be any gunfire, they murmured and some of them politely turned their backs to resume their games. The piano player took his cue and pounded the keys once more.

"Go on," I told the demon. "Walk toward the door." The red glow in the eyes faded and the tremors in the limbs subsided as the demon decided not to fight it anymore. He walked toward the door with clenched fists and I kept the sword pointed at him, asking people not to get between us. There was a table with a few down-at-the-heels miners chatting over drinks. I asked them if we could sit there and threw some uncashed chips at them as a naked bribe. One of them asked for more, but the other two told him not to be an asshole; they'd just come out ahead on what was otherwise a shit night.

I had him sit across from me, his back to the door, and Lucy came over to ask if we wanted drinks. I ordered two shots of rye, but neither of us had any intention of actually drinking.

It was time to use the other power of Fragarach: compelling the truth. "Let's get to it, shall we? I'm asking the demon possessing this human right now: What is your name?"

At first the demon was amused and a low chuckle burbled forth from Blackmoore's burned throat, but then "Mammon" escaped his lips, and the flaming eyes returned as the demon realized he didn't have a choice about answering.

"I thought so. Stefano Pastore was a fool to summon you. But what I want to know is this: Who helped you escape the summoning circle and kill Pastore?"

Blackmoore's face twisted into a nasty grin. Mammon was delighted to answer that question. "Some other fool entered the room shortly after I was summoned, because I bellowed. Pastore didn't protect against my influence on others. I prom-

ised the man incredible wealth and all he had to do was kick
a bit of salt aside for me. Pastore begged him not to do it, but
he was helpless to stop him. The man broke the circle and I
possessed him. Then I used him to break Pastore's circle of
protection and pay him properly for his arrogance. Who are
you?"

"I'll ask the questions. Did you keep your promise to the
man you possessed?"

"Yes. He had a fine run at faro and acquired more money
than he'd ever seen, before someone tried to stop me and guns
came out. But I took four more souls before I left his body."

That sounded like that first night, when Mr. Collins got
thrown across the room.

"And you've been doing something similar to that every
night since?"

Another smile from the demon. He approved of these
questions. "Yes. This is my kind of town."

"Well, not anymore. I need you to go back to hell." He
simply stared at me, and I realized I hadn't asked him a question. "You may speak freely so long as it is in English."

"You cannot send me back," he spat.

"Sure I can."

"You are no priest. You are not one of the host either."

"That's true enough. But your spiritual opposites are not
the only ones with an interest in keeping demons from roaming around this plane."

"This weapon you have used to bind me," he said, sneering
at it, "cannot do any lasting harm to me."

That was also true. I didn't have a nice set of arrows blessed
by the Virgin Mary, like that time in Mesa when we had to go
after the fallen angel. Fragarach could dispatch most lesser
demons, who had only a tenuous grip on their manifestations

here, but Mammon was one of the true badasses. How do you destroy a pure manifestation of greed?

"I never said I was going to stab you with it," I told him. "It's doing what it needs to do, which is keep you in place while I get hold of something or someone that *can* harm you. You've heard of Brighid, First among the Fae, who can cast Cold Fire?"

The confidence and condescension melted away. "Yes."

"She's a friend. So it's your call: Go back to hell of your own free will, where you will remain powerful and wind up paying no price for this little spree of yours, or stick around and be torn apart on this plane. You'll be scattered and weak for centuries, and your influence will wane—and actually, now that I think about it, that might be best for everyone but you. I probably shouldn't give you a choice, but I did say it would be your call."

Looking back on that now, I think that might have been one of my greatest cock-ups. What would this country—and, by extension, the whole world—look like now if greed had taken a backseat to other vices in 1850? So many implications I should have thought through. But I wasn't prioritizing the long term right then. I just wanted Mammon out of there and the short-term threat to the earth neutralized so that I could get back to hiding in Argentina.

"What's it going to be, Mammon? Go back whole, or get blown to pieces?"

He trembled and shook again and the red rage eyes returned, but he had to make a decision and answer. "I'll go back."

I awarded him a smile. "Thank you. Very cooperative. But I have to press you on the matter of *when*, because this isn't my first negotiation with folks who like to hide behind non-specifics. So, will you go back to hell when I open a portal to the plane?"

"Yes," he said through a clenched jaw. "But I swear I will—"

"Shut up now," I said, and Fragarach cut him off.

Sheriff Jack Hays strode through the saloon doors and I hailed him. He looked less than pleased to see me.

"Where the hell you been, Percy?" he said, and that reminded me to switch accents. "We've had men dropping dead every night for—Jesus Christ." He stopped once he took in the shaking form of Stephen Blackmoore. "Is this him?"

"That's him, Sheriff," I said. "And he's agreed to return to hell."

"Well, let's get him out of here, then."

"It would be better, I think, to get everyone out of here. Which is why I needed you. If we take him outside, there are too many things that can go wrong. We could be interrupted by most anyone—or witnessed by most anyone. We don't want that."

"Huh." Hays glanced around at the busy gambling hall. "It's gonna be a job to get them out of here when they're havin' such a high time."

I began pulling chips and coins and cash out of my pockets and put them on the table. "Pay them all off. The proprietor too. Greed is a powerful motivator." I smirked at Mammon as I said this, and he seethed.

"Jesus," Hays said again, and Blackmoore's body twitched as the sheriff began to gather up the money. He wisely began by visiting Perkins at the bar, then he told the piano player to leave off. He hollered until he could be heard, and once he had everyone's attention, he told them to finish their current round or hand in their games and then move along, the U.S. Exchange was closing for the night. The loudest grumbling came from the poker players who were currently down in their personal counts. The sheriff went over to them and quietly used my money to take the sting out of it.

Once everyone was out but Blackmoore, Perkins, the sheriff, and me, the lawman shrugged his shoulders at me. "Now what?"

"Now I need two things," I said. "I need a container or two of salt from the kitchen, Perkins. And, Sheriff, I hate to ask, but there's no helping it because I have to keep this sword holding the demon still. I need you to take off my boots."

Sheriff Hays's lip curled, and he looked like he'd rather dine on hog slop. "Why do you need that?"

"I need a solid connection to the earth. Again, I apologize. Please keep whatever money you have left as payment."

"Think I will," he said, shoving it into his coat pockets as he stomped over. "Don't tell nobody I did this."

Perkins disappeared into the kitchen while the sheriff pulled my boots off. "Ain't no earth in here, in case you didn't notice," he said.

"There will be." I addressed the demon. "All right, Mammon, get up. Walk straight backward until I tell you to stop." I wanted to do this away from the door in case someone came in, but to prevent that I asked the sheriff to stand guard and keep everyone out.

When Perkins returned from the kitchen, I used my left hand to sprinkle a generous line of salt underneath my sword hand, extending to either side, then gave the container back to Perkins. "I need you to continue to make a circle around this man, but stay out of arm's reach the whole way around him, okay?"

Perkins developed a crease between his eyes. "You been drinkin' my piano player's laudanum?" he said.

"No, I'd never do that. Laudanum's a hell of a drug."

"What's really going on here? Y'all told me this was a wanted man. Why don't the sheriff just take him away?"

"Because, Perkins, there's a demon inside this man, and we need to get him out."

Perkins stared for a few seconds, then turned to Hays. "Sheriff?"

Hays nodded at him. "Just do what he says."

"This is a damn crazy waste of salt," he said, but he did as I asked while I kept close watch on Blackmoore.

"Thanks," I said when he was finished. "Best get back behind the bar now." As he turned, shaking his head, I used the last of the energy in my bear charm to access more: I unbound the cellulose of the floorboards beneath me so that I could sink through the wood and make contact with the earth. Buildings back then didn't have cement foundations underneath them. They had stone and mortar foundations around the edges but just wood laid on top of earth in the middle.

With a fresh supply of energy from Gaia and contact with the elemental Sequoia, I told her I had captured the demon and needed to open a portal to return it to hell. Permission granted, I crafted a ward of containment around the ring of salt as a backup before I got to the really tricky part.

I had no idea what kind of person Stephen Blackmoore was when he wasn't possessed, but I couldn't simply toss him into hell while still alive. He should have his shot at life and a chance at redemption if he wanted to seek it. But to get Mammon out of Blackmoore, I would necessarily need to release him from the binding of Fragarach—and the demon knew it. He couldn't talk, but he winked and grinned at me. The chances of him meekly slinking back to hell were nil.

I checked my ward, which was stronger than the salt any-

way. I'd create the portal inside it. Nothing for it but to proceed: The longer I delayed, the greater the chance that someone
would come along to interrupt—as someone had interrupted
Stefano Pastore.

"When I release the binding, Mammon, you will exit Mr.
Blackmoore as promised."

"I never promised that. I only said I would go back to hell
when you opened a portal."

"You can't take Mr. Blackmoore with you."

"Oh, but that's precisely what I'm going to do. He belongs
to me every bit as much as that sword belongs to you."

"Not now he doesn't. He deserves to live his natural life
first, and you can have his soul later."

"Ha! You have no idea what this man deserves. But what
are you going to do? Destroy him to destroy me? You would
damn yourself in the process."

"No, I'm not going to hell when I die. I belong to the Morrigan."

The demon cocked Blackmoore's head to one side. "The
Morrigan? . . . Oh. You're one of *them*. A Druid. I thought
they were all dead."

"Clearly not."

Blackmoore closed his eyes, took a deep breath, and exhaled. When he opened his eyes again, he smiled at me. Or,
rather, Mammon did. "Very well, Druid. I will leave Mr.
Blackmoore when you release the binding and let him live his
life."

That was a bit too accommodating. "His natural life?" I
pressed.

"Yes."

"Fine. Do it." I released Blackmoore from Fragarach's grip,
and oily orange smoke began to pour out of his ears, nostrils,

and mouth. It swirled and coalesced behind him into a humanoid form, and when the smell hit me I threw up a little bit in my mouth.

Eventually the smoke stopped coming out of him, and Mammon manifested in his true shape—a grotesque starved thing of stringy muscles, like an Egon Schiele painting, except that he had a distended belly, pitiless barren eye sockets like mine shafts, and rows of serrated teeth in an unhinged jaw like some nightmare from the Marianas Trench.

His host wobbled and blinked as he came back to himself. "Stephen, come here," I called to him. All he had to do was step out of the circle and he'd be safe. "Stephen!"

"Huh? Gah! Damn, why does my asshole feel like it's on fire?"

Those were not, as last words go, particularly inspirational or profound. Mammon reached out from behind him, gripped his left shoulder, and then wrapped his long bony fingers around Blackmoore's neck, ripping off his head, hat and all. This he threw unerringly at a kerosene lantern resting on the bar, which shattered and immediately ignited the cherrywood. Blackmoore's head disappeared behind the bar and Perkins cried out in alarm, though I don't know whether it was at the fire or at the appearance of a demon in his place of business.

But Mammon wasn't done. He tore Blackmoore's corpse apart limb by limb and chucked them at other lanterns in the hall, setting fires elsewhere.

"You promised him a natural life!" I shouted as he dismembered his victim.

"And he got one. I killed him quite naturally, with my bare hands," Mammon said. "And it is natural for predators to tear apart their prey. Step into the circle, Druid, and I'll show you how natural it is."

"What the hell?" Deputy Kasey Princell stepped in to gape at the spectacle just then, and Sheriff Hays drew his gun and thunked the butt of it into Princell's shoulder.

"Damn it, the whole place is going to burn down! Go get help or the town could go!"

I turned and saw that he was right. There were so many fires now and there was nothing but wood in the place. The U.S. Exchange was done for. But Perkins plainly did not want to believe that. He was trying to contain the fire on the bar with a towel while the rest of the hall flared up.

"Perkins!" I shouted as Princell exited. "Get out of here! You can't save it!"

"We can stop it!" he replied. "Help me!"

"Perkins, we can't!" I struggled to think of something he loved more than the business he'd built from scratch and gambled on a guess: "Think of Felicity, Perkins! You have to save Felicity! Get her out of here!"

He ceased his flailing and looked up from his immediate area, seeing that it was true. The building would burn down no matter what we did at that point. The volunteer firemen and bucket brigade would never get there in time. We were both already sweating, and it was a cool early morning.

"I hope you all go to hell!" he said, throwing down his bar towel and dashing back to the kitchen to fetch Felicity. I think that poodle saved him just by being there; if she hadn't been, I believe he would have gladly burned with his saloon.

That, at least, was a silver lining to an otherwise legendary cock-up. As the flames popped and crackled and the heat and smoke grew, I realized what Mammon was trying to do: distract and delay until I had no choice but to leave myself. If

I never opened that portal to hell, he never had to step through it.

The sheriff wasn't distracted. He had something to kill and a fully functional firearm in his hand, and he'd just seen Mammon tear a man apart and toss his bits around the room. There was really no quibbling over the demon's guilt. Hays stepped forward into the room to get a better angle and started firing. The bullets were on target but simply passed through. Mammon had taken a shape but was not really flesh occupying space. He just laughed as the sheriff poured bullets into him and the flames grew higher.

Focusing on the space where Blackmoore used to stand, I chanted the words to first bind that space to its equivalent space in hell, then to unbind the veil separating the planes. Mammon responded to this by plunging his clawed hand into Blackmoore's headless, limbless torso, ripping out bloody ropes of intestine, and throwing them at me.

Such situations are a perfect example of why Druids must develop, at minimum, two different headspaces for battle. One must deal with the demands of the physical fight, while the other must remain undistracted to craft bindings.

I merely held up Fragarach with the flat of the blade presented to Mammon, so that nothing would hit me in the face, and continued. Stephen Blackmoore's digestive system smacked wetly against either the blade or my body before dropping to the floor, and I was splattered with his blood and shit, but it could hardly be worse than the smell of Mammon himself.

When the binding was complete and hell yawned before Mammon's feet, he roared and tossed Blackmoore's torso at me. I took the trouble to duck under that one.

"*Má ithis, nar chacair!*" I told him in Gaeilge, a fantastic curse for one such as Mammon, who always wants more: It means, "May you eat but not defecate."

He slid down through the portal as much as jumped into it, pulled by the strength of his own word, and I closed it up behind him. Sequoia would feel that and know that I'd done my duty.

//Harmony restored// I sent to her, and she replied in kind.

"I thought I'd seen everything," Hays shouted past the roar of the inferno, "but I reckon I better rethink that. Come on, Percy, let's go."

"I'm headed out back to make sure Perkins really left," I told him, pointing at the kitchen door, and he held my gaze for a moment, far too smart to accept that at face value, knowing he'd never see me again. Then a beam cracked above, and we nodded and parted ways. I escaped out the back door through the kitchen, making sure Perkins and Felicity were gone, and remembered to fetch Mustang Sally from where I had her stabled. I headed for the bound trees north of town, hoping I'd be able to shift out before my activity there drew a new batch of faeries from Aenghus Óg.

That episode turned out to be the second Great Fire of San Francisco, quite literally started by greed, which eventually consumed three city blocks and cost four million dollars in damages. Thanks to Deputy Princell's quick work, the alarm was spread in time to prevent any deaths other than Stephen Blackmoore's. And I was able to enjoy a year of peace with Mustang Sally in Argentina before she passed away of truly natural causes.

. . .

<You didn't give her Immortali-Tea?> Oberon asked.

No, Oberon, I told him via our mental link. *You're only the second companion I've done that with.*

<Why?>

Some people—and some creatures—don't handle long lives very well. It changes them for the worse. But you just keep getting better, buddy.

<Oh. Thanks. I would give you a snack for that if I had one. Hey, would you like some brisket? I still have some here.>

I briefly glanced at the slobbery hunk of beef underneath Oberon's paw. *No thanks; I'm full.*

<Who was the first companion you gave Immortali-Tea to?>

I'll tell you some other night, okay? It's a story in itself.

"That was quite a tale, Atticus," Granuaile said. "I'll be thinking about a world without greed for a while now. I think you might be right: Letting Mammon go back to hell might have been one of your worst cock-ups ever. It's greed that makes us destroy Gaia bit by bit."

I sighed and shrugged. "You won't get any argument from me. I could have done better, no doubt. But as the world's only Druid for so long, I've been living a life besieged. It's why Gaia could use more of us."

A slow grin spread across Granuaile's face, and her eyes reflected the light of the fire. "Yes. I'll be happy to help as soon as I'm able."

THE BOGEYMAN OF
BOORA BOG

❧❧❧❧❧❧❧❧❧❧❧❧❧❧

*This story, narrated by Archdruid Owen Kennedy,
takes place after* Staked, *Book 8 of* The Iron Druid Chronicles,
but before the events of Oberon's Meaty Mysteries:
The Purloined Poodle.

It doesn't matter whether we make love or war or both
when we go running together in the woods; Greta always
likes to snuggle up afterward for something she calls "pillow
talk," even though we never have any pillows with us. Perhaps
it's because we are so fecking savage when we play together,
and she wants a quiet time of conversation to set aside the
beast and reassert her humanity. I don't know; that might be
reading more into the bones of the thing than are really there.
But, like her, I have come to look forward to our talks as
much as the fighting and the sex. She has some wild fecking
stories, the kind of thing you're sure can't be real except in the
fevered dreams of a talk radio host armed only with a micro-
phone and two handfuls of batshit.

Hunting down wendigos in Manitoba, for instance. Negotiating with ghouls to make sure the pack has access to

efficient body disposal. And she claims they had to destroy an actual modern-day necromancer who had raised the dead in Phoenix just to make him tacos and margaritas, and he had to die before he decided to use his power for something more sinister.

She tells me it's me turn to share as we lie naked and bleeding on the slopes of Mount Humphreys near Flagstaff. She still shudders from the pain of her shift from wolf to human and clasps me hand as we stare up at a blue sky through the pickets of white-trunked aspens. Seen from the forest floor like that, they seem to be the clutching finger bones of giants long buried in the earth, reaching for one last fine day in the sun.

When I point this out to her, she squints up at them as if there's something wrong with her vision. "What if that were true?" she says, and nestles into the crook of me arm. "How do you suppose they would come to be here, lying in the cold ground?"

I snort at the question. "Might as well ask how we came to be here, lying on top of it."

Her head raises enough to look me in the eye. "All right, then. I'll ask: How did we get here?"

"What? Are ye serious? Ye already know that. Siodhachan fetched me off that fecking timesuck in Tír na nÓg, and we met at Hal's house."

"Right. And I was turned into a werewolf by Gunnar and Hal a long time ago. It's one hell of a chain of cause and effect. But you've never shared with me a crucial link of that chain."

"And what link is that?"

"How did you become the archdruid of Atticus O'Sullivan? Is there a story worth telling behind that? Or was it an ordinary thing, like your archdruid assigned him to you?"

"Ye really want to hear about Siodhachan and me? I thought ye would rather milk a cockroach than hear tell of him again."

She shakes her head once. "I want to hear about you. What brought you to cross his path and take him on as an apprentice? I mean, I know you said his father got killed in a cattle raid, but there was more to it than that, wasn't there?"

"Oh, aye, there was a right load of ox shite that led me to his blasted door, and that's no lie. That's a proper story for ye, I suppose."

Her head drops back down to the crook of me arm, her hands roam in the curls of me chest, and she calls me that pet name. "Tell me every little thing, Teddy Bear."

If I have it right, this would have been seventy years before this Common Era of yours began. Or something. We weren't thinking at that time that we would have an entirely new calendar in a few centuries; we were very much in tune with the seasons and solstices but didn't call the months and years what ye call them now.

I was a fairly young Druid, in me twenties, the younger and stupid side of it if I'm being honest, and me own archdruid had assigned me to tend to the needs of a village in what I believe is now County Offaly. They hadn't had a Druid around for some while, and they were doing some daft shite and turning the land into a giant peat bog. Clearing away trees, ye know, that were keeping everything balanced, sucking up all that rain, but with them gone, the soil turned acidic and the ground became waterlogged. I think ye have some modern term for it now . . . Yes! Clear-cutting. Does tremendous damage.

By the time I got there, the bog was already bigger than a king's ego and at night darker and more dangerous than a badger's arsehole—ye just really didn't want to be pokin' around in there. I was supposed to keep 'em from makin' it worse and maybe do something to heal the soil.

Problem was, the villagers didn't want to hear that they had anything to do with that bog. Way they told it, the bog owed them a few dozen head of sheep and cattle and maybe ten girls and boys over the years.

"Ye mean ye lost all that in the bog?" I asks them, and this red-faced knob of a man says no, ye giant tit, they were *stolen*.

"Stolen?" I says. "By who?" Or *whom*, whatever is proper—feck all the rules of this shite language ye have me speakin' anyways.

Well, the knob looks at his wife and she nods at him, and he looks at his friends and they nod too, which means he has everyone's permission to go ahead and say it out loud to a stranger.

"There's something out there," he says. "A bogeyman."

"Do ye mean one o' the Fae?" I asks him. "If it's one o' the Fae, there might be something I can do about that."

"Like what?" he sneers at me. "Are ye goin' to give us a hunk of iron? We're not as simple as ye think, Eoghan Ó Cinnéide. We've already taken all the precautions, and given all the of-ferings, and said all the prayers, and still it's been happening. And not just to us, not just here. All the villages near this fecking bog suffer, to the south and east and maybe the west too. During the night they lose a cow here, a sheep there, and every so often we lose a lad or a lass too. There's a gods-cursed bogeyman out there, sure as I have a cock to piss with, and if ye want us to give a single sad shite about your advice, which we never asked for, then ye will shuffle your bony arse into that bog and kill what's been killing us for all these years."

The others all grunted their assent and I saw that there was no help for it. I couldn't do Gaia's business until I attended to theirs. And in truth I thought Gaia's business could wait. Kids should be allowed to grow up in peace or else no one has any, do they? The desolate looks on those faces glaring back at me, well, there was only one way to fix them: justice. Whoever took those kids had stolen their parents' joy and their hope for the future along with them.

"All right," I says to them, and it's a good thing I did, because they were ready to tell me to feck the oldest goat in the meadow if I said anything else. "I want to hear some details, please. But one at a time. The more specific ye can be about times and places of property or children stolen—especially the children—the more it will help me. Because I do want to help ye, and that's no lie."

And that, me love, was what got me on the soggy, squelchy road to meeting Siodhachan, though I sure had no inkling of it at the time.

They gave me a lodge of earth and wood to work in, and there I received them, one by one, to hear stories of loss and mourning.

What grabbed me most was the tale of Saoirse, who had lost her daughter, Siobhan, not a fortnight before. A thin and underfed thing, as most of the villagers were, she wiped tears and snot away from her face as she sobbed out her tale in gulping fits and starts.

"'Twas thirteen nights ago, sir. I puts her to bed and gives her a kiss on the cheek and tells her she's loved, for she is. And I have me worries like we all do but I'm thinkin' she's safe, for who is sleepin' next to her but me an' her own da? She has the iron about her neck, and we says the prayers to Brighid and the Morrigan and all the gods below, and nary a peep out o' her all the night long. But when the dawn comes and the cocks are scolding the sun, she's gone! Her blanket turned down, her doll left behind, and no answer to our calls. We checks the grounds, ye know, to make sure she's not out relieving herself, but she is nowhere to be found, is she? Not anywhere. Nowhere in the village. We rouse the lot of it, but Siobhan is vanished. So what can it be, sir, but the bogeyman of Boora Bog what's been plaguing us for years now?"

"Are ye sure as ye can be in your most secret of hearts, Saoirse," I asks her, "that the Fae cannot be involved in this? Have ye, or perhaps your husband, done anything to draw down their wrath in years past?"

"I can't be positive, now can I, sir, when what offends them is so often a trifle what humans would never understand. But in me heart I'm sure I can't think of anything that would invite such a punishment upon our heads."

"I understand," I says, and nod to indicate that I'm in the same room, looking at the same facts. "Now think back to that morning ye found her gone; were there any footprints or anything at all unusual?"

"Oh, aye. We followed a pair of footprints right into the bog. But it wasn't a stretch of a hundred steps before we lost the trail. The waters, sir, are worse than clouds at covering up what ye wish to see."

"But these footprints, now: Were they a man's, a woman's, or something else?"

"Oh, it was too difficult to tell, sir, beyond they being human and full-grown."

"How old is Siobhan? Could they have been her footprints?"

Saoirse shakes her head. "I doubt it. She's fourteen and wee for her age. And she knows better than to go wanderin' in the bog anyway. And me husband said, look at the depth of those prints, now, for sure they was made by someone powerful heavy—or else someone carrying Siobhan! Me daughter could never make heavy prints like that."

The interviews with the others are all of a kind; whatever they lost, they lost in the night, and no clues except for the occasional footprints trailing off into Boora Bog before getting lost in standing waters. Well, that and the almost visible holes torn in their spirits. This wasn't like the mourning of men and women who'd lost their partners in a battle, where ye knew the risk and knew that death was to be expected and borne. This was the terror of the innocent, at the mercy of a world gone mad, and the way they looked at me, like I was the only one who could give them a reason to carry on in the mud and the rain and the infinite fog of their despair—well, it near stabbed me in the guts.

I'm still thinkin' it's some kind o' rogue Fae that's clever enough to glamour itself into a human shape, for I can't imagine what else might have an appetite for humans—unless it's a fecking vampire. Once I think o' that, the possibility grows in me mind. I had yet to meet one then, but the Druids on the continent said they were nasty and creeping north with some very disciplined armies—the Romans, ye know. The method fit with what I had heard about them: They hunted at night and had a strange ability to charm people into doing what they wished.

I had to hunt down this bogeyman regardless of what it turned out to be, and after a night's sleep that was about as restful as a Scotsman dancing on me stones and playing the bagpipe, I cadged a cheese here and a hunk of salted beef there and sloshed into Boora Bog, which is even bigger today than it was back then.

As soon as I'm out o' sight and I find a patch o' turf that's moderately dry and sprouting heather, I strip down and shove me clothes into me bag and shape-shift into a red kite. The bag isn't heavy by human standards—the food is the heaviest part of it, because I don't have a weapon—but it's still a boulder's worth of weight to me as a kite. I struggle to get off the ground with it, and I can tell I will have to land every so often to replenish me energy from the earth, but it's still far faster to look for trouble this way than wade through sucking mud and mosquitos.

It's miles and hours and clouds of midges like low-flying thunderheads before I see anything worth investigating. A lone figure trudges through the muck, heading roughly southwest, and when I circle closer he cranes his neck around and watches me. It's not long before he waves at me like we are old friends. That's stranger than a skunk dropping in on a Franciscan friar sex party, so I spiral in even closer. He holds up his arm, back of the hand toward me, and I see the familiar healing triskele of a Druid. He knows what I am because red kites don't glide over bogs with a bag of provisions clutched in their talons.

Disappointed and relieved at the same time, I pick a small rise of earth that practically counts as a hill out there and swoop down for a landing. It gives me time to shift and pull on me clothes while he jogs over to say hello.

He's older than me, a single shock of gray pouring down one side of his beard like he fell asleep with a mouthful of gravy and it dribbled out while he slept. He's taller and broader than me too, his frame packed with muscle, and he's got both an axe and a short sword slung about him, as well as a pack significantly larger than mine. With all those trappings he can't be shifting easily to haul them around, which is no doubt why I saw him traveling by foot out here, far from any grove that would let him travel where he wished. He greets me with a huge grin, happy to see another Druid out here.

"Well met, sir!" he calls when he's close enough to shout. "Gaia's blessings be upon ye!"

"Blessed be," I reply, and when we're near we clasp forearms and smile like we grew up together, though we had never met before. Up close, I see his face is grimy and dotted with what is either something nasty from the bog or dried blood. Poor lad hasn't seen a bath or his own reflection in a long while, I expect, nor even a river.

"Dubhlainn Ó Meara," he says, his voice bright as a child given a puppy to play with.

"Eoghan Ó Cinnéide," I says. Me eyes automatically stray to his right arm, looking at the bands around his biceps to see what animal forms he can take. It's always interesting, because Gaia chooses each Druid's forms, and they are often not animals ye might find in Ireland. His eyes do the same, dropping down to me arm. As always, I get asked about me water form.

"Your water shape is something with tusks?" he asks.

"Aye. It's called a walrus. I rarely use it."

"And your predator?"

"Ah, that's a bear. I like that one. What's yours, then? Some kind of big cat?"

"Aye. I'm told it's a tiger, though they don't live anywhere on the continent, much less here. Some part of the great wide world I'll never see, I suppose."

"Ah, now, don't be sayin' that. Looks like ye have it in mind to see a good portion of it. Where are ye headed, all loaded down like that?"

"Back to me camp. It's not far. Want to come along, share a cup and a story or two? I have some mead and root vegetables to munch on if we don't come across a hare or two for dinner."

"Sounds grand. I have some cheese and salted beef. But why would ye be camping out here?"

Dubhlainn shrugs. "I've been asked to do something about this bog. It's been growing and it will just keep at it if we don't amend the fecking soil."

"I'm to do the same. But I also have to convince a village to stop creating these conditions with their constant clearing of trees. How far is your camp?"

He squints into the afternoon sun. "Probably another hour's slog through the bog to the southwest."

"All right, let's go, then."

Turns out, as we waded through the slime and shared our backgrounds, that Dubhlainn grew up in Erainn, or what's called Munster now, near the southern port of Cork. And his archdruid knew mine—which made sense, since they had both sent their apprentices out to prevent the island from becoming one giant bog from coast to coast.

"Imagine," I says to him, "if there weren't any Druids around to tell people they're cocking up the earth and teach them how to fix it. Everything would be shite."

He shudders and agrees. "Shite in the air, shite in the water, folk getting sick because there's no end to the shite. May the Morrigan take me before I ever see such a day."

And o' course I remember him sayin' that now because the Morrigan made sure I *did* see such a day, skipping over two thousand years just so I could see how badly humans could cock up the planet without Druids. Dubhlainn had been right, damn his eyes.

His camp, when we reach it, is largely underground, built no doubt with the help of the elemental, solid stone all around to prevent water from seeping in. For a good fifty paces all around, the land is solid and balanced. He even has a garden.

"It looks like you've been at it a while," I says, and he nods.

"More of a home than a camp at this point," he admits. "It's slow work. It took hundreds of years to get this bad, and I can't fix it in a week or three. I keep calling it a camp out of optimism, but it may turn out to be me life's work."

"Ah, I can see where ye might be worried. But I'm on it now too, and I would wager there will be more soon, and before too much longer ye may be able to move on to someplace drier."

He takes a large ceramic jug down from a shelf and tears the cork out with his teeth, spitting it into a corner because we'll presumably be finishing the whole thing. He pours two cups of mellow yellow, hands one to me, and says, "May the gods below make it so."

"Sláinte, lad," I says, and we drain our cups, being more thirsty than a whale swimming in the Sahara, and he refills them. I look around and see a wee straw tick for sleeping, some odds and ends, what looks like a woman's fancy jewelry box, and some wicker baskets of vegetables, kept cool and dry in the usual darkness. He also has a hearth and a stack of wood next to it for fires, though I saw a fire pit aboveground that looked like it got more frequent use. He follows me gaze and shrugs when he next catches me eye.

"Not much to look at, I know. The chief luxury here is staying dry and warm when it's cold and wet outside. I prefer it out there, honestly. Shall we build a fire up top?" he asks, and I quickly agree. After the open sky, a shelter can seem like a prison when it's fine out.

We haul up an armful of wood and get the lot of it popping and crackling before the sun goes down. The cheese isn't going to last long, so I offer him a wedge and he gives me an onion that I eat like an apple, which was perfectly normal back then.

"Are ye familiar with the village up north of here, on the edge of the bog?" I asks him when we have filled our bellies.

"Aye. They keep clearing land for their cattle and goats."

"Right. But they seem to be mighty vexed about something in the bog. I nearly cut meself on the sharp words they had for me; never heard so much as a 'good day' when I came to town. Have ye seen any Fae in these parts what would give these people fits?"

His bottom lip juts out and his brows come together as he considers, then he shakes his head. "Not for years. There was a bog troll some years back, but I convinced him to relocate."

"Some natural predator, then? Though I don't know what it could be. An animal wouldn't fit the facts."

"What facts do ye have, then?"

"Missing cattle. The stray goat or sheep."

"Animals could do that. Though wolves are scarce now and on their way to dying out on the island if I'm not mistaken."

"Aye. The wolfhounds are too fecking good at their jobs, eh?"

We have a chuckle about that and I ask for another refill of that honey mead of his. He left the jug below, so he goes down to fetch it while I grab an iron poker to stir up the fire a bit and throw on another log. I notice he's got quite a deep bed of ashes in the pit and he should empty it soon. There are bits of charred bone in there, which I don't think is unusual, until it registers that these aren't the bones of a hare or even a sheep or goat. They're undeniably human.

Even with the evidence in front of me, I can't believe it. Me first thought is, Who put these bones in Dubhlainn's fire? As if it weren't himself all along. And then the facts assemble themselves like a well-made boot and it fits him perfectly.

If the Fae weren't responsible, then it had to be a man; neither wolves nor trolls left human footprints, and neither can sneak a child out of her village without someone seeing or hearing something. A Druid can, though, and Dubhlainn was the only one living in the middle of Boora Bog with bones in his fire pit. He'd been there for years, and he could strike at any of the villages surrounding the bog whenever the fancy took him.

I toss down the poker and rise, stepping away from the fire as Dubhlainn returns with the jug of mead.

"Ah, that's what I need," I say as I hold out me cup, even though I have no plans to drink another drop. I wouldn't put it past him to have poisoned it while out of me sight.

He pours himself another and raises his glass to me. "*Sláinte.*" I mirror him and bring the cup to me lips and pretend to drink, while asking the elemental through me tattoos if there are any bodies buried nearby, specifying human remains.

//Yes// the reply comes, and far too quickly for me comfort. //Many juvenile humans//

I lower the cup and drop my pretense with it, watching his eyes.

"Is Siobhan still alive?" I asks him, and for a wee fraction of a second his eyes widen in surprise, but then he tries to deflect.

"Siobhan who?"

I throw the cup at him, mead spilling out and splashing his face. Those spots on his cheek I thought might be the dried blood of some animal were probably the blood of poor Siobhan.

"I'm talkin' about the girl ye took from that village two weeks ago! Is she still alive, ye poxy pair o' bollocks, or have ye already eaten her, ye feckin' heartless monster?"

For a small moment, there's fear in those eyes. Maybe a flash of guilt too, for he's been caught and he knows it. I'm expecting him to lash out at me, but instead he throws back his head and laughs, and ye could have shoveled me jaw off the ground, I was that surprised.

"You're so young and full of yourself!" he says, and beams at me. "I'm doing Gaia's work out here and nothing else matters, ye see? This goat, or that cow, or that girl Siobhan— they're all just meat to Gaia, and ye know it to be as true as Brighid speakin' in three voices. If Gaia gave a damn about what I ate one day and shat the next, I wouldn't be here now, would I? The earth wants to be healed, Eoghan, and who's makin' it hurt like this? Those same fecking villagers on whose behalf ye come here, all full of outrage. Where's the outrage for this great big bog, lad, that we are supposed to fix because they're too stupid to think of the long term?"

"We can fix the land and we can educate the villagers and we can sacrifice when we have to, but we can't become the horrors we're supposed to be fighting. There's a reason that Druidic law overlays the laws of Gaia! How can ye stand there and tell me it doesn't matter?"

"Because it doesn't," he replies, his voice cold as a penguin pecker in an Antarctic winter. "And besides: Children are delicious."

Well, after that, there wasn't much use for talking. It was going to be a fight and nothing for it, except it's not often that two Druids try to end one another. If we face off in a cattle raid, we don't do much apart from trying to give our side an advantage or make things tough for the enemy—summoning some fog or softening the earth, that sort of thing. We rarely attack one another directly, because the truth is we are bound to Gaia, not this king or that warlord.

But Dubhlainn had somehow decided this meant he was no longer bound to humanity. I knew he had to be torn from the world before he could tear apart any more lives.

I shift me shape into a bear and he shifts to a tiger and we try our best to rip up the other guy's flesh faster than he can heal it—for what else can we do? If we cast camouflage, the aura is still visible in magical sight.

He scratches up an eye and blinds me on one side, but I back up and keep the other eye on him while it heals. He keeps coming, thinking to press his advantage, but he's never fought a bear before and doesn't realize I'm perfectly happy to swipe at him while I'm back on me heels. He charges right into a timed haymaker, and me claws—powered by a whole lot of muscle and more than me usual store of anger—take off most of his nose and knock out a tooth as well, spraying his blood into the fire, where it sizzles and hisses. That makes him pull back and think some.

While we circle and regroup, I contact the elemental and ask that Dubhlainn's access to energy be cut off. It asks me why and I explain that he's broken Druidic law by eating the children of those he's supposed to protect. The answer is basically, //So what?// and it chills me—changes me too.

Dubhlainn had been right: He hadn't used bindings to commit murder, and he was doing what he could to amend the soil, so according to Gaia he was finer than a frog's hair. It threw into question all the pillars of morality I'd been taught: Me archdruid had presented everything as if it had been received wisdom from Gaia herself.

If I wanted him dead, I'd have to somehow prove to be more savage than he was. And if I failed, he'd probably not be bothered, much less challenged, for years, free to prey on all the villages around Boora Bog.

I charge at him, head cocked to keep me good eye on him, thinking I will take whatever he wants to dish out so long as I can give him an answer. Tough to anticipate whether he will try to sidestep and come at me blind side or take a swipe at the target of me other eye—he'd surely love to have a blind opponent, but maybe he's the type of fighter to attack weakness every time. I try to be ready for either: I'm going to be taking claws to the head regardless, so it's kind of like choosing whether to place your head in a hippo's mouth or up its arse.

Just before I reach him, his muscles bunch and give me a tell: Tigers aren't built to sidestep, and that blow's going to come at me good right eye. I rise up on me back legs a bit and lift a paw in time to take the brunt of his attack. It knocks me near off me feet, but he's committed to it so hard that the follow-through has him out of guard and vulnerable. He sees me left coming but can't avoid it because I still have plenty of momentum left from me charge. It catches him square on the side of the head, ear to bottom of the jaw, and there's a crunch and a deep gouge left behind, no chance of him opening that mouth to bite me for a while, and he tumbles over besides.

I press in before he can regain his feet, me teeth at his

throat. He tears into me with all the claws, ripping open me belly in a desperate bid to repel me, and I back away all right, but not without taking his jugular out for some fresh air.

That proves too much for him and he bleeds out before he can heal it up, and I spit out the flesh in me teeth before I can vomit.

As I collapse and try to focus on me healing, a crow spirals down and lands on Dubhlainn's face. It wastes no time but plucks out the eyes and swallows them. I'm thinkin' that crow better not try such shenanigans with me when a scratchy voice enters me head, as if in answer.

Ye have nothing to fear from the Morrigan today, Eoghan Ó Cinnéide. The head turns and the eyes glow red and I realize I'm looking at the Chooser of the Slain herself. Me hackles rise and I shudder in fear, no help for it. And then I wonder if the Morrigan had anything to do with me victory.

I may have helped a bit, she says, answering me thoughts again. *But it was still you who found him, and it was your choice to fight.*

I want to shift to human so I might be able to talk, but I worry that it might slow me healing or make something worse if I do. I'd really like to know if other Druids had found Dubhlainn, seen what he was, and chose not to fight him. I needn't have worried; the Morrigan read that in me mind as well.

Two others found him, knew him for a villain, and left him alone. They do not have much longer to live. The next time they fight—and I will make sure it's soon—I will take them and eat their hearts, for they looked this evil in the eye and did nothing but let it pass them by and grow. But you, Eoghan, will have a long, productive life. I know this to be true. We will speak again, years hence, well before it is your time to move on. Harmony until then.

That was the only hint she ever gave me that she planned to park me arse on a time island later. She takes off after that, apparently only interested in his tiger eyes. I hoped she stowed Dubhlainn's spirit somewhere dark.

It's no small thing, killing another Druid and having a death goddess give ye an "attaboy!" I take a few days to heal and think over what it all means. I search Dubhlainn's house, such as it is, and find that he's been keeping souvenirs in that jewelry box: It's full of finger bones. I haven't trusted men in bogs ever since, nor any other hermit out in the wilderness.

I leave the tiger's body for carrion and fly back north, bag of clothes gripped in me talons. On the way to the village, I figure I'll only stay long enough to give them the news and assure them that the bogeyman is dead. They're to give me no welcome after I tell them it was a Druid that had been feasting on them all this while. Even if they believe I'm nothing like Dubhlainn, every time they see me they will think of who and what they've lost, and that's no way for any of us to live.

With me guts back in their proper place and me left eye healed up, I have no trouble seeing there's a cattle raid in progress when I arrive—or, rather, a raid that's nearly over, and failed to boot. The attackers have been routed and they're scrambling away from the bodies of the fallen. The defenders aren't keen on pursuing, but I'm keen to know where those attackers might hail from.

Ignoring the village for the moment, I fly ahead of the three men headed home and land in front of them, shifting to human so that they know right away I'm a Druid. They veer away to either side, terrified, but I hold up a hand and call out that I merely wish to talk, their safety guaranteed.

"Would I be right in thinking," I asks them, "that your village could use a Druid on its side now? Because ye sure don't have one, judging by what I saw back there."

They admit I would have been most welcome a few minutes ago.

"If I'd been here a few minutes ago I would have been on the other side, and every fecking one o' ye would be dead," I says. "But I'm looking to move on and give help where it's needed. So what do ye say? Will ye put up a Druid and let me teach and honor the gods below? I won't come where I'm not welcome."

They agree, and I tell them to wait while I say me farewells to the villagers and help them bury their dead as well as the dead raiders.

Saoirse screams and attacks me with her fists when I tell her Siobhan is dead—that they're all dead, the livestock and children alike. I don't blame her; there's no one else to receive the rage she must set free before it gnaws away her insides. Some of the other parents who lost their children much earlier well up, shed some tears, but wind up thanking me, because at least now they know. But no one is sorry to see me go.

As I take me leave to join the three surviving raiders, I think that Dubhlainn was only half right: Gaia might not give a damn about human laws, but that doesn't mean human laws are meaningless or serve no valid purpose. On the contrary, we can hardly serve Gaia and be stewards of the earth if we do not have law and civility.

The survivors lead me back to their village, on the eastern side of the bog, a wee poor place of half-starved citizens with hollow cheeks and haunted eyes. Unlike the other village, which was more prosperous, they are quite ready to accept help and instruction.

Some of them are wrecks when they hear that their fathers or brothers or husbands fell. One woman and her fire-headed son, however, are not sorry at all. They trade a look of relief, and maybe there's a glimmer of hope in their expressions too. Whoever they lost, he must have been a shite father and husband. The purpling under the mother's left eye tells me more than enough.

I meet the lad formally the next day. He's seven, sharp as a knife's point, and curious about everything. I can hardly finish a sentence without him asking me another question, and when I take him to task for it, he grins at me. "Sorry, Archdruid," he says, even though I wasn't one yet—he knew how to flatter and manipulate straightaway. "It's just that I haven't had anyone around who would answer me before."

So that's how I met Siodhachan Ó Suileabháin and took him on as an apprentice. I'd buried his father back there and his life would have been shite, sure, and his whole village would have suffered too, if I hadn't come along to help them through those lean times. His life would certainly have been much shorter, and I imagine the world would be much different without him swinging his cock around for two thousand years. But just different, mind: no way to know if it would be better or worse.

But looking back on it now, it was what happened at Boora Bog that made Siodhachan turn out the way he did. Because I didn't train him the same way as I'd been taught, did I? I didn't present Gaia's law and Druidic law as one big monolith that must be followed at all times. I taught him that sometimes ye could break those Druidic laws—or other laws, for that matter—and get away with it if ye truly needed to, because Gaia wouldn't care.

So that's why he had the stones to steal Fragarach from the Tuatha Dé Danann and make this deal and that awful bargain. If he was going to be the best Druid he could be, he needed to stay alive and grow powerful, and if he broke all the rules and cheesed off all the Fae in the process, well, it was justified to his way of thinking, because he always served Gaia.

Greta props herself up on an elbow and stares at me. "Are you telling me that you're responsible for his behavior?"

"Nay, he's responsible for his own bollocks. I'm to blame for teaching him to question authority, its priorities and motivations, and to fight that authority when he saw it conflicting with Gaia's interests."

Me love frowns and gives a tiny shake of her head. "Why would you do that when it could turn him into the same kind of monster that Dubhlainn was—a lawless predator?"

"Because I didn't want him to become a bitter cynic like me, disillusioned and questioning me whole training like it was all a lie! I wanted him to have the whole truth and be a skeptic, which is a very different thing. And besides, I knew going into it that if he *did* turn out bad, the Morrigan would make sure he got cut down. But that's clearly not what happened. The way he tells it, the Morrigan actually wound up protecting him for a long time."

Greta blinks, trying to absorb that information and make it fit with her experience of him.

"It comes down to the fact that he serves a different value system than any human one. I pointed out that Gaia was interested in protecting the vitality and variety of life on the whole planet. Broadly speaking that's difficult to argue, because unless you're falling prey to this predator or that, that basic value is pure and good and beneficial to all concerned, if ye take the long and wide view. But humans, I taught him, rarely take that view. Human laws think of protecting humans first. Though if ye look closely at most human laws, they tend to benefit a narrow few over the good of all humans. I'm sure ye can think of a law or three that protects someone's personal profit rather than what's good for everyone."

Greta rolls her eyes. "That's easy. The tax code protects the rich, and lots of voting laws protect a white majority, and arbitration clauses protect corporations from getting sued when they rip people off, and we could go on all day."

"Good, so ye see me point. That's basically the core of what I taught him: Protect Gaia first, protect humans second, and question everything else. That probably led him to construct a strange moral compass. And looking at Granuaile, I wonder if he might have taught her in an even more extreme fashion— that Gaia's law is all that matters and human laws are just shite to carefully step over in pursuit of defending the planet."

"Huh. We kind of think that way too. The pack, I mean. We step around the law constantly to protect our own interests. What I want to know is this: Are you planning on teaching your current apprentices the same way?"

"I don't know. Well, no—it's already different. I'm not half so angry as I used to be. I'm still boiling over what's been done to the planet since the Morrigan put me in long-term storage, but I think I understand that all people are protecting what's theirs and rarely think beyond what they're going to eat in the next week. And I understand that training minds to think differently is a long road, but at least I have the time to walk it. These are good kids and we're in a good place now."

"Yes." Greta pats me chest a couple times, falls back and looks up at the sky with me, and sighs her contentment. "That we are, Owen."

"I'm glad I get to walk this long road with you, love."

Greta giggles, which is not the reaction I'd hoped for. "Are you getting sentimental on me, Teddy Bear?"

"Nah, I just injured me gob. I have no idea what the hell just happened. I was trying to grunt and it came out all wrong."

She chuckles and drapes a leg across me, planting a kiss on me cheek. "I think someone's told you about foreplay."

"I thought the fighting was the foreplay."

"Ha!" She kisses me again. "You're not still bleeding anywhere, are you?"

"I'm good to go."

She shifts all her weight on top of me, cups me face in her hands, and says nose-to-nose, "Let's have that long walk, then."

cuddLe dungeon

This story, narrated by Perun, takes place after the events of
Staked, Book 8 in The Iron Druid Chronicles.

When I am invited to this thing called "Cuddle Dungeon," I am thinking perhaps my English still not so good, or maybe these are very strange peoples. Dungeon is prison underground and full of many unpleasant things—rats and bad smells and moist coughing noises. Cuddles is soft and warm times before or after sex. I would not think to put these things together, but these modern peoples do.

My lover, Flidais, tries to say is ironic, a kind of joke, but I am not understanding. So she shrugs and says, "Is Scottish," which she says about everything I do not understand. But she also says this for things she does not want to explain. Like who invited her to bring me to Cuddle Dungeon: "Some Scottish lad."

Is very confusing being old Slavic thunder god in modern

world, but is good that there are new kinds of dungeons, I suppose. Is consistent with technology culture obsessed with upgrades. They upgrade everything now: even dungeons.

We join line in wet city of Edinburgh, down narrow cobbled alley between old brick buildings where there are stairs leading belowground. Man at front of line holds out hand, and Flidais gives him tickets she buy somewhere before. Man looks at me and laughs and says, "Ye have no fookin' idea what you're doing here, do ye?"

I point to downstairs door. "Am cuddling," I say, and he laughs again and says stream of words in Scottish accent so thick I am not understanding.

I ask Flidais as we go down, "Why does small man laugh at me? What is going to happen?"

"I don't know, Perun," she says. "That's why I'm here. I want to be surprised. I want something new."

She is old Irish goddess of the hunt, maybe older than me. We do not speak of our many years, of our boredom with routine. We seek new experience instead and see if humans can surprise us. Is very long battle, fighting boredom. Is why when Flidais saw me in leather shop in Prague with the Druid named Atticus she thought we should try leather for sexy times, and I agree very fast because is novelty for me. But leather clothings is only outward sign of a certain kind of play, Flidais tells me. There is rules and behaviors and many, many toys. All we have now is the clothes: We have leathers under long jackets that cover us up, and other peoples in line are covered up too.

I am hoping is much fun behind door. Already going down steps I feel more alive. Anticipation is sweet thing. I am wishing staircase is longer just so I can anticipate for longer time.

Door is metal and loud creaking on hinges. When we open we hear people laughing. Also screaming. Maybe some moaning too, and thumping music. Wall ahead is white and padded like marshmallow room. We have hallway to walk down, and lights get dim as we go. Bright near door, a bit darker down the hall. But wall stays white and fluffy on all sides.

Screaming and laughing get louder as we go, and Flidais looks at me with smile on face. She enjoys anticipation too.

We turn corner and find selves in another hallway going both directions. There are doorways but with no doors in them on either side. Is like maze.

"Which way?" I ask, and Flidais shrugs again.

Choice is made for us when very large and broad man emerges from doorway to our right and charges, yelling battle cry. Is bigger than me, and is naked except for black mask around eyes and black leather around groin. His body is oiled and jiggles very muchly, and his arms spread wide like he is coming for crushing bear hug. We run away but join the peoples we hear laughing. In place where good times are to be had, is fun to be chased and not know what is happening.

Flidais darts around corner into twisty passage and I follow. After three turns it is dead end and we turn around, smiling. We take two or three steps back the way we came, sneaky moving, thinking maybe running oily chubby man will pass us by. But then he turns corner and crashes into fluffy wall, out of breath.

"There you are!" he says, straightening up. He does not have Scottish accent. Sounds more American. "Thought you'd lose me, eh?" Flidais giggles at that. If she had not wanted him to see us, he would not have. "Why'd you run? I just wanted to dance for you." He makes *oontz-oontz-oontz* noise, puts hands behind head, and thrusts hips in time to his own music. His flesh ripples and flaps around and is so unexpected we lose our good manners. Flidais laughs so hard she sinks to floor, unable to stand, clutching her middle and her eyes all scrunchy and teary at the edges. I am almost same, roaring louder than I have in many years: I have to stagger back and lean against wall for support. I know Flidais has never laughed so hard since being with me. Cuddle Dungeon is already worth price of admission.

Funny dancing man finally has mercy and stops thrusting hips. "Right," he says, smiling very big smile at us. He is not offended by our laughs; is what he wants. He takes couple of deep breaths. "I'm Paul. I'm going to be your guide and take you to the shop in case you need any last-minute items, and then you can go from there to the main play area. While we walk I can go over the house rules—even if you already know them—because failure to abide by them will get you thrown out."

We flick tears away from eyes and thank him, and I hold out hand to Flidais to help her to her feet. She is wearing tight thing called corset under her coat and cannot bend so well.

"Please lead on, Paul," she says.

"Right! This way, please." Once we turn corner behind him, he says important rule speech from memory over his shoulder and is very serious now, no more smiles.

"Consent and safety are of prime importance in everything we do here. Do not touch anyone without their express verbal consent or you will be asked to leave. Likewise, if someone touches you without your express verbal consent, report it and they will be asked to leave. Do not talk to a sub without their domme's permission. Watch all the scenes in the dungeon you like, but if you want to play yourself and be watched in turn, make sure you have your safe word settled and, of course, *red* is the universal one. If either of you says that, a dungeon master will come to make sure everything's okay."

He says more things like this, but I am already unsure what he is talking about. I hope Flidais knows. He says "dungeon" a lot and says no pictures are allowed but nothing about cuddles. At least is easy to remember not to touch other peoples. I am here for Flidais only.

Soon we go through door and white marshmallow walls end. We enter room with black walls that must be shop. There are many things on walls made of black leather and metal, and there are shelves with items I have never seen before and do not know what they do. But there are peoples there who know these things and also know exactly what they want. Like us they wear not much clothes, except they do not have coats covering them up. Paul points to right side and says the counter there is coat-check area, and door past cash register is entrance to play area; then he tells us to enjoy our evening.

A man with many piercings in face and chest stands at the coat check, with bands of spiky leather around his neck and wrists. He also has tattoos on most of his skin; these disappear beneath tight pants like rock star wears.

We take off coats and hand them to him. His eyes linger on me more than Flidais, so I assume he must like men, because Flidais is goddess in all senses. Other eyes in shop see what I see: She is most beautiful. But since I am also god I get my looks too. I am very hairy and not so beautiful, but peoples have different tastes and some of them like muscles. I am told American word for me is *beefcake*, though I am not made of cow flesh and am also nothing like frosted sugar pastry.

I am wearing collar with a metal ring in front. Flidais takes chain out of coat pocket before man hangs them up and clips one end to my collar. Tonight, she says, I am her pet. She also takes small money purse from pocket.

Coat-check man asks for our phones and we say we have none. He does not believe at first, but Flidais points to her clothes and mine. She has black corset under bust and nothing above it except fulgurite talisman dangling between breasts to protect from my lightning—when I am excited my touch can be electric in literal way. Below hips is thin bikini underwear and then thick-soled boots with many buckles up to knees. I have harness across chest and back that makes letter X under my collar and then a leather jock with front that opens as needed. "Where do you think we'd be hiding them? I don't even have a place for my purse." Man admits we have zero pockets and no phone-shaped bulges and gives her ticket for coats.

We turn and see many heads in shop look away from either my backside or Flidais's. We both chuckle at this. But I think we are both excited too. There is much skin on display, many curves and cleavages, silvery studs and spikes on black leather wrapped around so many soft lines and hard edges, attractive on all shapes and skin colors. These clothings are made to be seen.

Flidais leads me to place on wall where different whips are hanging. She buys a kind called a riding crop, with money from purse, but nothing else.

"Crop is for what?" I ask, but she does not answer question. Instead, she says for rest of evening I should not speak unless she gives permission first. Is part of the experience, she explains, and so I do not ask about all the other things I see.

We go through door to play area and the music changes. Is not slick thumping electric pulse anymore but loud angry metal guitar. And this is where the screaming is.

Room is very large and dark, with only lights coming from kind you see in dance clubs—cones of rage-face red and urine yellow and fake raspberry blue shining down on scenes.

A slim woman dressed the exact opposite of Paul welcomes us. She has leather on entire body *except* for eyes and happy place. There is zipper over her mouth, but this is open to allow speaking.

"Is this your first time in our dungeon?" she asks Flidais in Scottish English, ignoring me. My lover nods and woman points at lighted scenes, naming them. "We have a standard bondage table there, a punishment bench, a jail cell, a set of bondage chairs next to it, and on the back wall on the other side of the center stage is a row of stockades of different kinds. On this other wall we have lockdown systems and pillories and a couple of bondage horses. You're welcome to use anything not currently being used by others."

Much is being used already. Some men, some women, bound to these things with steel clasps or rope, are being tickled, slapped, pinched, and more by partners. They make many noises above loud music, but this treatment they are wanting. And other peoples are watching.

Zipper Woman says, "I was also told to tell ye she's not here yet but will be once the center-stage scene begins. She's always here for that."

"Thank you," Flidais replies, and I forget my instructions.

"Who will be here?" I ask, and Flidais flicks my chest with crop, stinging my nipple.

"Do not speak!" She watches me to see if I will respond, but I keep mouth shut. Satisfied, she turns to woman and says, "When will the center-stage scene begin?"

"Soon," she says.

"Okay. I think my partner and I will be playing."

"Great. Ye have settled upon a safe word, haven't ye?"

Flidais looks back at me. "Perun. You may answer. What's your safe word?"

"What is safe word?"

"We will be playing and having a good time, but if it stops being a good time for you, or if you want or need to stop for any reason at all, you say the safe word and I will stop and let you go. And the observers will make sure I do."

"Let me go?"

"I'm going to tie you up, Perun. I think you'll like it. So what's your safe word?"

"Um." I try to think of something I would never say during sexy times. "Beefcake."

Flidais looks at Zipper Woman and she nods, satisfied. "That's good."

"Who will be here later?" I ask Flidais, since she has not told me to be quiet again. But my question earns whip from crop and new command to be silent. Maybe person she waits for will be part of our play later. Maybe is surprise for me so she does not want to say.

Flidais says farewell to Zipper Woman and tugs gently on my chain. We walk around stage to left, taking in scenes, and some peoples who are watching turn to watch us. Flidais must turn down many invitations to play with us as we circle the stage. Is very polite.

When we get to far side opposite door, perhaps small bit to right, Flidais points with riding crop to strange wooden posts with cuffs and straps hanging from them. No: not cuffs like police have. These are wider and black steel. I remember now: Word is *manacles*.

"Let's begin," she says. "Stand in front of that, facing me."

I feel my excitement start with only these words. The anticipation has been building, and now I am thinking most of our play will be anticipation too.

Since I am tall man, Flidais must adjust this thing to fit me. She must bend and stretch to do this, and some peoples are attracted. They begin to drift our way, leaving other scenes to watch what we do.

Flidais places my right wrist into manacles so my arm points northwest if I am person lying flat on compass. My left arm goes into other manacles pointing northeast. More manacles near floor lock around my legs above the ankle. My limbs are like chest harness now, shaped like X.

As she does this to ensure I cannot touch her, she is constantly touching me, her fingernails tracing with light pressure my arms and legs. And she tells me how I will be teased and turned on in front of all these people—more are gathering to watch—until I am ready to explode. But I must not— I cannot—until she gives me permission.

This happens mostly like she says it will. Mostly.

She opens front of jock and my arousal is very much plain. But her fingers never touch me after that. Is all talking and touching with riding crop. But not having control—the anticipation and surprise of where I will next be touched, and how, with a sting or a caress—is much more exciting than I would have thought. And I did not expect to have peoples watching or to see on faces how much they like it, and this feels good to me also.

While Flidais brings me to edge and keeps me there, I

glimpse peoples behind watchers moving about on center stage. Short time later, strange man pushes to front of watchers, dressed in suit, no leather on except maybe shoes. He is not in Cuddle Dungeon for sexy times and does not look interested in me or Flidais or anyone. All the naked hotness is very boring to this man with white mustache all waxy at tips. He clears throat and says to Flidais, "She is here now and watching."

"Thank you," she says, turning her head only little bit to answer. He pushes back through crowd and disappears.

"Who—" I begin, but crop whacks me before I can say more.

"Never mind that now, Perun," Flidais says. "I think you've been very good and deserve to let go now." She drops the crop and presses herself against me, uses her hands, and is so different, so wanted, that I feel myself building to point of no return. Sparks light in my eyes, and electricity makes hairs on my body stand up. "Don't you want to lose control? I want you to. These people want you to. You have permission. Come on."

Is only seconds and shiver of ecstasy lights up spine, everything tightens, muscles clench, and then—nothing. Or, rather, something but not orgasm. Muscles go slack and I slump as much as manacles allow. They are in fact all that keeps me standing. All my strength is gone and head spins like pinwheel, colors firing in vision but all blurs, no shapes.

"Got you," Flidais says, but does not sound like she talks to me. I feel her at my right leg, undoing manacle.

"What happens? Something wrong." I try to remember safe word. "Cake!"

"Yes, we're finished playing. Time to go hunting."

Right leg free, my knee tries to flex and buckles. Other

manacles keep me standing. Vision clears enough to see Flidais working on left leg, but blotchy like looking through window in rainstorm.

"Hunting what?"

"Hunting whoever just siphoned your energy at the point of orgasm."

"Was it strange man in suit?"

"No, that was Aloysius MacBharrais, the Scots wizard." She says like I should know the name. "He's the one who told me there was a problem here."

Left leg is free and I wobble like walking on noodle. Muscles do not want to work. Flidais notices. "Am I going to have to carry you?"

"I should maybe lie down and eat whole chicken. Maybe five."

"No, Perun, we have to go after her," she insists, unlocking left arm. I try not to fall, but I topple forward. Flidais pushes me back to post.

"Thanks," I say, trying to lock knees and stay upright. Legs tremble beneath me. "Go after who?"

"The mad nymph who did this. She's trackable now. She's one of my daughter's."

"Fand sent nymph here?"

"No, I doubt that. She simply fled Tír na nÓg after Fand failed to overthrow Brighid, and she found a way to live in the iron world."

The woman with zipper mouth comes forward and asks if I am all right, if we need help.

"Maybe," Flidais says. "Help keep him standing for me if he needs it when I undo this last manacle."

Zipper Woman puts shoulder underneath my left arm. "What happened?"

"He's just having an episode," Flidais says, which is true but hardly whole story. She undoes other arm, and I would have fallen except that she and Zipper Woman hold me up. Never have I been so weak. "We need to get him to coat check. I have some medicine in my pocket." I am thinking this must be lie. How could she have medicine for this? But I stagger to coat check with their help, past the stage and peoples who continue to do sex under lights and loud music.

Vision clears more, but I do not see this nymph. I want to ask Flidais more but do not think is good time when Zipper Woman can hear.

Pierced tattoo man gives us coats, and Flidais takes small glass bottle out of pocket and removes cork. "Drink this," she says.

Is like chocolate sludge with alcohol and maybe handful of sand. I choke it down, cough a few times, eyes watering. And as I look down I see I am not so excited anymore. Penis droops like very sad snake. I put it away and close up flap of jock.

"Better?" she asks, nodding her head to give me hint at right answer.

"Yes," I say. "Much better now."

"Thanks for your help," Flidais says to Zipper Woman. "We'll be fine. Enjoy your evening."

Zipper Woman also takes hint and leaves us. We put on coats and move away from counter so we can talk in privates. My legs steady now but I move slow.

"Tell me about nymph. And what I drank."

"The drink is something Goibhniu brewed up before he died. It was a gift to me, to restore my energy should I need it when hunting in cities, cut off from the earth. But I thought it would help you out in this instance. You should be feeling better very soon."

"Already feel better. But how did you know I would need?"

"A couple days ago Aloysius MacBharrais informed me that one of the Fae had been preying on sexual energy in the Cuddle Dungeon, violating some very old treaties that the Tuatha Dé Danann have with the Scots. As a courtesy he contacted me to ask if I'd like to take care of it, and I said I would. Because whoever it turned out to be might know something about Fand. And I'd like to know what started her doing this."

"I would like to know this too! Nymph is maniac."

Flidais snorts and grins as if I say something funny. "Are you ready?"

"No, I have important question." With my wits returning, I am realizing that she uses me. She planned to or she would not have brought potion. She knew from start that nymph would be here. "Why am I bait for nymph without asking me first?"

"Because you wouldn't have enjoyed yourself if you knew we were hunting while playing. And because you'll be fine."

"I did not get to enjoy myself and am not fine, Flidais. You bring me here under false pretense."

"No, I didn't. I said we were going to play tonight, and we did. I left out the part where I'd be mixing a bit of business with our pleasure, but the pleasure will resume soon. You will be better than before, and I promise I will make it up to you. But we have to catch her first."

"Why?"

"You want to be a god of thunder again, don't you?"

"I am god of thunder now."

"In name only, I'm afraid. She didn't just rob you of an orgasm. She stole your thunder."

I scoff at this. "Impossible." But I try to feel the clouds and moisture in air and cannot. Is worrisome, but I remember this happens sometimes when I am underground. "Is she still here?"

"No, she left the building as soon as she could. But we'll find her."

"Let's go." We make way through maze of marshmallow wall to stairs and then dark alley, my mood souring like goat milk in sun. Scots wizard with mustache is waiting there. He dips head to our left.

"She went that way," he says. "Very unstable."

"Thanks, Aloysius," Flidais says. We jog down alley, and body feels much better now but no longer like god. I cannot feel clouds or winds. Nymph really did steal powers.

"If that Scotsman can find her, why not have him help you hunt this nymph? Why let her take my strength?"

"Because nymphs are nearly impossible to hunt unless you mark them somehow or know exactly where they like to hide. They just disappear into whatever element they're kin to. Fill her up with thunder god, though, and she won't blend in no matter what she does. Can you smell it? Singed air and burned hair. She got more than she bargained for."

Is fair to say I also got more than I bargained for. Or maybe I get no bargain at all. I come to dungeon for good time—which maybe is problem, I admit—but I get bad time instead. Is very uncomfortable to feel stripped of what made me Perun. If nymph has my power and I confront her now, will I still be immune to lightning?

I am seething as we follow trail through wet cobbled streets of Edinburgh. Is good English word, this *seething*. Very much anger but very much hidden. Because this should not be happening. I should not be casual means to some end.

Especially an end I am not knowing. Flidais continues to hide true purposes from me. The end I want is to feel the lightning again.

"She's heading to Holyrood Park," Flidais says, nostrils flaring, following scent. "We have to—wait, there she is!"

She points ahead to staggering person under streetlights. Looks like tiny dark-haired woman fighting bees around her head, except there are no bees. Is only madness and sparks of lightning. Peoples give cry and move away from her on street because she frightens them. She is in clear pains. Small Irish nymph is not meant to hold powers of old Slavic god.

She is also close to park—lights end ahead, and that must mean large place of nature.

We pick up paces because target is now clear. Flidais is faster and tackles nymph just as she reaches first grass of park. Nymph roars like me, not making noise one would expect from tiny person. Lightning strikes Flidais, not from sky but from nymph, and surrounds her in forking tongues of blue and white. She is protected by fulgurite talisman and shouts at nymph to stop, she just wants to talk. She flips nymph onto back and pins her.

But nymph has no control of this power. Head shakes back and forth, roar keeps going with rage of modern boy playing video game, and eyes glow with fire of angry sky.

Flidais asks about Fand and about Manannan Mac Lir. About their plans. Their defenses. How she learned to siphon energy. To all these questions nymph only screams and struggles. Peoples begin to look our way, which is not good.

Is clear nymph has lost most of mind, and I grow frustrated. Is all wasted effort, and I feel like pawn sacrificed in meaningless game. In truth is not even my game: Is Irish game and I should not be involved.

"Nine bloody hells," Flidais mutters, and pulls hunk of cold iron out of inside coat pocket. "It wasn't supposed to go this way." Is mercy when she presses iron to nymph's forehead.

Nymph gives short scream, turns to ash, and power she took from me crackles in air and returns where it should. My body is strong again, the wind whispers in my thoughts, the thunder and lightning booms and cracks too. Is like dive into refreshing pool, swimming in health. I have not felt this fine in ages. Is good to be reminded of my gifts, of what my peoples granted me with their beliefs. And Flidais thought these gifts were hers to play with.

The never-ending summer of Tír na nÓg is pleasant but is perfect example of how the Tuatha Dé Danann manipulate natural order of things. I am Slavic god of that natural order, and I too was manipulated. Is time to be free again, to let rain wash away resentment and renew my peace of mind.

We have to spend short time waving away peoples who come to investigate screaming and lights. We assure them all is well. The nymph is scattered in wind, or her remains are invisible in darkness. There is nothing to see. When they go away I look at my lover and do what I must.

"You remember what Paul, funny dancing man, said?" I remove coat and unclasp harness, leaving on collar and jock. "He said, 'Consent is prime importance.' He was talking sexy things, but applies to other things also. You did not have my consent to do this. You thought it okay to use me. Is not okay, Flidais."

She stretches out hand to me, shaking her head. "Perun—"

"No. I am very thankful for good times with you. Will always be, in fact, for they are truly good times. But I think is over now. Weles is dead and Loki cannot find me. So I stay on earth and enjoy stormy weather again. Please do me favor and leave my axe with the Druid Atticus. I will pick up later. Goodbye."

As Flidais protests, I change my shape into eagle, step out of jock and duck out of collar, then take wing into cool moonlight sky darkening with thunderclouds. I bank east to make flight across oceans and plains and mountains to neglected land of my peoples. I have been gone for very long time, and now I want nothing so much as to be home.

Blood Pudding

This story of Granuaile's takes place after the events of Staked and Oberon's Meaty Mysteries: The Purloined Poodle.

i have had only one tutor for so long that having thirteen is like learning that ice cream comes in more flavors than plain vanilla or feeling the delicious chill of a swelling chorus that touches the soul where a solo voice cannot. There is richness and variety and a shared joy—they love to see me learn and I exult in their approval. Learning Polish not only from the words of Wisława Szymborska but from the Sisters of the Three Auroras and the many customers at the pub where I work now in Warszawa is so rewarding. I pretty much come home to Oregon and do little more than collapse, for which I feel guilty, but fortunately Atticus is a patient man who can take the long view. He has given me no grief over my hours spent abroad. He had me all to himself for twelve years, after all, and a little more besides, and he knows very well the importance of developing multiple headspaces.

I smile when I think of the concatenation of events that led me to bartending again. When I worked at Rúla Búla, it was a prelude to becoming a Druid. I wonder what grand adventure awaits me now at Browar Szóstej Dzielnicy?

The brewpub is busy and I have a good co-worker, Oliwia Żuraw, who's bilingual and happy to help me improve my Polish when I need it. She spent some years in the UK, so her English is a delightful blend of Suffolk and Warszawa.

But the customers are equally happy to help. The men, especially, are eager to first correct me on my pronunciation and then, when I say it precisely the way I said it the first time, tell me I'm getting better. I field plenty of questions about my tattoos—*tatuaże*—and I've found it's difficult to give an answer anyone will like.

If I say it's just personal, they feel like I'm blowing them off. If I tell them the truth—that I'm a Druid and the tattoos bind me to Gaia—they kind of smile uncertainly, nod, and then very carefully order their next round from Oliwia. Same reaction if I tell them I got inked in prison—though one guy does ask what I did time for.

"I killed a man . . . with this thumb!" He doesn't get the reference to *Ratatouille*. He thinks I'm being serious and squints at me.

"You were in for murder and you're already out?"

"Shh. They didn't let me go. I escaped. But don't tell anyone, okay?"

He finally understands I'm kidding at that point but isn't amused, and apparently he's a regular. "Hey, Oliwia, who is this new girl?" he says.

"Just another American hiding from all the other Americans with guns," she tells him, and he cracks a smile at that.

"Well, she kills people with her thumb!"

After that particular shift I head to Malina Sokołowska's house, across the river in the Radość neighborhood, to continue my Polish-language studies with the coven. I work mostly with Anna, who enjoys Szymborska's poetry so much, but I make a point of posing a question to Agnieszka, who's very accomplished at wards and took the lead in cloaking me from divination.

"Do you think it would be possible to put some kind of cloak on my tattoos?" I ask. "People keep asking me about them at the brewery and it's annoying."

"This is merely a visual cloak, yes? Not something that would cloak the powers or the bindings in any way?"

"Right."

"Hmm." She taps her chin as she considers, and Roksana pokes her head around the corner to speak up, her curls spilling free for once instead of bound up behind her head.

"Not to eavesdrop, but I overheard your question. What if we did a reverse charm instead of a cloak?"

"What? Encourage the eye to look elsewhere instead of 'look specifically here'? I'm afraid that would make people look away from her altogether. And what about the part of that charm that affects desire? If we reverse that, then we could be encouraging people to be revolted."

"Well, obviously I don't have it all figured out," Roksana replies, blinking rapidly through her glasses. "I'm just offering a starting point."

"Oh, yes, I understand. There's certainly plenty to consider." Agnieszka turns to me and asks, "Give us some time to think about it?"

"Of course." It's only a couple of days before they come back with something, and they try it only on my healing circle to make sure they don't mess up anything on my forearm, which is what allows me to shift planes and go home.

"This isn't going to be a charm or a reverse charm or anything," Agnieszka explains. "It was a fascinating conversation and we might use some of the ideas elsewhere, but for you, we think we've come up with a cloak."

Berta first smears a clear but smelly goo on my hand. "Cooked it up myself," she says, though I'd already assumed as much. It wasn't the sort of thing one finds at CVS.

I thought Berta just enjoyed cooking when I first met her but it turns out that she and Martyna are the coven's experts at potions and ritual ingredients. They cook and bake in the mundane sense as a way to one-up each other and often make me judge the results.

"What is it?"

"That's a binder for the cloak. The cloak will attach to that binder, not your tattoos, but then that binder is being absorbed into your skin, so the cloak should stay there and conceal your tattoos without affecting your actual binding to the earth."

"In theory?"

"Yes, in theory."

The rest of the coven arrives and Agnieszka leads them in attaching the cloak. It's much faster than the ritual for shielding me from divination, and when they're finished, the healing circle on my hand fades from view.

"Oh, that is wicked cool," I say, grinning at them.

"But you need to test it," Malina says, handing me a knife. "We need to know if you can still heal."

"Right." I give myself a small cut on my left forearm, just enough to start the blood flowing a wee bit, then command my body to knit up the skin. The cut closes and you'd never know there was a wound. It works.

"Victory! Fist bumps all around! And mandatory preening at this evidence of your awesome skills!"

Success confirmed, the coven cloaks my forearm too, but I leave the shape-shifting bands on my biceps alone. I really like those. I give everyone hugs and have to judge two celebratory chocolate cakes before my shift begins at the brewery.

A couple of hours into it, around eight o'clock, a handsome man with a long-distance-runner's physique approaches the bar, his cheeks falling away like the white cliffs of Dover and his jaw sharp as the edge of an anvil. Hair and clothes look like he has a date with a catalog photo shoot in a couple of hours. He's crisp and clean and might not mind going shopping for a few hours. Pretty dreamy, if I'm being honest.

I ask him in Polish what I can get for him. His eyes flash down—not to my chest, which would be typical male behavior, but to my arms, which I have stretched out, leaning my weight on the bar. He's looking in particular at my right arm.

"Is there an American working here, red hair like yours, but with tattoos on her forearm?" he asks. And the specific nature of that query creeps me out instantly. He's come looking for me but is obviously a stranger, or else he would know that I'm the one he's looking for. Someone told him to look for a redhead with tattoos; the cloak that the sisters put on them may have just saved me more than a minor annoyance at work.

"She's not here yet but should be any minute," I say, grabbing a bar napkin and placing it in front of him. "I can get you something while you wait."

He looks uncertain, then lets loose with a sheepish snort and a grin. "I'm not much of a drinker." His head turns to the man sitting at the bar next to him, enjoying a dessert that I wish I could find in the States. "What's he having?"

"That's beer pudding," I tell him. "It's outstanding. Shall I get you one?"

He shrugs a shoulder. "Sure," he says, and pulls up a seat next to the other customer, whose name is Maciej. He's become my first regular, a metalhead with a scraggly blond beard and a studded leather jacket. Occasionally his head will bob up and down in time to some sick riff he has looping in his head. He thinks I'm of his tribe because I know who Yngwie Malmsteen is and can even name a few of his songs.

"What's it taste like?" I hear the newcomer ask as I turn to punch in the order on the computer.

Maciej pauses to answer. I'm sure he's considering something epic, because he's given to excess when it comes to description. I'm expecting him to say, "It tastes like the sweet desperate cries of your enemy as you burn down his house and then dive headfirst into a lake of his tears," but apparently he's decided the posh man wouldn't appreciate it. "It's plum pudding cooked in stout, so you get a little bit of that chocolate malty flavor mixed in with the plum. Very good."

"That was a nice description, Maciej," I say, flashing him a smile as I grab a glass of water for the newcomer. Maciej's eyes look a bit worried when they meet mine. He's getting a bad vibe off the new guy too, and he didn't give me away when I lied about some other American girl with tattoos working here. Maciej had asked me where the tattoos went when he came in tonight, and I told him they were concealed because I was getting too much unwelcome attention from them. He hadn't thought that would be possible—tattoos were a good thing!—but now he understands perfectly.

I use the noise of scooping ice to cover the fact that I'm casting magical sight under my breath. I don't have a store of energy on me at the moment, but it's not a high-energy binding, so I figure it's worth taking the dip in my own reserves to figure out what I'm dealing with.

Maciej has a multicolored aura that suggests a preoccupation with sex and violence underneath a thick film of loneliness. Nothing surprising there. The handsome newcomer, however, has a dull gray aura with two pinpoints of red: one in his torso and one in his head. Which means he's a vampire. And he has exactly one day to get out of Poland for good. The treaty we signed with Leif Helgarson in Rome states that starting tomorrow I can unbind any vampires I find in Poland on sight.

I place the water down in front of him, already knowing he won't touch it or the beer pudding he ordered either. "What's your name, sweetie?" I ask him.

"Bartosz."

"I like it. Can I call you Bartosz with the Good Hair?"

He looks helpless at my question. He's obviously not a Beyoncé fan, which means he's out of step with most of the world. But I've seen that expression before: It's exactly what Leif Helgarson looks like when he doesn't understand what young people of today are talking about. Bartosz is from another era. "If you wish," he says, waving slim fingers to dismiss something unimportant. "What did you say the name of your coworker is?"

"I didn't. What do you need from her, if you don't even know her name?"

He reaches into his jacket and pulls out an envelope. "I am merely a messenger. I'm supposed to give this letter to the redheaded American with tattoos on her forearm."

He places it on the bar: classy linen stationery in an ivory cream, not addressed to anyone. "Oh. Well," I say, adopting what I hope is a casual, helpful tone, "I can give it to her if you want, no problem at all, if you're in a hurry."

"A kind offer. And what is your name?"

I don't want to give him my real name or my current alias either, so I make one up: "I'm Delilah."

"Delilah. Excellent. Delilah, please look at me." I do, and he immediately uses eye contact to attempt to charm me. I know what he's up to, because the cold iron talisman resting out of sight beneath my shirt presses against my chest, warding off this direct attack. And I *do* consider charms an attack, something I've discussed at length with the sisters: They're a subversion of the will, a mental assault, no matter how benign they're supposed to be.

"If I give this letter into your care, you will be sure to give it to your co-worker as soon as she arrives, won't you?"

"Yes," I say, and nod for good measure, doing my best to play along and sound dazed. But I mess up somehow, because he doesn't believe me. His head tilts to the side and he frowns.

"Are you sure? You sound uncertain."

I do a rapid calculation in my head: A letter delivered to a signee of a treaty banishing vampires from Poland on the eve of that provision taking effect cannot be anything positive. It's not a fond farewell, a "So long, and thanks for all the blood!" It's a challenge and a provocation. And if I don't meet it immediately—if Bartosz decides to get physical—I'm not going to survive, because he's seconds away from figuring out I'm not like other humans, not easily swayed and controlled and consumed. But I don't have my staff with me, and there's no easy access to the earth's power either. I am a weak human at the moment, with only one advantage: the ability to unbind vampires. Well, maybe two other advantages: surprise, and the American talent for bullshitting.

I flash a grin at him and nod, maintaining eye contact as I switch my language to Old Irish, reciting the unbinding that will separate his component parts and turn him into a slurry of minerals and blood. His frown deepens, because he doesn't recognize the language, and halfway through he tries to interrupt. "Wait, what? Speak Polish." I keep going, and it dawns on him that regardless of what I'm saying, I'm not charmed, as he thought I would be, and in fact something very untoward might be in progress. He might have been warned to expect something like it. His eyes go wide as the thought registers that I'm chanting something, not really speaking, and then he hisses and pops his fangs, lunging out of his chair to grab me as I complete the unbinding.

Those fine chiseled features shift and melt as the bones lose their shape and get pushed around by the liquefying muscles inside. I sidestep quickly to avoid an anticipated gush of blood from his open mouth—it vomits forth and drenches the drink-prep containers of citrus wedges and maraschino cherries. He deflates for a moment like an emptying bladder and then the skin comes apart, letting all that liquefied mess spew where it will. It fairly erupts out of his neck along with some chunks of tissue and brain, raining down on poor Maciej and plopping wetly into his beer pudding.

A goodly number of screams tear through the bar at the sight of this—most people don't see it all but catch the end, where a dude just appears to explode, and their fight-or-flight instinct takes over and there's an exodus for the door. Maciej lets out a raw, panicked yell and cringes a bit but otherwise doesn't move. He sees I'm still standing and the creepy guy is toast, and that's good enough for him, though after a couple of deep breaths he does start to shout, "Fuck! Shit!" over and over. I use the chaos to dart forward, snatch the blood-soaked envelope off the bar, and absorb the worst of the gore with a bar towel before cramming it into my back pocket.

Oliwia comes over from her end of the bar and says, "Oh, my God, what happened?"

"I don't know; that guy just exploded."

"What do you mean, exploded?"

"I mean he exploded."

Maciej stops his cursing, looks at his jacket, now all gules, and begins to laugh. "That! Was! So! Metalllll!" he shouts. I step away from Oliwia and lean over the bar to speak to him in low tones.

"When the police come, I need you to say nothing about why he was here or what he wanted. He just sat down, ordered pudding, and told us his name was Bartosz before he died."

"Hell yes," Maciej growls. "That is exactly what happened. I will say that I asked him about his job and he just exploded. Must have been a very stressful occupation."

"Good, that's good. I'll say the same. Your tab is on me today. Order whatever you like. Need anything now?"

"A shot of Żubrówka and a beer. And maybe a bar towel."

"Coming right up. And let me get that out of your way, because eww." I reach for his pudding goblet, now ruined with a small pond of blood and bits of brain in it, but Maciej stops me.

"No, no, wait, I need to take a picture first," he says, taking out his phone. "Blood pudding is the most metal pudding of all, ha ha!"

The manager emerges from the kitchen, takes a brief look at the scene, then says we're comping everyone's tab because it's not good business to make people pay for their emotional trauma. He closes the pub until the police arrive, and then for hours I'm busy pouring drinks and answering questions— from my co-workers, the police, and even the press, though I insist on no photos or images of any kind.

When I'm finally released, Scáthmhaide, my staff, is waiting for me in the employee area behind the kitchen. As soon as I pick it up, I draw on the power stored in the silver end and feel better; those two small bindings had wiped me out.

With a sliver of privacy at hand, I take the bloody envelope out of my pocket and open it. I read it twice and then dial a stored number on my phone, more pissed than I've been since I last saw my stepfather.

"Hello, Granuaile. I expected a call from you tonight," a cultured voice purrs in my ear.

"Fuck you, Leif. You knew he was coming?"

"I knew who . . . ? Excuse me. Has something happened?"

"Yes, something's happened! I had to unbind a vampire in my bar tonight!"

"Did you get his name?"

"Fucking Bartosz."

"Hmm. I do not know a Fucking Bartosz, but I can consult my roster."

"He's not why I'm calling. Before I unmade his ass he gave me a letter, which I just found time to read. It's signed by someone named Kacper Glowa. You recognize that name?"

"Oh, yes. Unfortunately. He is the reason why I expected

your call—I heard a rumor he would not be leaving Poland as per the agreement."

"That's not a rumor. It's a fact. Let me read you this shit verbatim."

"Please do. I would like to hear what has made you so upset."

"It reads: *To the young Druid bitch and her upstart Viking boy: I will not be leaving Poland, and neither will my friends. We do not recognize your treaty or the leadership of Leif Helgarson and do not consider ourselves required to obey the demands of children. Instead, obey your elders: Leave Poland, and indeed leave Rome. You may think because you surprised some ancient ones grown stale in their thinking that you deserve to lead. That is not the case. You may both leave or die. That is all.*"

"Ah," Leif said. "Well. What is the modern parlance for that? Cheeky? Saucy? Clumsily stumbling over one's own testicles? I think I have that right."

"What? Do you mean 'tripping balls' or something? Gods, stop trying to sound hip, Leif. You're even worse than Atticus led me to believe. What I want to know is why he called you a boy. Didn't you tell us in Rome that you were the oldest vampire in the world now?"

"I believe I used the phrase *as far as I know.* I did not know at the time that Kacper was still walking the earth. I thought he was unmade in World War Two. Obviously I was in error."

"So how old is he? I mean how much stronger is he than you are?"

"He is my elder by a hundred and thirty years, born into a tribe in the ninth century living near modern-day Krakow, before Poland became any sort of distinct political entity."

"Which means his claim to leadership among other vampires is legit."

"It is. He is a genuine threat. The vampires of Poland are certainly listening to him. Some have left, but I estimate that he has fifty to sixty more rallying to his banner, and perhaps others are coming in, urging him to contest my leadership."

"Nobody rallies to banners anymore, Leif."

"Old vampires do. His call to reject our treaty is reverberating around the globe, I assure you. I just learned of it myself today; he has picked his moment to emerge from obscurity. Tell me, has either Atticus or Owen received similar communication?"

"I don't know yet. I need to check in with them. But I bet they haven't, and you haven't either, am I right?"

"You are correct."

"I thought so. Because Kacper wouldn't call Atticus and Owen anything demeaning, would he? Atticus is eight or nine hundred years older than he is, and while Owen hasn't lived that long in subjective time, he was born before Atticus and wouldn't stand for such language."

"Surely you will not stand for it either?"

"Hell no, I'm going to unbind him just like his buddy Bartosz. As soon as I can find him. I don't suppose you know where he might be?"

"My information on him predates the rise of Hitler. He used to hold properties in and around Krakow. He may have shifted his holdings elsewhere after the war, but I imagine he simply transferred ownership to a new alias unknown to me."

"All right. I need you up here to help take care of this."

"I could not agree more. This challenge must not go unanswered."

"Call me when you're in the country."

I already had the next couple of days off, so that was fortunate. It might take more than that, however, to get the job done, and since the vampires were able to find me, my position at the brewery might be compromised. How *were* they able to do that? I wonder. I've only been here a couple of weeks and hadn't done any obvious Druidic stuff in that time, and I'm protected from divination now. I should have been completely anonymous. Somebody at the brewery—either a customer or an employee—knows a vampire.

It's late and I don't feel like reviewing the story again to the coven, so I jog to the bound tree in Pole Mokotowskie, take off my shoes, and shift home to Oregon. The coven could hear about it in the morning.

My sweet hound, Orlaith, greets me with such happiness that her body shakes in all directions. <Granuaile! Guess what! Guess what!>

What is it, Orlaith? I reply through our mental link.

<You're home and I'm happy! But guess what else!>

I can't possibly. Tell me.

<Atticus said I have six puppies coming! He looked in my belly and said there were six auras. Can you believe it? That's like five . . . plus one!>

You're right, it is! Wow! That's a lot of puppies!

<Oberon says it is because he is magnificent, but I think it's because *I'm* magnificent. Who do you think is right?>

Can't you both be magnificent?

<Well, yeah, that's what Atticus said, but, come on, I'm doing all the work here. And I know that five plus one equals six.>

That's an excellent point, Orlaith. Let us say, then, that you are magnificent and Oberon is kind of okay as far as dudes go. You can tell him I said so.

<Oh, that's going to make him growl! Hee hee! You are the best human and I love you.>

You are the best hound and I love you too. Are Atticus and Oberon inside?

<Yes! And Starbuck too!>

Oh! Of course! I'm embarrassed to have left him out, but Starbuck is such a new addition to our home; he's a Boston terrier that Atticus rescued in Portland and I'm still getting to know him.

<Atticus is preparing several chickens for our delight.>

He really said it just like that, didn't he?

<He did!>

Let's go see them. I take six happy steps, one for each puppy, before a message shoots up through the sole of my foot from the Willamette elemental. There is something that demands Druidic attention in Tasmania, and I hurry in to call Atticus outside so he can get the message as well.

After a quick hello and turning the stove down low, he joins me outside.

"Don't give an answer yet," I tell him. "We need to talk about what happened today."

"Okay."

We work it out so that he'll go to Tasmania on the earth's business, returning each night to make sure Orlaith and Starbuck are okay, and I'll return to Poland to enforce the treaty.

"Don't ever turn your back on Leif," he tells me. "His allegiance is only to himself. You're safe only so long as he believes you're of more benefit to him alive. And watch out: The ones you're after might be using infrared if they know you're coming."

He was referring to the single reliable way to penetrate camouflage—and, I assumed, the invisibility conferred by Scáthmhaide. The vampires had used it successfully against him in Germany. "Thanks for the reminder," I say, and we leave it settled and enjoy the delightful chicken and, later, some private time together, with the hounds firmly instructed to leave us alone for a while. I sleep in until noon, local time, and wake to my phone buzzing. Atticus and Oberon are already gone.

"I'm in Krakow," Leif says. "It is eight in the evening here."

"Okay. I am shifting into Las Wolski forest above Old Town in a half hour. Where will you be?"

"At Stary Port, a sailor-themed establishment where they serve grog and sing sea shanties. The address is Straszewskiego twenty-seven. Please hurry. The singing is already intolerable."

"I will be there soon after I shift, depending on how long it takes to run there from the bound tree."

A quick shower and some kisses to Orlaith's belly, some scritches for Starbuck, and a snack for them both, and I'm off. I shift into a forest on a hilltop above Krakow and descend, well rested and Scáthmhaide in hand, and give Malina a call to catch her up.

"Basically anything you can tell us about where Kacper Glowa or his alias might be would be helpful. We want to make Poland free of vampires as promised but could use some intel."

"And where is Mr. O'Sullivan?" Malina asks. "He's the one who made the promise."

"He's been called by Gaia to attend to something in Tasmania. I'm going to handle this with Leif Helgarson. He has a vested interest in making sure this gets done, and once it is, he'll be out of Poland too."

"And if Kacper Glowa is not in Krakow?"

"Then we'll go wherever he is, if you can give us a lead."

"The undead defy divination, so we'll try to divine his thralls. I'll call as soon as I have something."

Stary Port, I find, more than lives up to its nautical theme. Dark wooden tables with thin tapering candles in the center of them line the walls, and the place is generally decorated in warm tones. Portraits of old-timey ships in gold frames beckon to drinkers, like Tennyson's *Ulysses*, that "'tis not too late to seek a newer world." Leif Helgarson has seated himself upon a square-topped stool, delicately crossing one leg over the other in a place that practically shouts he should be manspreading. He looks intensely uncomfortable as a group of red-faced drunken men shout their way through a raucous Polish sea shanty about rope burns, with what I think might have been a double entendre on the word *rope*.

"I am so grateful you are here," Leif says as I take a seat. "They keep looking at me to join in. Do you know where Kacper is?"

"Not yet. Waiting for a clue from Malina."

"So it may be a while."

"Yeah. We should order something."

"Please get two of whatever you wish and then you may have mine as well."

"Have you, uh . . . eaten?"

He nods but provides no details, for which I'm thankful. I order two grogs with clove, cinnamon, and orange, and we pass the time reviewing what little Leif has been able to learn about Kacper and his Polish cronies.

I've started on the second grog when my phone beeps: It's Malina.

"He's in the Nowa Huta district, which got developed

after World War Two," she says. "He owns several homes that look like humble abodes built by the Communists on the outside, but they really serve as entrances and exits to an extensive underground complex. We've located two of the houses that contain thralls and can tell you where the hidden staircases are, but we doubt that those are all of them."

"Okay, give me the addresses."

What follows is a scouting mission where we take care not to be seen by anyone in the two houses Malina points us to: The Polish vampires themselves, never mind their human thralls, could be prowling about.

I notice that the houses, both dreary and in need of paint, are fully three blocks apart from each other, putting the complex underneath them at three blocks at minimum. They don't look like anything much; a couple of decrepit cars with rusted fenders rest in the driveways, providing a disguise. No one rich or powerful could be living there.

"Okay, I need to try something," I tell Leif. "I might be able to get a sense of the complex's dimensions through the earth. The absence of living earth—the negative space, I guess—will sketch out the boundaries for me."

"Good. Might you be able to sense the staircases as well, thereby establishing the locations of the other entry and exit points?"

"Hmm. Depends on how they constructed it, I suppose. If they built the staircases to drop straight down in flights or spiral from the foundation of the ground-level houses, I won't be able to tell which houses are entry points other than the ones we already know. If they slope straight down, however, away from the foundations, in toward the center, I think I'd be able to pick them out."

"I am confident you will find it to be so," Leif says. "There is a saying along these lines . . ."

"Please don't."

"No, I assure you it is amusing! It is by way of asking a rhetorical question that the correct answer is rendered. Should you ask me if their staircases slope down at a forty-five-degree angle, I would reply, 'Does a bear defecate in densely forested areas?' Eh? You see? The answer is obviously yes."

"Gods, Leif, no. You are incapable of blending in."

"But still I labor, like Sisyphus."

"Why are you so confident about this?"

"A straight narrow space offers nowhere to hide. Vampires are confident they will win any confrontation face-to-face."

"Okay. Be still and let me see what I can see."

There is a small stretch of turf nearby, a sad attempt at a greenbelt, and I kick off my sandals to communicate with the earth. With the elemental's help I seek underground for the edges of Glowa's bunker, and it indeed sprawls for blocks underneath us, far too much space for a single person, and judging by the stark straits leading to and from, it also features more escape routes than the two that the sisters identified. Leif was right: The staircases angle down from the surface houses to the secret complex.

"There are four more bolt-holes," I tell him, and he gives a low whistle.

"Can you identify which houses?"

"Yes."

"Let us investigate them and see how they are guarded." We walk along the streets as if we had some club to visit or some coffee to inhale at a hip café.

I nod at each house as we pass, and they appear not to be guarded at all. Or at least not guarded by thralls.

"These houses contain no humans," Leif says in low tones, after staring at each in turn. "Their defenses are either automatic or undead. That is useful information. Let us move out of the vicinity to discuss it further."

"All right. Back to Stary Port?"

The vampire winces. "If we must. Though I find the atmosphere jarring, it should certainly provide us ample privacy."

The earlier collection of jocund fellows has been replaced by another set, but they are no less loud and proud of their singing voices. I order a couple of grogs, and once they arrive, Leif leans over to plot with me.

"I think the compound is too big for us to handle alone. We cannot possibly cover six exits, to begin with."

"Agreed."

"So I suggest that I call in some mercenaries to clean out the nest during daylight hours."

"Yewmen?" Though expensive, Atticus had used them to great effect.

"No, human mercenaries. I've employed them before and they are used to this work. They know what's involved. Expendable and therefore perfect."

"If this is during the day, where will you be?"

"Sleeping somewhere else."

"While I will be expendable and perfect?"

"No. We send in the mercenaries through all the entrances but one. That will be their escape route. You wait for them to emerge. Thralls will either bring Kacper out, where you can dispatch them all, or he will die down there."

"Unless he and his defenses mow down the mercenaries and run over their bodies to exit one of the other five ways."

"Yes, unless that happens. But perhaps we can instruct the

mercenaries to seal the exits behind them. Everyone must come out the one exit we wish or not at all."

"That might work. Can you get the mercenaries here in the morning?"

Leif pulls out his cell phone. "If not, then certainly by the afternoon. This can be Kacper's last moonrise."

"All right. Let's do it."

I listen to him coldly arrange the arrival of a significant paramilitary strike force and then call Switzerland, rattling off bank-account numbers to pay for it all and get them mobilized. He has the kind of resources that Atticus used to have. We're finished by midnight.

Twelve hours later I'm meeting the mercenaries at Stary Port with maps and objectives and warnings to look for booby traps and make sure no one gets out the way they came in.

"This ain't the first nest we've cleared," one guy says, probably the only American in the bunch. He bulges and glistens like an eighties' steroid movie; all he's missing is the stogie in his mouth, chewed up and tapered like a fresh dachshund turd. The rest of the mercenaries are square-jawed Euro lads who speak to one another in accented English.

"Fine. But it's probably the biggest. Each squad leader has his breach address. You go in hot at thirteen hundred hours and either terminate all hostiles or push them to the single exit. Questions?"

There are none. They really have done it before, and they act like the paid professionals they are. They move out to their appointed positions and gear up. I get a nifty Bluetooth headset thingie so that I can hear what's happening with Squad A. I just stroll into the front yard of the one house we're leaving open, trigger the invisibility binding on Scáthmhaide, and hunker down near the door, out of sight of any windows. The silver reservoir of my staff is all filled up with energy, and the front lawn will provide all I need in real time.

The chatter of the mercenaries in my headset increases as one o'clock approaches. They copy and roger a lot of stuff and tell one another that everything's five by five.

None of the other entry houses is in my line of sight, so I don't see anything but a quiet working-class neighborhood, but I hear plenty through my earpiece when the breach happens. Commands to get hands up, knees down. Shouts of surprise, defiance, and a few quick bursts of gunfire, then shouts of "Clear!" as each room is inspected for hostiles.

Squad A waits for the other houses to report clear, and then they check for booby traps or security measures around the staircases—all accessed through the back of a closet in one of the bedrooms.

Once they're satisfied, the second coordinated breach begins. They open the doors and descend those staircases, and the firefight starts early. There's screaming and hissing and some dying going on, but I can't tell who's producing the death screams. I don't know how well the other squads are doing, but the A team sounds like they are making progress.

Squad A finds at least two occupied coffins in one room and stakes the vampires sleeping inside them. They meet up with Squad C and proceed. No word on the others.

But the strategy is effective. I hear some cursing and noise from within the house. Thumps and the squeak of rubber soles on the floors, a heavy thud. Someone or perhaps many someones have come through the trapdoor. Silent and empty before, the house suddenly has loud tenants, cursing creatively in Polish and shouting at one another.

Panicked thralls. Lugging something awkward.

Clanking. The hollow rushing of hard plastic wheels on tile. "Go! Go!" someone shouts. The wheels whir toward the door, and I tighten my grip on Scáthmhaide in my left hand and draw out a throwing knife in my right.

The lock clicks, the door opens, and a gun barrel pokes out past my head. A pale human thrall steps out, quivering on adrenaline, eyes darting up and down the street but not on me, invisible behind him and to the right. I let him go. He turns and signals to the others that it's clear.

A gurney rolls out with a damn heavy coffin resting on it and four anxious dudes guiding it with sweaty hands. They're heading for a huge black SUV parked on the street. Behind them trails the rearguard, armed and keeping an eye on any pursuit from the mercenaries. I first throw the knife into the back of the vanguard, then attack the rearguard with my staff. A sharp whip against his wrists disarms him and maybe breaks a bone, and then I clock his jaw and he goes down with a squawk as the first fella cries out and tries in vain to reach the knife in his back.

The gurney guides whirl around, looking for who's doing all the damage, but never see the knotted wood that smashes their noses and lays out three of them. The last guy runs and I let him, deciding to chase down the vanguard with the gun instead and make sure he doesn't use it. I smash his elbow and his hand drops the gun as he screams, but I do pull out the knife for him before slapping the backs of his knees and putting him on the ground. He'll be fine eventually.

That's not the case for the slumbering occupant of the coffin. It's a lovely clear day with full sun. I sheathe the knife and pull out my cell phone, thumbing the camera app. I open the coffin lid and snap a quick picture of the milk-white face before the sun starts to fry him and he wakes up to the sound of his own sizzling cheeks.

He screeches and sits up and I swing full force at him, taking him in the throat and knocking him back into the coffin. He can't really die of a crushed larynx, but the hit does stun him for a few seconds more, letting the sun work its justice upon him. I back up, stepping over the thralls' bodies, and block the door. The vampire vaults out a moment later and heads straight for me, visibly aflame and desperate for shelter. I think it's going to be a simple matter of batting him away again, but he stops, picks up the gun of the rearguard, and points it right at me. He knows where I am; he can hear me or smell me if he can't see me. And he pulls that trigger fast.

Two punches to the chest and another lower down drop me like a lunch lady's mashed potatoes on a sad cafeteria tray. But I lever up one end of Scáthmhaide from the ground, mostly by reflex, as he keeps coming, determined to run right over me into the house.

He runs onto Scáthmhaide instead. His fragile papery skin, already on fire and melting, allows the wood to punch right through his flesh, and his shirt is drawn into the wound, surrounding it like a prophylactic. He's skewered underneath the ribs and stuck, and he shrieks as his strength fades and the sun's fire consumes him all the quicker. He crumbles to ash in an orgasm of flame, and the weight is gone as he blows away, leaving only some scorched clothing behind, which is good because my strength is fading fast too. I drop Scáthmhaide and become visible as Squads A and C stomp up the stairs inside the house. They drag me out of the doorway and over to the lawn, where I can draw on the earth easily to heal; my breath comes in short gasps as I try to lock down the pain and then address the wounds. Nothing passed through. They were hollow points and had expanded, tearing up my left side underneath the collarbone but high up on my breast. The lower one on my side just missed a kidney but nicked a renal artery, which I mend first. Removing the bullets is going to suck.

The mercs start hauling the unconscious or moaning thralls inside to hopefully prevent a call from a neighbor. I'm hoping no one saw or heard much; all it takes is one curious retiree to bring the authorities.

Realizing that a bleeding woman on a lawn might also cause comment, I cast camouflage while I heal.

Once the front yard is clear, I hear more mercs coming up from the compound. The over-muscled one—the Glistening American Hulk, who is now chewing the stogie he was missing earlier—comes out the front door, looking for me.

"Hey, Red. Where are ya?"

"Name's Granuaile," I say, after dismissing camouflage.

He gives me a manly toss of the chin to say hello. "I'm Dirk."

"Of course you are."

"You gonna be all right or do we need a medic?"

"I'll be fine. Are your men okay?"

"Mine are. But we lost two from Squad B, and somebody in C got wounded. One of the suckers was awake in the dark. So, hey, I'm supposed to ask if we got Casper."

"You mean Kacper?"

"That's what I just said, isn't it?"

It wasn't, but I suppose he didn't hear the slight difference in pronunciation. "I don't know if we got him. I took a picture of the one that cooked, before he disintegrated. We'll have to check with the money man."

Dirk grunted and shifted his nasty stogie to the other side of his mouth. "He'll have plenty more money after this."

"How is that?"

"We kill 'em and he takes all their stuff. That's how it works."

"You mean they have vaults of cash down there or something?"

"Nah. They have computers, though, and a habit of writing down their passwords where we can find them. He gives them to his circuit jockeys, and it gets him money or intel or both."

His voice sounds awfully bored and it makes me wonder. "How many nests have you taken down now for him?"

"I think this gets us to twenty-one."

"Twenty-one? All this year?"

"Well, in the past three or four months. Wouldn't want to do this forever—risk is too high—but if I make it another couple of months at this rate, I can retire to an island somewhere and drown in rum."

I frown, wondering if Atticus knows about this. Perhaps Leif was inspired by the use of yewmen to take out nests in Rome but decided to add a profit angle. He profits doubly doing it this way: Every nest of older vampires taken down increases his power as well as his wealth.

"So what are you anyway?" he asks. "Some kind of witch?"

"I'm a Druid."

"And that means you can take some bullets and not need a medic."

"Sometimes, yeah."

"That's badass. How do you become a Druid?"

"Twelve years of study in languages and martial arts and

memorizing poetry until you're magically bound to the earth in an excruciating three-month ritual."

"Oh, shit. Fuck that, then."

"Dirk!" a voice calls from inside. "Report."

"Duty calls," he says, and this time I get a full nod of respect from him rather than a mere chin toss before he clomps back into the house, sunlight gleaming on the acreage of his triceps.

I'm blissfully forgotten and left to the unpleasant task of removing the bullets. I go for the one down low first; it caused the most damage. They're jacketed rounds, meaning they're composed mainly of lead and copper, and I won't have trouble binding because of iron content.

Since they mushroomed inside me, they'll tear me up even more on the way out if I leave them as is when I bind them, so I first take the time to reshape the bullet into a smooth, thin cylinder of an even-narrower diameter than its original manufacture. That doesn't mean I don't feel it as I bind the back of the round to my palm, but it does mean I'm not tearing myself any new holes. After it's out, I bind up the skin and let the tissue healing commence.

I repeat the process with the other two bullets. It takes me an hour to get them out, sweating and weakening all the while, but I feel better immediately afterward. And ridiculously thirsty. I holler at the house and convince Dirk, when he emerges, to bring me some juice or whatever's available. He leaves and returns fifteen minutes later with an entire liter of OJ.

"What're you doing after this?" he asks, squatting down on his haunches beside me.

"You mean after I'm done healing up?"

"Well, yeah. After this gig."

"I'm memorizing the collected works of Wisława Szymborska. How about you?"

"Maybe some Netflix. But a documentary! Animals or something. You wanna . . . ?"

"You're seriously giving me the Netflix-and-chill line?"

He doesn't look particularly embarrassed to be called out on it; a tiny shrug and a smirk are all I get by way of apology. "That's about as subtle as I get, unfortunately."

Hmm. Aside from the stogie, he *is* handsome, and I think perhaps the acronym for Glistening American Hulk—GAH!— is appropriate when considering the fun we could have. It's not as if Atticus and I have an exclusive arrangement; the desire for variety is hardwired into our genetic code, and monogamy is a patriarchal construct anyway, so I'm inclined to disregard it. But that doesn't mean we don't have high standards.

"I'll give you a chance, Dirk. Recite some poetry for me right now. And I'm not talking about a dirty limerick or something you read on the bathroom wall. I mean a poem by a real poet. Go."

"What?"

"Ah, sorry. That's not a poem."

"Well, wait, I can learn some—"

"I'm sure you can, but that's not the point. I wasn't asking for poetry as a stepping-stone to my pants. I wanted to see if your mind was as well rounded as your biceps. Turns out it's not."

He bristles. "What does that have to do with sex?"

"Quite a bit. I will have poetry in my life, Dirk. Poetry and asskicking. You *can* have both, you know. There's a certain poetry to violence, don't you find?"

He shrugs and agrees in case it will get him somewhere. "I guess."

I caught his gaze and held it. "There's a certain violence to sex too. Penetration. Screaming. You know."

He licks his lips, realizing that there's a whole lot he's been missing. "Jesus, at least let me have your phone number. I'll work on it and get back to you."

That earns him a laugh. "Attaboy. But you should know I have a boyfriend. He's a Druid too. He got shot in the head once, but he's fine now and can recite the complete works of William Shakespeare from memory. He kills gods on Saturdays."

"Holy shit. For reals?"

"Yep." I give him the same tiny shrug and smirk he gave me. "That's about as far as you're gonna get with me, unfortunately. Thanks for the juice, Dirk."

"Yeah, no problem." He shakes his head before he gets to his feet and mutters, "Damn."

Leif arrives after sundown, in a sharp tailored suit, and I'm still sitting on the ground, weary but feeling as if I can move again.

"Good evening, Granuaile. I trust all went well?"

"A couple of your perfectly expendable mercenaries died, but the nest is toast."

"Excellent." He's carrying a pad and pulls it out, showing me a checklist of names. *Kacper Glowa* is at the top. "Shall we see who we have?"

"Let's start with this guy," I say, pulling out my cell phone to show him the photo I took. "I gave him to the sun and he shot me."

"Hmm. That is not Kacper, unfortunately. That's Arkadiusz Koziol. Six hundred years old, very powerful, and on my list." He taps his screen and a check mark appears next to the dead vampire's name. "But not someone who would ever challenge me on his own. Let's see who's inside."

He offers me a hand and I take it, wincing as I get to my feet for the first time since being shot. It's tender in there, but my legs work just fine.

The thralls are lined up against the wall. They've been given first aid by the mercs, but they could use more help. Leif isn't going to give them any. He descends upon them and charms each in turn, forcing him to reveal who else was in the nest and whatever they know about passwords or hidden intel or even the location of other nests. He checks off names, but I can hear just as well as he can: Kacper Glowa wasn't there, though most of his thralls were.

"I will confirm the kills and see if there is anyone they missed or simply did not know about," Leif says, "but it appears Kacper sent his thralls here to help defend the nest, without occupying it himself."

"He knew we could divine his thralls but not him."

"I suspected he would prove to be a challenge. But we shall not have to face him tonight anyway. You should go home and get some rest. We eliminated twelve vampires here in accordance with the treaty. That is fine progress and should send a clear message that the treaty will be enforced. I may be able to find out the locations of other nests once I search their files. I will contact you when I know more."

I have no will to argue. I want a shower and some sack time more than anything else. I still have another day off from the pub, and I might as well use it to recuperate.

Halfway through my hike up to the bound tree above Krakow, I snort to myself. I guess I now know what my grand adventure will be as a bartender at Browar Szóstej Dzielnicy: I'll be a vampire hunter. And a student of Szymborska.

Honestly, that suits me perfectly: I do not see a path I can walk on the earth that is not strewn with beauty and horror in equal measure. My road ahead is poetry and blood, and after today, I know I'm prepared to walk it.

Haunted Devils

This story, narrated from Owen's point of view, takes place after the events of Staked *and* Oberon's Meaty Mysteries: The Purloined Poodle.

Back in me own time—I'm fecking allowed to start like that because me own time was two thousand years ago—elementals never asked Druids for help with the environment. Humans weren't sophisticated or numerous enough then to cock up the planet on an industrial scale. So when a call shudders up through me bones and it's the elemental Colorado, asking me directly for help on behalf of another elemental, ye could knock me over with a spider whisper—and I'm talkin' about one o' those giant, silent, brooding bastards that lurk in your house high up on the walls and wait for ye to see them and ruin your pants.

The elemental wants me to save a species on the path to extinction, and that's even stranger. Animals go extinct all the time and Druids never hear so much as a sad trombone noise. But some species are key to the healthy functioning of their ecosystems, and sometimes, in small places, Druids can help out. I hear Granuaile helped clean out an invasive species of crawfish from an Arizona river while she was still an apprentice, saving some native trout that were getting all their eggs eaten. That kind of thing makes sense: The invasive species is still vital in its own space, and balance is restored where they were causing trouble. This job sounds different, though.

The request for help comes from an elemental I've never even heard of: Tasmania.

//Devils dying from disease / Mutated cancer / Contagious / Must cure//

Images flood me head of what a Tasmanian devil looks like: the size of a small dog with a face akin to something in the rat family, black fur with a white stripe crossing at the collarbone and again on its back near the tail, which did have hair on it like a dog instead of naked like a rat. And Tasmania emphasizes that the devils are important to keeping its ecosystem balanced—Greta tells me the popular term for that nowadays is *keystone species.*

I get the idea that it's not going to be a nice afternoon's work: It's going to take a while, because I'll have to cure every devil individually until the disease is wiped out. I can't leave me apprentices for so long—but then it makes me wonder if I can bring them along.

//Query: Can apprentices help?//

//Yes / Harmony//

//Harmony// I says, and then I have to hunt down Greta. We can't shift there: For some reason there are no bound trees on the island, and I'm not confident that I know the kids well enough anyway, so we'll have to fly. That's going to take money. And of course it would be best to have the parents along, so that's more money. But at least the full moon is recently past and the werewolves can travel safely.

Greta is excited by the idea and welcomes the idea of a trip to the other side of the globe. Especially since we'll probably be there the next time a full moon rolls around and the pack can run together in the woods there. She says she's going to charter a private flight for us—using either the pack's funds or her own, I don't know which. I have a project to complete while she's at it: something to keep the elemental spheres the apprentices use to talk to the earth safe. I'm thinking they're going to need both hands for this project, and holding the spheres in one hand won't be effective anymore.

Back up in the woods on Greta's property, I have a small patch of hemp I'm growing—stupidly illegal in the United States, but a fantastically useful plant for all sorts of things because ye can use every bit of it. I started the patch to teach the grove the beginnings of botany and how plants can help us as we help them. Tuya, especially, seems keen to learn more about plants, and since her father passed, I'm keen to make sure she's engaged in her apprenticeship.

Right now I want hemp fibers. I harvest one plant, and it's more than enough for me purposes. Using me fingers and a little bit of binding to maintain the shape I want, I weave a spherical cage made of triskele knotwork, separated in halves with a hinge on one side and a clasp on the other. I coat this in gold—helpfully supplied by Colorado—and when it's finished I have a locket suitable for an elemental sphere. We can string a chain or maybe a leather strip through the clasp end, and the apprentices can wear the spheres like a necklace and keep in contact with elementals that way, while also reducing the chance of losing the spheres. They'll get new ones in Tasmania, of course, but for now they can practice communicating to animals with Colorado's help.

I make five more lockets out of gold-coated hemp and run into Flagstaff to get some chains, figuring they'd be a bit sturdier. Then I call me apprentices together with their parents and the few translators and announce our plans.

"We have to heal all the affected Tasmanian devils and wipe out the disease, one by one," I tell them. "It will take some time, but it's going to be worth it."

Ozcar's mother, Rafaela, is a pre-med student at the university and wants to know more about the disease.

"It's called devil facial tumor disease, and it appeared—or was first reported—in 1996. I've looked into it a bit, and your scientists think it originated in a single devil and got transmitted to others, mostly through biting. Devils like to bite and scratch one another quite a bit, but especially during mating season, and this disease is getting transmitted from the bitten devil to the biter as the tumors get punctured. Those tumors grow and swell up on the face until eventually the devils can't eat and they starve to death. Or else the cancer spreads throughout the body and they die of organ failure."

Ozcar casts a worried glance at his mother. He knows she's not going to like this. I catch him often watching other peoples' faces, evaluating expressions, and trying to say something positive when he thinks it's needed. "We'll fix it somehow, Mama," he says. She puts a gentle hand on his head to thank him for the reassurance but doesn't take her eyes off me.

"So it spontaneously occurred from a single source?" she asks.

"Aye. Genetic tests confirm this. But since then it's evolved or mutated into four different strains."

Rafaela can't go with us because of her classes, but Ozcar's father, Diego, can make the journey, and so can the other kids' parents. None have landed jobs since coming to the United States.

"Greta says we have a couple days before we can fly over there. In the meantime, we're going to practice bonding with animals here first. Do ye all have your spheres from Colorado?"

They all nod at me and I tell them to get them out. As the sandstone appears in their tiny fingers, held up as proof of their responsibility, I give them the lockets. This is utterly delightful to them, and there is some spontaneous dancing as they put Colorado's spheres in the lockets and then fasten them around their necks. They tell me thank you in tiny kid voices, and it's so fecking cute I can hardly stand it.

"Welcome," I says. "Right. We're going to learn a couple of different bindings today. Normally I wouldn't teach you these until you were much older, but we have to save some animals on the other side of the world, so we can't wait."

"Are we going to give them medicine?" Ozcar asks, clearly thinking of what his mother was learning in her pre-med training.

"No, we're going to cure them with bindings. Come on, I'll show you."

Normally, Tuya, Luiz, and Amita need translators, but they are getting pretty good with basic English and I figure we can muddle through without help. What we can't do is expect other animals to hang around with werewolves nearby—and all the translators are part of the pack. So it's just me and the six apprentices crunching into the pine needles uphill from the house, headed for a small herd of deer that have been keeping their distance since more of the pack started hanging out at Greta's. I stop the kids as soon as we're in far enough to startle a squirrel and some birds cry out an alarm. The deer can wait a wee while: basics first.

"I'm going to do this one at a time now. Your eyes only see part of the world, ye know: You're filtered from seeing all there is to see by default." As soon as I say it I realize that the kids aren't going to know about filters and defaults. "I mean your brains are only ready to see a small piece of the world. Like looking through a dirty window. Ye can't see as well as ye should until ye do something about it. Most people *can't* do anything about it, but Druids can. We can see better at night, for example. Or ye can see the bindings between all things in the natural world. It's what allows us to create new bindings or unbind what's already there. And that's what you're about to do: See the world for how it really is."

They all look excited by this, but I notice Mehdi's eyes especially, because they're wide and shining. He's normally a levelheaded lad, much like his father, Mohammed, extremely polite but rarely showing ye what he feels except for being interested or bored. He's more than interested now, and it gives me a clue about him: His wonder is reserved for mysteries.

"Some people call it magical sight, and I've even heard it called faerie spectacles, because it allows ye to see what the Fae are doing, but I call it true vision. Call it what ye want; I'll know what you're talkin' about. But I have to warn ye now: It's a lot of information. It's not the way you're used to looking at things. You're going to have to learn to focus on what's important and ignore the rest. Is there any one of ye who would like to go first?"

All six hands shoot up, of course. Being the first to experience a new binding is going to be fecking cool and they know it. They also know how they get to go first.

"Quiz time." I point at a ponderosa pine. "These pines feed both squirrels and fungi. Squirrels eat both parts of the tree and the fungi, and the fungi give the tree phosphates and nitrogen to grow tall and strong. The squirrel spreads fungi spores around to other trees and sometimes spreads the tree seeds as well. All of them benefit. What kind of relationship is that?"

"Symbiotic!" Amita says first, though the others are close behind. Amita is learning her English very well, I see.

"That's right, Amita. Well done. I'm going to have Colorado give ye true vision first. Don't try to move anything but your neck, okay? I mean, look around, but don't try to walk. First time I saw the world with true vision I fell down. Ready?"

"Yes!" She jumps up and down and then remembers her manners, goes very still, and folds her hands together in front of her. "Yes, please, Archdruid." Those aren't any manners I've taught her: She must be hearing her father's instructions on how to address me. He's very strict about proper behavior, but he was smart to teach Amita first that behaving properly means she is in the right and can face the world with confidence, even if the world seems to disagree. Whenever she knows precisely how to behave, a calm settles about her shoulders and she is at peace. New situations can stress her out a wee bit, but she immediately seeks clarification on how to proceed and then executes her instructions flawlessly, trusting that she's been told the truth. I think that's going to be trouble for her once she's a teen, but for now it makes her a fine student.

"Okay, here we go. And the rest of ye be patient; ye will all get to see this."

I can cast night vision on other people, but not true vision. It's a tougher binding to peel that veil away from your senses;

ye need the earth's permission to see the unfiltered version of nature. Since me apprentices are twelve years away from being bound to the earth, I have to ask Colorado for help—which will eventually allow us to help Tasmania.

Amita blinks and jerks when the true vision kicks in, the binding applied through the sphere in her locket.

"Ah! Uh, what? Whoa." Her head can't stop moving as she tries to match what she sees now to what she saw before. And then a stream of her native language comes out as she looks around, trying to get her bearings. She's seeing how everything's tied together, and my warning not to move is forgotten. Overwhelmed by what she sees, she takes a step back, and that shift in balance is too much for her brain to handle on top of everything else: She falls over, just as I did, but laughs about it with everyone else.

"Maybe ye should all sit first while I do this." Once they're all seated and all bound, I switch to true vision meself and direct their attention up to the trees, where that squirrel is high up in the branches.

"Do ye see the life of the tree, kids, and the life of the squirrel? Colors around them both. And a connection, yes? Do ye see how the tree is aware of the squirrel, and the squirrel is aware of the tree? They know each other. The tree is not mere bark and wood, needles and pinecones. It has its own intelligence. Different from the squirrel, and different from us, but it's there. It's aware."

"I see it!" Tuya says. "I like the tree."

"Yeah!" Mehdi agrees. "There's green between them. I mean connecting them. Like vines tied in knots."

The others tell me they see it too. "Good. That green you see can mean many things, but it's all positive. The tree is glad the squirrel lives in it and near it and will therefore be able to make new trees. The squirrel is glad the tree feeds it and gives it a safe place to run from scary creatures like us. Now let's try something. I want you to very carefully, very slowly, get to your feet and walk to that tree. Hands out in front of you, and then put them on the tree. Watch how the colors and knots and everything you see changes once you put your hands on the trunk."

They rise and stagger on uncertain feet toward it, arms outstretched, and once their wee hands plant themselves against the trunk, they see new patterns expand and flourish underneath their fingers.

"Whoa," Thandi says. "What is that? What does it mean?"

"It means the tree knows you're there. It can feel ye against its bark, sense the carbon dioxide you're breathing out of your lungs. And o' course ye can feel it underneath your fingers. You're seeing the magic of our shared existence together and much of the science as well. Ye can tell the tree you love it and that you're glad it's growing here—just ask Colorado to relay the message. The tree won't understand your words any more than Colorado does, but the emotion will get through just fine."

They spend a few seconds doing this, and they get a response from the tree through the spheres at their neck—a combination hello and welcome—and they squeal their excitement. Tuya throws her wee arms as wide as she can and hugs the pine. "I love you, tree," she says.

"Good. Now I need to turn off that true vision for a bit. I don't want you to get headaches. We're going to find some deer and see if ye can talk to them as well. Ye need to learn how to connect with animals first before ye can heal them. There's a laying on of hands needed to heal, but ye can't do that if the animals don't trust ye first."

They blink and rub at their eyes when the true vision leaves them, but there's a new sense of wonder there, floating in the waters of their eyes. They've seen a glimpse of the hidden world, and they know that what they perceive is only a small fraction of what's really going on all around them.

"We have some running to do. Quietly, now. We don't want the deer to hear us coming."

I set off at an easy jog, which is a fine clip for the kids, but I ask Colorado to provide them with some stamina, and they're able to keep up easily over three miles uphill to a high mountain meadow ringed with aspens and pines. I hold up me hand and they stop, breathing heavily.

"Where are they?" Luiz whispers. I look down at him and his mouth is slightly open, showing off the gap between his front teeth. All me apprentices love animals, but I think Luiz loves them the way Tuya loves plants.

"They're bedded down for the day on the other side of the meadow, hiding in the tall grasses. I'm going to have Colorado urge one to stand up, but be quiet now—we don't want to scare them off."

After a few moments, a big buck rises above the grasses, and the kids give tiny little gasps.

"Okay, I'm going to give ye true vision again. I want ye to watch and listen to how I reach out to the deer and form a basic mental bond that will let me tell him I won't hurt him and he shouldn't be afraid. Ye create this binding in Old Irish, not English or Latin, so listen carefully."

I speak the words slowly, laying out the targeting, the effect desired, the draw of power, and the execution. The stag is startled when the binding's made and jumps a bit, but I soothe him and ask him to cross the field to us. While he's doing that, the kids are seeing the new binding in the air between us, and I point out features of the knotwork and what they mean. I review the language needed and have them repeat it back to me without actually drawing any power from Colorado to make it work—and it won't work unless they say the words correctly, because that's part of the craft, part of the binding itself.

Without prompting, a few of the other deer have risen to see where the buck has gone. He's nearby and I ask him to stop, thanking him for his courtesy while I teach the young humans how to appreciate all creatures. He's not especially impressed but gives me the equivalent of a friendly "okay" while he munches on a bit of grass. Might as well graze.

But now the kids can try to form their own bindings. Thandi seems to have the language down best, so I ask her to kindly go first, and I warn the others that if she makes mistakes, we can all learn from them.

She does make a couple of small errors on pronunciation in the drawing phase, but they are enough to make the entire binding fizzle. I coach her again on the troubling passage and she tries again, targeting a doe. This time it works, the binding executes, and everyone grins as the knotwork forms in the air between Thandi and the doe.

"Ah! Hello, deer," she says in her own language, and then looks to me with doubt in her eyes, as if she's made a mistake. She's often anxious about doing something wrong; her father, Sonkwe, says this is new behavior for her since her mother left them, and he suspects Thandi blames herself for it even though there's no reason to. But he is perhaps the most patient and kind man I've ever met, and he shows me exactly how to handle Thandi: constant reassurance. She will find her confidence again in time.

"The language you use now doesn't matter, Thandi. Your

thoughts and emotions will be communicated, not the words themselves. Go ahead. Just ask the doe to come say hello to us and tell her we're friendly."

She does, and then the other apprentices follow her example, one by one, until we have seven deer standing in front of us, some curious about us, some grazing. We don't pet them; our scent might bother the rest of the herd.

I teach them how to unbind the connection. "Say thank you, wish them good health and farewell, and we'll let them be about their business."

We back away and the deer wander off to rejoin their herd, some of them nodding at us first, and then I remove the true vision from my apprentices' eyes.

Ozcar squints and pinches the top of his nose. "Ay, *mi cabeza!*" Then he switches to English. "Archdruid, I have a headache."

Some of the others agree—they're all strained by the experience. But they are still in a good mood, and as we hike back to Greta's house, I tell them they're a fine wee grove and learning so quickly, but we'll work on languages the rest of the day, to give their eyes a rest, and practice binding with other animals tomorrow until it's time to travel.

It's me first time on an airplane. Greta tells me that by having a private charter we're missing a lot of nonsense at the airport that most people have to suffer. No real security check, no endless wait for baggage, very little in the way of dehumanizing shite. I get me fair share of that at customs, though, once we all deplane in Tasmania and have to show passports and declare why we're there and provide some guarantee that we're going to leave soon. I note that Mehdi and Mohammed get quizzed more carefully than the rest of us.

"Why are they so suspicious of Mohammed?" I asks Greta, once the rest of us are through and we're looking back, waiting.

"Because that right there is racial and religious profiling."

"I still don't know what you mean."

"Well, you skipped over a lot of history on that time island of yours, including 9/11, so I'll have to catch you up on it later. What they're doing is wrong and illogical, but if we want to get on with the work we're here to do, we'll have to put up with it for now."

I want to stomp on the nuts of every damp and frowning government toad there.

"Gaia's one planet," I growl in a low voice to Greta, because she's told me that whenever I get frustrated about modern life I should complain to her and I'll get in less trouble that way. "We're all on it together, and we should all be able to live and work and play where we want, ye fecking brainless, poxy shit-gibbons!"

Heads turn in my direction, and I realize me voice might have grown a bit too loud at the end there.

"Sorry, he wasn't talking to you," Greta says to the immigration officials, flat-out lying and smiling as she does it. "Keep it *down*, Owen," she whispers to me, even as the kids ask their parents what a poxy shitgibbon is and they shrug because it's more convenient to pretend they don't understand me either. Me temper still gets the best of me sometimes, but I figure it's fine so long as I never blow up at the kids. I really don't want to cock that up.

We can't get out of that airport too soon to suit me. But when we do clear customs, we rent a couple of vans and drive toward Sorell and the Sandspit River Forest Reserve, which is in the general direction of where the first case of the devil cancer appeared. Greta finds a place to park, and once I get me feet in the soil I'm ever so grateful.

They have some mighty huge trees in Tasmania. Bunch of eucalyptus varieties—one in particular, called the swamp gum or mountain ash, is a towering thing, only second in height to the giant redwoods of the California coast. But along the Sandspit River you have blue gum eucalyptus, under which live ferns and shrubs that look mighty lush and inviting until ye remember those are home to poisonous spiders and snakes and some vicious ants called jack jumpers that kill people more frequently than the spiders and snakes do.

I get all this knowledge from Tasmania, the elemental, once I finally make contact and ask about dangers. Then I have the apprentices line up in front of me and take off their shoes so Tasmania can sense them.

//Apprentices will help// I say. //Need stones to talk / Work through you//

//Harmony// Tasmania responds. //Bring forward one at a time//

"Tuya, please take three steps forward," I asks her, and she does. "Kneel down. Tasmania will give ye a stone, and I want ye to put it in your locket and give your Colorado stone to your mother. When that stone appears, pick it up and say hello and learn about the animals here while the others get their stones."

She obeys, and after a few seconds a pale-green sphere emerges from the earth—the bright yellow-green of algae drying on rocks after water has receded. And there are little droplets and veins of rich violet in there too. It's as attractive as any stone I've seen, and I find out later that it's a combination of green serpentine stone and stichtite that occur naturally together only in Tasmania, so it's called tasmanite.

Once Tuya picks it up and begins the joyful process of getting to know a new elemental and all the things it loves about the plants and animals living there, the other apprentices step forward, one by one, to receive their spheres. Ozcar has a blissful half grin on his face; Mehdi is solemn and reverential; Amita projects an air of tranquility, as if this is where she's always wanted to be and she now wants for nothing; Luiz shows off his wide, gap-toothed smile; and Thandi, who is so often worried about something, finally relaxes and lets the corners of her mouth turn up a wee bit.

I give them some time with Tasmania—and the reverse is true: I give Tasmania some time to acquaint itself with the kids. Then I ask where to find the nearest devil that needs help. The answer is only a half mile away—there are several in a den in need of attention.

//On our way// I tell Tasmania, and then its reply gives me pause.

//Druid is on way also//

Well, ye could run the business end of a lawnmower over me arse and I wouldn't be more surprised. "Druid" is what the elementals of the world call Siodhachan. He's been the only one protecting them for so long that he earned the basic title from them. They call his apprentice, Granuaile, "Fierce Druid," but I'm not sure about me own current title. In the old days they called me "Avenging Druid" because of an episode with a dodgy man in a bog, but that's hardly who I am now. I've had no proper vengeance since I came forward in time. Maybe I'll ask Siodhachan what they call me now when I see him.

//Query: To see me or to help you?//

//To help// Tasmania says, and I get the feeling that I had just asked a stupid question. Except it's a bit of a problem for him to be here. Or at least to be within the sight of Greta. Right or wrong, she blames him for the death of Hal Hauk and Gunnar Magnusson, the wolves who saved her life and brought her into the pack many years ago. All the parents of me apprentices, well, they're part of the Flagstaff Pack now, and they rightfully see Greta, not me, as their leader. They're going to follow her lead. Which means this peaceful mission is going to explode like a shitcan on fire if I don't do something quick.

Truth, methinks, will serve me best.

"Greta, love?" I says to her as we jog toward the den.

"Yes?"

"The elemental just told me that Siodhachan is here to help cure the devils."

She stops running and glares at me—and everyone else stops and watches, expecting to see the equivalent of a car wreck in progress.

"What do you mean by 'here,' exactly?" she asks, placing hands on hips.

"I mean here in Tasmania. Heading for the same den that we are."

Her hands drop to her sides and clench into fists. "Well, he can—"

"Hold on, love," I says to her, holding up a pleading hand. "He's here on the same business as I am. Tasmania asked all the Druids for help, and he answered. He's not violated your banishment nor caused trouble in the territory of any pack here. Is there even a pack in Tasmania?"

"No," she admits. "But I don't want to see him."

"That's fine. We can arrange that. It's only a quarter mile now to the den. Why don't ye and the other pack members wait here, or hereabouts, and I'll take the kids on to deal with this first batch of devils and let Siodhachan know he should steer clear of us from here on?"

She closes her eyes, takes a deep breath, and exhales before she opens her eyes and responds. "All right. Try to make it quick."

I hurry forward with the apprentices to the den Tasmania wished us to visit. There are only four devils there, but one of them is as yet cancer-free. I figure that will be a good visual contrast to show the kids how the devils normally look.

I tell the kids to turn on their true vision through Tasmania and ask four of them to call out the devils from the den. When they emerge, the diseased animals look sad enough to make ye cry. The tumors growing on their faces have swollen their eyes shut, and they must feel unending pressure and pain.

"All right, that was good. Luiz, Thandi, Amita, have your devils wait, and, Ozcar, I'm going to heal yours first. I want ye all to watch carefully how this is done, then I'm going to have ye all practice healing these other two."

I show them that the trick is to make the devil's immune system recognize the cancer cells as disease rather than an acceptable part of its body and, once that's accomplished, to boost the immune system so it's hopping like a man on twelve cups of coffee.

"Ye first work in close on one wee cell by zooming in your vision," and I walk them through the steps of how to do that, then how to alter the proteins on the cell walls to create antigens. "And ye only have to do that once, because then ye create a macro and apply it to all cancer cells in the animal. That will basically do the job by itself if ye give it time, because the immune system will begin to attack the cancer. Thing is, the poor devil is already weak and might not have the time or strength to fight it out. So ye can feed it some energy and things will happen very quickly. Ye just have to monitor your patient to make sure things proceed well."

And things do proceed well for about ten minutes. The devil shudders and makes some tiny screeching noises as a war rages inside his body, but the tumors are beginning to visibly shrink when Siodhachan shows up with his smart-ass slobber hound. I can tell by the look on Luiz's face he wants his own hound as soon as possible.

"Hello, Owen," me old apprentice says, nodding at me, and I nod back.

"Ye didn't run into Greta, did ye?"

"No." His head turns, eyes searching the woods. "Is she here?"

"About a quarter mile away, with all their parents," I reply, gesturing at the kids.

"These are the apprentices?"

"Aye." I introduce them to Siodhachan and I'm not sure if they're more impressed with him or the hound. I think maybe the hound, because he talks to them once Siodhachan says it's all right for them to reach out, and it's mere seconds before they ask me if I have a snack to give him. While the kids are distracted by Oberon, Siodhachan squats down next to me and checks me progress; the way his eyes are focused I can tell he's using true vision.

"That's going nicely."

"Aye. But this is going to take a while. Fifteen or twenty minutes per devil. If ye take off and don't accelerate the healing, they can still infect others or be reinfected themselves."

"Right. It's why I wanted to talk to you. Perhaps we can coordinate. Thought we'd start at the point of origin at Port

Arthur and secure that peninsula, then go from there, you heading west and me heading north, then we spiral in."

"I can just head down there with the kids and you head north now."

Siodhachan shakes his head. "I don't think you want to take the kids down there."

"Why not? We got a damn fine pack to protect them."

"I've been talking to Tasmania about the origin since I got here. I'm not so sure it's natural."

"What, now? Cancer is natural, even if it's a fecking bastard."

"No argument there, but single-origin transmissible cancers are rare. There's something strange behind this."

"Now, hold on, lad. You're handing me a bowlful of batshit and calling it beans, and I'm not about to eat it. Ye think someone woke up one day a couple of decades ago and said, 'I know how to lure the Druids to their doom. I'll start a transmissible cancer in Tasmanian devils!' and then they laughed a cruel supervillain laugh and just waited for us to show up?"

"No, no. I don't think there was a specific motive or that it's a trap or anything. I think the cancer was a side effect of something else."

"Like what?"

Siodhachan looks at the kids, at least a few of whom are not petting the hound but listening to us. "I'd rather not speculate here. But humor me, for safety's sake?"

I shrug at him and says, "Sure, lad. I'll need to work it out with Greta, but we have to get these kids trained first regardless. Help me do that. This first devil's good now. I'll send him back in. Luiz, send your healthy one back in the den too. Two more diseased ones, and we can split up the apprentices between them. Walk them through the steps, make sure they got it?"

Siodhachan nods and I assign him Ozcar, Thandi, and Tuya, while I work with Luiz, Mehdi, and Amita. It takes us another half hour to heal those two devils, with the kids learning how to craft and visualize the bindings properly.

I overhear Siodhachan giving them praise: "You know, this is really advanced stuff you're doing. I didn't teach my apprentice this until she was in her eighth year, and here you are doing it in your first few months. You are building impressive minds already. That's because you have the best archdruid."

"Really?" Thandi says. "How do you know he's the best?"

"Because he was my archdruid too. What he taught me saved my life too many times to count. You're in good hands."

Damn sneaky of him to say that. Now when Greta wants to beat the shite out of him, I'll feel like I have to step in between them.

"And these devils are in good hands too," he continues. "You three just saved this one's life. Feels good, doesn't it?"

They agree, and I congratulate my three on their work as well, and we let the devils return to their den, all of us feeling better.

"Glad ye like it, because we'll have to do it a whole lot more. Let's go back to your parents and make some plans for how to proceed."

Siodhachan wisely hangs back out of sight when we return, so it takes Greta a while to catch his scent and realize he's nearby—the excitement of the apprentices helps with that. When the nostrils flare and the eyes widen, though, I step right up.

"Aye, he's here. He'd like to discuss with us how we're going to split up duties on the island, if that's okay. May I let him approach?"

And that's just enough warning and courtesy to prevent her from turning on him. She still has cords standing out on her neck and her teeth bared at him, but her skin isn't rippling in the first signs of transformation.

She's well aware Siodhachan didn't kill either Gunnar or Hal, but since getting involved with him was a precondition for their deaths, she doesn't want any of the pack associating with him anymore. And apparently that includes me.

"No," she says, when she hears we're heading to Port Arthur together. "There's no way I'm letting you go off with him after something dangerous. People who run off with him don't always come back."

"That's why we're leaving the kids behind," I says. "But if there's something causing the infection down by Port Arthur and thereby disrupting the balance of Tasmania, we need to eliminate it. It's why we're Druids, love."

She grinds her teeth together and her jaw flexes so hard I'm afraid she's going to start changing, but she takes a deep breath and growls instead, "Then I'm going with you."

I glance at Siodhachan and he shrugs first, then nods, so it's not a problem for him.

We drive down to Dunalley, which is right at the top of the peninsula, and check in to an inn there. Tasmania says there are a few devils nearby, and the parents are content with escorting the kids to do some healing on their own. By the time they're settled and we've eaten dinner—Siodhachan and his hound eat by themselves outside, and I feel bad—the sun is setting and we climb into the van, casting long shadows.

Greta's projecting a cone of silence and it's fecking boring, so I reach out with me mind to connect with Siodhachan's hound, Oberon, and find out that there's at least a conversation there, even if it's beyond my understanding—and I'm only hearing his side of it anyway. I can't hear what Siodhachan is saying.

<So I can't use the phrase *Netflix and chill* as a verb? But why not, if you can tell people to just chill? Oh . . . so I should definitely not use it as a command?>

Fecking modern slang. I have had plenty of conversations like that with Greta.

We have the windows down—a hound and a werewolf practically make that a requirement—but even I am noticing that the air here is much different. There's no pine, for one thing, but plenty of dry grass and eucalyptus in the wind, and a hint of salt from the ocean. Damn loud bugs drone on about their desire for sex, and the occasional chatter of mammals or the chirp of birds whips past our ears.

Siodhachan's driving, and he pulls us into a parking lot that's almost deserted, some lights giving us just a dim glimpse of what lies beyond. I see some brick buildings, painted white or maybe a sickly cream, and they must be old or have suffered a disaster at some point, because they look like they might be ruins, with roofs and chunks of the walls missing. The lawns in between them look like they're better kept.

"What's this place, then?" I says.

"This is Port Arthur."

"Not much of a port. Or am I unclear on the concept? Where's the boats?"

"Port Arthur was a penal colony for the British. One of the worst."

I know I can't be hearing that right; I'm still building me English vocabulary. "Penile colony, as in lads walking around with their cocks out?"

"No, penal, as in penitentiary, as in prison."

"Ah. So it was a colony of prisoners, then?"

"A favorite practice of the British. They would ship their undesirables from England to Australia's main continent and use their forced labor to establish infrastructure for settlers. The worst of those prisoners they sent here to Port Arthur. They practiced 'advanced' methods of rehabilitation here."

Greta tilts her head to the side and speaks civilly to him for the first time. "You mean in the same way the United States used 'advanced' interrogation techniques?"

"Yes, very similar. It was thought at the time that if prisoners were forced to reflect on their crimes, this would somehow inspire true repentance. So they were given the silent treatment for an hour every day: a black bag over their heads and an admonition not to speak but just reflect. Naturally, few of the men could remain silent in such conditions, so they made some noise, and as punishment they were thrown into a dark cell for solitary confinement. This drove many of them mad, and they had an asylum built right next door."

"Gods below, why didn't they just club them with a branch and get it over with? Fecking cruel."

"Why are we here?" Greta says.

"Aye, lad, I know ye didn't want to speculate earlier, but I think now is the time."

"Let's head over to the grass," Siodhachan says, "and get in touch with Tasmania. See if there are any devils around."

"Fine. But fecking speculate already."

"A lot of people died violent deaths here, Owen. The prisoners, yes, but the native Tasmanians before that—the British pretty much wiped them out, so there are no longer any full-blooded natives, and nobody talks about it. Regardless, I don't think anyone who died here was in a happy place, you know? Not even the guards. It wasn't the time or place for peaceful living. There are more than fifteen hundred bodies buried on a little island over there," he says, pointing to the southeast, "called the Isle of the Dead. But they all died right around here."

"So you're suggesting this area is haunted," I says as we step onto the grass. "Big fecking deal. Maybe one of those unwashed crews of nervous lads can film a ghost-finding show here in the dark and jump at every little noise they hear."

I really should not have said that, because right then a chorus of ragged, smoky screeches tears through the night all around us, as close to the harrowing cry of a *ban sidhe* as anything mortal might get, and if we hadn't all clenched as tight as we could, I'm sure we would have shat ourselves, and that's no lie. I have never heard anything so fecking awful, like claws on steel, shearing away me sanity and all me muscles strung tight as a harp string, expecting a brief final visit from the Morrigan before the darkness takes me.

I'm not the only one who feels it. Siodhachan's eyes practically pop out of his skull, and Greta crouches and snarls as if she were cornered, and the hound barks.

<Atticus, are those wombats or what?>

"Those are Tasmanian devils," Siodhachan says, answering the question for all of us.

"They didn't make noises like that when we were healing them," I says.

"Something has them upset."

<Maybe it's the ghosts. There are more than two and less than all of them, but not by much.>

"You're being serious, Oberon?"

\<Serious enough to ask, "Who ya gonna call?" We could use Holtzmann's ecto-blaster thingies right about now.\>

"You can see them?"

\<Yeah, can't you?\>

"Not yet. Which direction are they?"

\<Uh.\> The hound turns around in a circle. \<All directions. Where the devils are. Flying low to the ground—harassing them, I think.\>

I can hardly think with all that racket going on, so I asks Tasmania to calm down the devils in the area and stop them screaming. When the night goes quiet, the hound's ears lie back flat against his head.

\<Atticus, what did you just do?\>

"Nothing, Oberon."

"It might have been something I did," I says.

\<Incoming ghosts!\>

"What?"

We see them, finally, a few seconds before they're on us, silent pale wraiths with yawning mouths gliding across the grass from all directions. We're in the eye of a fecking spectre hurricane, but it's a quiet, creeping menace coming for us instead of howling fury. Greta shucks off her pants and curses because she knows she'll be changing when they hit us, and they *do* hit us. Ye wouldn't think they could, not physically, but they hit ye in the ether, where they exist entirely and we exist only partially.

"Quick, Siodhachan, summon a mist!"

"What? Why?"

"Because o' the ghosts, ye blistered tit! Didn't I teach ye that?"

"No, you didn't."

They slam into us then and pass through, one by one, and then circle around for more. We're chilled to the core by every pass as the cold of the void they occupy seeps into all the tiny in-between spaces within us, and it fecking hurts, a burning freeze that tears cries out of Siodhachan and Greta as I begin to chant a binding to collect a fog about us—though maybe Greta's cries are the first pains of her transformation, because her skin's rippling and bones are starting to pop and rear-range themselves.

Perhaps I *didn't* teach him after all: Spirits are beings of the ether, a netherworld between planes, so that they are half here and half somewhere else. Water impedes them, which is why ye don't find a bunch of ghosts haunting the ocean. I've seen some o' these modern movies with water spirits in them—those elven lads in the fecking bogs outside Mordor, for example: That was all bollocks. The truth of it is, back in me own time, if we didn't want to be haunted by some shite of a human, we'd bury him in a bog. Water kept that spirit inside or, if it was already out, from reaching its anchor or safe harbor before dawn.

The water in the air begins to condense and fog around us when I complete me binding, and then I'm simply rocked by the pain of the spectral attack, and I give voice to it as well, my throat joining Siodhachan's. That's why the devils were screaming: The fecking ghosts were attacking them, and as far as I can figure, they did it precisely for those screams, to make living creatures give a voice to their long-suffering pain. Those mad prisoners given the silent treatment would want nothing so much as a voice now, and they had figured out how to make living creatures give them one: Tweak them hard enough in the ether and they'd feel pain in the physical world.

Except why now exactly?

The hound is immune to the attacks, and once Greta is in werewolf form, so is she. They tear into the apparitions and their substance dissolves, unbound by whatever innate ability hounds have to affect spirits. Seeing this, Siodhachan sheathes his sword, strips, and shifts to a hound himself, leaving me the only human plagued by the haunts. Oberon is actually having fun, and I hear his cheerful voice in me head as I freeze from the inside.

<Hey, Atticus, did you know that a group of phantoms is called a rumpus? If these are phantoms, then this would be a rumpus bringing the ruckus.>

The attacks slow down once the fog forms and the hounds and Greta take their toll, thank the gods below, but it's not enough; there are too many apparitions. I know they're chewing through the ghosts as fast as they can, but it feels like maybe all fifteen hundred o' the tortured souls buried on the Isle of the Dead are having a go at me. I can't stop shivering and feeling little ice picks of pain stab through me guts as clouds of dirty dishwater pass through me with silent screaming faces on them. Soon I'm convulsing too much to keep me feet, and I'm helpless to heal what's happening. I collapse to me knees and the canines form up around me, which does help, but some ghosts are still getting through and the assault continues.

The only thing I can think of is to bind vapor closer and condense water on me skin, letting it bead up like a sheen of sweat—it's either that or run over to the ocean and jump in. Except I don't think I can make it. Nerves fire involuntarily and muscles contract unpredictably. I shove the pain into one headspace and use the other to craft the binding. The fog thickens and collects about me, and I hear the hound complain about it once to Siodhachan—hard to pick his targets in such soup, or something like that. But soon the mist settles about me, seeps into my clothes, and I feel like a hand towel that's been used too many times, discarded on the floor, an unwanted mess.

The spooky shites don't want me anyway, and that's the point of it. The stabbing cold stops, the hounds and Greta move away in diminishing growls—chasing stragglers, I guess—and I'm left alone to shudder in me own private cloud, trying to recover and warm up.

At first I think there's no use in trying to heal anything, because I'm cold more than anything else, but after checking meself out I realize that I *do* need to heal. That prolonged assault with multiple ghosts tearing through me did have some side effects: Mutated cells in me pancreas, liver, lungs, and spleen. Cancer.

I see what Siodhachan was getting at now: The cancer in the devils spawned from a malignant spectre looking for a way to scream his defiance into the night. I say as much when Siodhachan returns some time later and shifts back to his human form.

He nods and says, "I figured it was something like that."

"Where's Greta?"

<She's eating a kangaroo and doesn't want to share.>

"Ah, yes. She gets hungry when she goes wolf. Siodhachan, didn't ye say this devil cancer appeared in the nineties?"

"That's right."

"How could there be that many ghosts around here since then and no one ever noticed?"

"The obvious answer is that there weren't that many actively haunting the area. Just one or two ghosts could have started it all back then, and that would be considered almost normal for a place like Port Arthur. This mass haunting, though, with so many spirits delighted to attack anyone near the prison, must be a recent development."

"How do ye fecking develop a rumpus like that, and why would ye bother?"

"My guess is that Loki has been busy stirring up trouble in the planes—him or one of his surrogates. He's preparing for Ragnarok. The more chaos he can create to distract from his true objectives, the better. I think we'll start to see much more of this sort of thing. I would bet there are already all kinds of unusual things happening, but this is the first one to interfere with Gaia's wishes and therefore the first we've really seen."

"Do ye think ye got 'em all? The ghosts, I mean."

Siodhachan shrugs. "We'll keep an eye out. In the meantime, if you're up for it, we can start healing the devils on this peninsula."

"Oh, I'm up for it," I says to him, though I'd much rather lie down with a blanket and a bottle of fiery whiskey.

We get to work, going in opposite directions to heal the nearest devils. I head in the general direction of where they say Greta is doing her thing, and once I find her she spends the night guarding me from any further ghosts as I work, though we do not see any.

Working quickly and running between our patients, we heal most of the peninsula's devils before sunrise, and Greta shifts back to human at dawn and gets dressed.

We meet up with Siodhachan and Oberon at the inn in

Dunalley, where they tell us over a breakfast of sausage and eggs that they did find a couple more phantoms and destroyed them.

The apprentices healed a den of devils each in our absence and have plans to move farther afield after breakfast, while catch some much-needed sleep.

Siodhachan and I attend to the rest of the peninsula's devils that afternoon and wait for nightfall to see if any of what Oberon calls the "Ruckus Rumpus" shows up. A few do, and Oberon sends them to whatever cold oblivion awaits them. Should the cancer reappear on the peninsula after we've gone, we'll know that we didn't get all the ghosts and we'll return.

It's a good start—and I don't just mean for the wee ones. It's a good start for me, to learn how fecking huge this planet truly is and what an astounding variety of creatures live on it, because Arizona and Tasmania are about as far from Ireland as bull bollocks are from a popular breakfast food.

It's also a good start for Greta, methinks, to realize that maybe Siodhachan isn't all bad.

Or maybe I'm imagining a shred of goodwill there when in fact there isn't so much as a firefly's bright arse winking in the darkness. She may be simply putting on a mask of civility because she knows he'll be going in a different direction from us soon.

He does that a lot—go in a different direction, I mean. I sometimes think if it weren't for Oberon, Siodhachan would be the loneliest man alive.

But I wonder if he can't be thought of as a sturdy bridge, who connects people for good or ill but always remains, unshaken by storms or floods, serving his function.

The idea, once I have it, sticks with me, and after we've

said farewell and separated to tackle the devils on the island as a whole, I look at me apprentices already serving Gaia and see that he's a bridge between the old Druids and the new. We would none of us be here if it weren't for him.

Greta may only see what he's destroyed, but I see what he's created too, and I have to admit: It makes me proud.

tHe enɒ oſiɒyLLs

*The events of this story, narrated by Atticus,
take place immediately before the events of Scourged,
Book 9 of The Iron Druid Chronicles.*

i have never thought that winds howled so much as
moaned. My imagination gives them reasons: They moan
because they're weary of their never-ending journey around
the globe and are haunted by what they've witnessed—
species extinction and coral-reef death and miles of trash
floating in the ocean and a strange collection of humans who
keep saying the earth is doing just fine, in spite of clear evidence to the contrary.

And the weather has been vicious in recent years, Gaia's
way of forcing people to consider that maybe there will be
some consequences for their careless behavior. The moaning
began in late afternoon after first sliding through the eucalyptus leaves of Tasmania in a dry whistle. The sky roiled with
thunderheads colliding like rams, and the boom rumbled for
miles. Lightning flashed and speared the ground with blue-

white pitchforks. The rain would come soon, and not a wee sprinkle either, dribbling out a few drops like an old man with an enlarged prostate: It would gush down and splatter like a diuretic rhino voiding his bladder on a flagstone.

Oberon and I were near the eastern shore of Tasmania but nowhere near adequate shelter. We had left Owen and his grove of apprentices behind the day before; they were moving to the west, curing Tasmanian devils of transmissible cancer at the elemental's request, while I was moving north on the same errand. Together we'd save a species, but it was going to be a project of weeks or even months. No need for us to get wet when we could shift planes home to Oregon and wait it out for a couple of hours. Besides, there were friends to be met. And it was past time Tasmania got tethered to Tír na nÓg. To get here I'd had to shift to Australia and then take a ferry to the island.

"Let's go home for a little while, Oberon," I said to my hound. "We need some camping gear if we're going to keep at this the way we should, and we have to check up on Starbuck and Orlaith."

<I was wondering about them just now! They'd probably like to chase a wallaby or five. Do you think we can bring them back here with us?>

"I'm not sure, buddy. Orlaith probably shouldn't plane-shift much now that she's getting closer to having puppies. That's why we left her and Starbuck together at the cabin, so they'd have each other's company."

<Oh, I remember that. But maybe one more shift wouldn't be so bad? If we're going to be staying here for fifteen decades or sixty years or whatever—>

"More like two months, Oberon."

<But that's sixty years, like I just said—>

"No, that's sixty days."

<Days, years, whatever! What I'm saying is that we can all have a good time out here chasing wallabies and wombats and nobody has to spend any time away from humans who provide necessary services like gravy-dispensing and chicken-frying and steak-grilling and sausage-making and stuff like that.>

"Gods below, Oberon," I said, shaking my head, "you've become too pampered. We're going to be hunting and cooking over the fire when we cook at all. Very basic meals. Nothing gourmet. And no gravy."

<Well, look, I understand if we can't do gourmet, but no gravy? There's no need to get primitive, Atticus.>

"*Au contraire:* That's exactly what we need to do. We have to go where the devils are, and most of them aren't going to be living in close proximity to full kitchens."

<Wait. So that means . . . that means the devils have never even had gravy? Not once in their lives?>

"Nope. They don't live a privileged existence like you."

<You're making me sad, Atticus! All those poor devils!> He warbled a mournful dirge at the thunderheads to make sure I got the point.

"What is all this melodrama? Just because they've never heard of your favorite thing doesn't mean they hate their lives or they need your sympathy or need you to come along and show them how to fix it. In fact, it's kind of arrogant of you to think that. Imperialist, even."

<Wait, what? You mean like the Empire? Am I supposed to be a Moff or something in this analogy, like Grand Moff Oberon, and I'd wear a starchy uniform and look angry all the time and sneer at rebel scum?>

"If you like. Think about it for a while. I have to bind this tree to Tír na nÓg, and I can't be interrupted. We'll talk when we get home."

It took about fifteen minutes to tether the tree, and the rain had begun before I finished. Oberon smelled like wet dog already and probably needed a proper bath. When I said we were all set to go and to put his paw on the tree, he asked me to wait a minute.

<Atticus, I thought about what you said for that whole fifteen centuries, and I'm sorry. I don't want to be an Imperial guy who oppresses planets. I want to be like Rey and save planets.>

"I think you've made an admirable decision, Oberon. That's what I'm all about too."

<Thank you. So what I want to know is, will you be my BB-8 droid?>

"Wow, uh . . . that's an intriguing offer. Let me think about it for fifteen centuries, okay? Come on, let's go."

When we shifted to our cabin near the McKenzie River in the Willamette National Forest, there was of course a few minutes of ecstatic doggie homecoming festivities. Jumping and running and flapping tongues, playful nips on ears and back legs, and plenty of happy barking.

Starbuck the Boston terrier had quite the vertical leap, which allowed him to vie for attention against the much taller wolfhounds. He was just beginning to pick up a few words of language from the hounds and myself, and he employed every single one of them when Oberon and I appeared.

<Yes no play squirrel happy gravy food!> he practically shouted in my head. His mental voice was a bit higher-pitched than those of the wolfhounds—not shrill or anything, but

more like a fine tenor who'd gradually ruined his singing voice with years of alcohol and cigarettes.

"Hi, Starbuck. I'm very happy to see you. That's how you greet someone. Can you say that back to me? Say 'Hi, Atticus'?"

<Yes hi Atticus happy play! No squirrel!>

"That's much better. You're learning very fast. Hi, Orlaith."

<Hello, Atticus! I am so full of puppies now! They are hungry, though. And me too, of course.>

"They'll be running around here soon before you know it," I said, giving her some scritches. "Shall we go for a run in the woods to work up an appetite, and then maybe some sausage?"

The hounds all agreed, and I ran into the house to shed my clothes and sword and everything before shifting to a hound and leading the charge into the forest. We scared up some deer and a couple of wild turkeys and annoyed the everloving hell out of some squirrels, which automatically counted as a Glorious Outing in the minds of the hounds.

But I did note that Orlaith was close to delivering and shouldn't be shifting anymore. I had to get back to Tasmania, and Granuaile would be occupied in Poland for a while enforcing the treaty we signed with Leif Helgarson: All vampires were supposed to be out now, yet some were being stubborn about it and staying, challenging both Leif's leadership and us. We really needed someone to stay at the cabin and look after Orlaith and, eventually, her puppies while we took care of business abroad. We didn't have any solid friends in the area, but I did think of a potential lead: Earnest Goggins-Smythe, the owner of Jack, the purloined poodle Oberon and I had tracked down and returned during the same caper that resulted in us adopting Starbuck. He was a

British expat who lived in Eugene, but that wasn't so far away as to make it inconvenient.

I gave him a call once we got back to the cabin and I had dressed and put some burgers on the grill.

"Hey, Earnest. Connor Molloy here," I said, using my current alias. "How's Jack?"

"Oh, he's brilliant!" I almost laughed aloud because I'd forgotten how hoity and toity Earnest's British accent sounded. "How is Oberon?"

His question perfectly summed up why Earnest was an excellent choice: He didn't give a damn about me, but he couldn't wait to hear how my hound was doing.

"Very well, but hoping I could ask you for a favor. The well-paid kind."

"Training Oberon for the circuit?"

"Oh, no. I'm not interested in showing him. But I do need another wolfhound and a Boston looked after for a while. I wondered if you'd like to come out to the cabin and watch over everyone. Jack's welcome too, of course, and your boxer, Algy. Plenty of room for them to run around out here, and you can even work from here like you do at home."

"I can?"

"Well, we have great Wi-Fi." Earnest wrote code and only left the house for groceries and trips to the dog park.

"That's very tempting, and in theory it's possible," he said. "I'd need some more details, though." We talked those through, and since I'd recovered quite the hoard of gold from Arizona recently, I was able to make him an offer he couldn't refuse. He showed up in the morning with his dogs, and they got on famously with Orlaith and Starbuck once the compulsory round of polite ass-sniffing had been observed. I gave him the keys, showed him around, and he was engaged for an indefinite time. I hoped I'd be back before Orlaith's litter dropped, but if not, she and her puppies would be looked after until either Granuaile or I could return.

Orlaith and Starbuck were so distracted by the two new hounds and a kind human who was ready to feed them that they hardly noticed when Oberon and I shifted back to Tasmania.

Nine days into our healing project and more than two hundred devils cured of facial tumor disease, the Morrigan visited me in my dreams. It tore me away from a nightmare where I was trying to teach high school science to a room full of creationists, so I was mightily relieved to see the Chooser of the Slain.

"Your idyll is almost at an end, Siodhachan," she said, a tiny smirk on her blood-red lips. If she was amused, it meant I was in for some pain.

"Huh? What idyll? I was trying to explain to my students that they were all going to believe in evolution when an anti-bacterial-resistant supermicrobe infected their spleens, and it wasn't going well." I looked around at my new surroundings. The Morrigan and I were sitting across from each other in the healing pools of Mag Mell. Birds chirped in hedges, and nymphs frolicked and giggled close by. We were neither of us clothed. "I think this is much more idyllic," I concluded.

"This idyll is almost at an end as well. I am paying you a courtesy by informing you that Loki will cease his scheming soon. He's going to act."

"Act? As in begin Ragnarok?"

"Yes. He has just left the hell of Christians after speaking with Lucifer. Since I know you have numerous affairs, I thought you might like to put them in order. I can't protect you as I once did. I'll see you soon, Siodhachan."

"Wait, Morrigan—"

My protest did me no good. I woke up under a canopy of swamp gum trees with a shout, and Oberon leapt straight out of his slumber, ready to fight.

<What is it, Atticus? Cybermen? Borgs? Frakkin' toasters?>

"No, it was the Morrigan."

<So I wasn't even close.>

"Not even. What were you dreaming about there—*The Matrix?*"

<Cyberdyne Systems Model T-1000. He had turned into a murderous liquid metal Chihuahua. I'm telling you, Atticus, the machines are gonna get us eventually. An entire genre of dystopian film can't be wrong.>

"Well, maybe we won't get to that point. The Morrigan just told me we're all going to die from fire and ice and the World Serpent."

Oberon looked around as if those things would appear at any moment, then, when nothing happened and there was naught to battle but the drone of insects, he sat down.

<Go back to sleep, Atticus. I will stand guard.>

"No, I don't think sleep is possible now. Might as well build a fire and have a talk I've been putting off for a while."

<Oh, suffering cats. That doesn't sound good.>

"It's actually for your own good."

<I'm not convinced. Is this about getting more fiber in my diet?>

I snorted. "No, it's more serious than fiber," I said, getting up and throwing a few dry branches onto the glowing embers of the fire we'd let burn low earlier. "Be patient while I build this up again. It's a fireside kind of chat."

<Okay.> Oberon inched closer to the fire, sat down again, then thought better of it and stretched himself out as I poked and prodded the fire back to life. There was no use dancing around the subject, so I just said it.

"I'm going to need you to stay with Orlaith and Starbuck at the cabin until further notice."

<Until further—does that mean I'm suspended without pay or something? What did I do? Was I snoring?>

"You've done nothing wrong. This is a safety issue. You'll be safe with Earnest back at the cabin while I take care of something."

<Take care of what?>

"The end of the world, possibly. The fire-and-ice business I was talking about. Plus a really big snake and maybe Lucifer, I don't know. The Morrigan kinda shorted me on the details."

<Well, you shouldn't be doing that alone. I can help!>

"I'm sorry, Oberon, you really can't. Do you remember me telling you a story when Granuaile was a new apprentice, about a wolverine companion I used to have? His name was Faolan."

<Faolan . . . hmm . . . oh, yeah! He was in a swamp with you and you met the last Bigfoot or something, right?>

"That's right."

<I asked you what happened to him and you said you'd tell me some other time.>

"Now is that other time. Are you ready?"

<Ready as a three-toed sloth!>

"Ready as a . . . ? Never mind."

• • •

Faolan was my companion during a good portion of the time I was binding the New World to Tír na nÓg. He was surly and easily angered and I loved to tease him. For some reason he stuck with me even though he claimed I drove him mad— well, I should amend that. He told me one night during a hurricane on the Gulf Coast why he didn't just take off and return to the north, where it was cooler and populated by far fewer alligators: It would be boring.

<It'd be peaceful and lazy, no doubt, compared to running around with you,> he said, <but I'd be dying to argue about mushrooms or just about anything after a week. Because there'd be no one to talk to! First wolverine I saw would jump me for intruding on his territory without discussing it first. So as much as I hate the heat and the humidity and the sucking mud and the way you smell and this unbelievable storm trying to blow us away like some god's spiteful fart, I have to stay.>

"That's really sweet, Faolan," I told him, because for him, it was. He didn't invite belly rubs or pay me compliments— wolverines just aren't like that—but I could feel through our bond that he was intensely loyal to me.

In the ninth century, we were down by the Yucatán Peninsula, which is in modern-day Mexico, and he had occasion to demonstrate that loyalty.

Back then the Mayans had built an impressive civilization throughout the region, with cities of up to fifty thousand people supported by advanced agriculture. They had the most astounding architecture, which persists to this day, a complex mathematics system, and a firmer grasp on astronomy than anyone in Europe at the time. I was awed by the Mayans and was one of the very few Europeans to see their civilization while it was still mighty. I had so much to learn from them that I stayed in the region a bit longer than strictly necessary and learned their language. And as I learned that, I started to absorb bits of their religion too: It was rich and complex, populated by many gods. And once I heard some details about their plane of the afterlife, Xibalba, I became curious to see at least part of it.

There were supposed to be three rivers the dead had to cross into Xibalba. Rivers in the underworld are common to many cultures. Tír na nÓg has one, and the Norse have thirteen rivers under the spring of Hvergelmir, and the Greeks had the River Styx, and so on. All of these rivers typically symbolize the boundary between the living and the dead, and the dead must cross over them, never to return to the land of the living.

Xibalba had three: a river of scorpions, a river of blood, and a river of pus.

<Time-out, Atticus: a river of pus?>

"Heh! I thought you were going to question the scorpions."

<I can imagine a lot of scorpions, because we lived in Arizona. But I can't imagine a river of pus.>

"You see why I was intrigued."

<Well, yeah. I mean, if you're going to have a whole river full of pus, don't you need a heck of a lot of infected wounds or boils or zits or something?>

"Or maybe just one giant, legendary wound like a spring, oozing pus into the darkness . . ."

<Maybe? You mean you don't know where it all came from?>

"Some things are best left as mysteries, Oberon. In any case, I wanted to see these rivers if I could, because when you live for as long as I have, every new experience is something to be treasured. And this would be next-level amazing, a land created by human imagination rather than geologic forces."

I sat down under the canopy of the rain forest and contacted the elemental Yucatán: //Query: Can Druid visit plane of Xibalba?//

It's a good idea to ask such things. Realms of the dead often have rules about the living walking around.

//Yes// the elemental replied. //With protection//

I asked for such protection for a short trip, and Yucatán agreed, directing me to a cave in modern-day Belize that would serve as the portal to the plane. Once there, I bound a tree to Tír na nÓg and told Faolan that he had two choices: I could shift him back to the north, where we first met more than a hundred years before, and say farewell, or he could wait for me outside the cave, for a possibly very long time. Under no circumstances could he follow me into Xibalba.

He challenged me immediately. <Why not?>

"Because it's a land of the dead. The living don't go there without protection, and Gaia will only protect me."

<Is this because I smell bad?>

"No, it's because this is the kind of favor Gaia does only for Druids. You simply can't go. Stepping into a land of the dead means you're dead. So what's it going to be: Wait here, where there are jaguars and too many bugs to count, and I might not come back and you'd be stuck here—"

<You might not come back?>

"It could be very dangerous for me even with protection. I could run into something awful, and I'm just being honest. However, I hope it won't take me long. But to finish my thought: You can wait, or you could just go back to the north, where you frequently say you'd rather be, and not have to put up with my annoying attacks of curiosity."

<And do what? Fight with other wolverines? Get mauled by a bear? No thanks, I'll stay here and you'll come back fast,> he said.

<Aww! I'm kinda sorry I never met Faolan,> Oberon said. <I think we might have gotten along. He had a sensible attitude about bears anyway.>

"He didn't like squirrels either."

<Wow. I bet we would have been friends!>

The yawning mouth of the cave had moss hanging from the top like green fangs. I stepped past and through, bare feet on cold stone, and cast night vision to help me see in the dark.

To the living, Xibalba's cave was normally just a cave, but to the dead it extended and changed. Yucatán opened that portal for me at the appropriate point, and the temperature, already chilly compared with that of the jungle, cooled further. The floor was strewn with skeletons, calcified and broadcasting a warning in their eternal repose.

For a hundred yards or so, I simply descended into the shivery damp and worried about my footing.

And then a clicking and dry, raspy susurrus warned me that something waited ahead; the passage turned and opened wider and I came to a river of black scorpions, strangely lit from below. No bridge, no ferry, just a wide expanse teeming with poisonous dudes—an apt metaphor, now that I think of it, for my few brief attempts to understand social media.

The river extended in either direction into darkness, and the scorpions seemed content to stay within the confines of their riverbank.

Yucatán helped me bridge it, creating a thin strip of stone to walk across. It was as awesome as it sounds, and I even said it aloud in the middle, with a goofy grin on my face: "I'm walking across a river of scorpions right now."

I smelled the river of blood before I saw it—that sorta nasty metallic scent, you know, from the copper and iron in there, like dirty pennies. It burbled a bit, and parts of it were bright and oxygenated like arterial spray, and other swirls and eddies were darker as if spent from veins. It was more blood than Lady Macbeth ever had to deal with. Another stone bridge grew across it courtesy of Yucatán, and I stepped lightly over.

And then I saw the river of pus.

As with the others, something in the riverbed provided illumination, so it was glowing pus I was looking at, a pale-yellow flow with twirling fingers of darker yellow in it. The smell was of moist rot, the kind that blowflies grow fat upon, and indeed there were churning fists of squirmy maggots floating upon it, and clouds of buzzing flies hovering above it.

I felt no desire to move past it, and not only because the flies would probably pester me to the point of falling in the river. Nightmares waited on the other side: toothsome bats shrieking in the dark, and who knew what else. The Lords of Xibalba, no doubt. By all accounts they were not the hospitable type, and I didn't want them to figure out I'd popped in for a nice long gawk.

But it was magnificent: three fantastic, impossible rivers imagined by humans and maintained by their belief. Sights like that renew my sense of wonder at the world, which flags from time to time.

Feeling rejuvenated and blessed, I returned across the rivers and picked my way past bones, ascending to the surface. But just at the open portal connecting Xibalba and earth, where I could see the slightly different cast to the stone of the subterranean cave in Belize, I spied a body lying on the floor on the Xibalba side.

It was the body of Faolan. Against my explicit direction and no doubt thinking he was going to protect me, or acting out of loyalty, or maybe just hurrying after me to say he had changed his mind, he had followed me into the land of the dead. And in so doing, without any protection, he had died.

He looked like he was sleeping, and the brief flare of hope that maybe he was still alive only increased my pain when I confirmed he wasn't.

I carefully cradled Faolan's body in my arms and bore him out of Xibalba, all my joy turned to regret, and under that bound tree, where there were birds and insects and life all around me, I just cried for him a while, remembering his favorite insults and his adorable tendency to argue for about thirty seconds max before tearing into me with his claws or teeth. He'd come a long way, honestly. When I first met him he'd lasted only five seconds before resorting to violence.

He wouldn't have wanted to stay in a jungle, so I shifted us back to where we first met, on the shoreline of Lac Seul in Ontario, and I buried him there and told him I was so very sorry for my many personal faults but mostly for my stupid thrill-seeking and carelessly allowing him to come to harm.

• • •

"After that I didn't bond with any animal for more than a year at a time, until I met you, Oberon. I only taught them some basic words, never gave them Immortali-Tea, and parted ways to let them live their natural lives. I couldn't stand the thought of being responsible for their deaths."

<But you weren't responsible, Atticus! You told him not to follow and what the consequences would be, and he did it anyway.>

I shook my head. "I shouldn't have given him the choice. I put him in a position to make that mistake. He never would have been there if it weren't for me. So that's why I can't give you the choice to come with me to face Ragnarok. Frost giants and fire giants and those *draugar* we faced that one time are just the beginning, I'd imagine, of what lies ahead. It's far more dangerous than me spelunking in Belize to get my kicks. This is an entire underworld—who knows, maybe more than one—coming to the surface to start some shit. I'd never forgive myself if they hurt you."

<Okay, I understand all that, Atticus.> He inched forward on the ground and looked right at me to emphasize his point. <I do. But I want to be wherever you are. Especially if you aren't coming back.>

"I plan to come back, Oberon. And I plan to do my best to save a bunch of innocents from becoming casualties of Loki's ambition. All I'm trying to do is make sure you're not one of them. And, besides, you won't be alone. You'll be with Orlaith and Starbuck, Jack and Algy, and maybe you'll get to see your puppies be born."

Oberon put his head down on his front paws and offered up a disgruntled whimper, his eyes turned up pleadingly.

<You leave me no choice but to deploy the puppy-dog eyes, Atticus. These come with +10 charisma and I'd have to

roll a 1 on a 20-sided die to fail. You are helpless to repel this assault of cuteness and will agree to take me with you into battle as it was foretold in days of yore.>

"Ohhh, no. Not the puppy-dog eyes! Do you even remember how much sausage that look has earned you over the years?"

<Well, I'd certainly like to, but you know I'm not very good at adding up big numbers. Hey—hold the tofu! You're trying to change the subject to sausage!>

"It usually works, doesn't it?"

Oberon's expression fell and he heaved a heavy sigh. <You're not going to let me win this time, are you?>

"I'm sorry, buddy. But you know it's because of love, right?"

My hound snorted. <Well, duh, of course! It's the whole reason we're having this argument!>

"C'mere, you," I said, holding out my arms. Oberon rose to his feet and moved forward until his head rested on my shoulder and I could hug him around the neck. I leaned the side of my head against his. "You've been the best friend ever."

<Oh, I know, I mean—hey! That sounded like a goodbye. You just said you were coming back!>

"I said I *plan* on it. But I'm quite sure that others have different plans for me. So, you know, just in case my plans don't work out, I didn't want it to go unsaid. You've kept me sane and grounded since the day we met, and you renew my appreciation for the little things in life, like food and naps and smelling things."

<I think those are the *big* things in life, Atticus.>

"I know that, buddy."

<And defying squirrels. That's crucial.>

"Couldn't agree more. Come on. I bet there's time for one last big blowout feast before I have to go do my thing. What do you say we head back to Oregon and get cooking for everyone?"

<I bet you can't set up a salad bar that's a meat bar instead, with different gravies at the end rather than salad dressings, and you will serve us whatever we want on giant platters with little tongs and ladles and then give us belly rubs afterward.>

I laughed at his imagination. "You might have hit upon a fabulous new dining concept there. Okay, challenge accepted. Let's eat."

acknowledgments

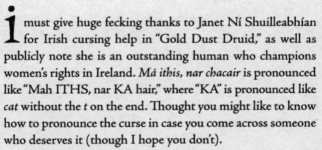

i must give huge fecking thanks to Janet Ní Shuilleabhían for Irish cursing help in "Gold Dust Druid," as well as publicly note she is an outstanding human who champions women's rights in Ireland. *Má ithis, nar chacair* is pronounced like "Mah ITHS, nar KA hair," where "KA" is pronounced like *cat* without the *t* on the end. Thought you might like to know how to pronounce the curse in case you come across someone who deserves it (though I hope you don't).

I'm deeply grateful to Simone Alexander for advising me on the customs and ethos of BDSM culture in preparing to write "Cuddle Dungeon." Consent is the underlying foundation to the whole thing, yet many narratives tend to focus on what might be kinky rather than how such kinks can be safe. Any errors or stretches of the truth in the story are of course mine and not hers. I also wish to thank author Jaye Wells for uttering the very phrase "cuddle dungeon" in a car on Camelback Road in Phoenix a few years ago. Clearly I found it inspiring. I titled the story thus with her permission.

Thanks to Adrian Tomczyk in Poznań, Poland, for his help with the Polish bits, and to those spiffy readers I met at Pyrkon who gave me a copy of Wisława Szymborska's poetry in translation.

And thank you, of course, for being a spiffy reader!

Read on for a sneak peek at

SCOURGED

We hope you have enjoyed *Besieged*.
We're pleased to present you with a sneak peek
of the next book in the thrilling Iron Druid Chronicles,
Scourged, releasing in April 2018. Enjoy!

i f ye give the world half a chance it'll turn to shite. We knew that thousands of years ago, but Siodhachan tells me there's a fancy law about it now. Kind of like if ye have a basic cracker and ye feel okay about it, but put some fecking nasty fish eggs on top and call it caviar, now it's *fancy*.

The fancy law is the Second Law of Thermodynamics, and it says if ye have an isolated system then entropy will increase and—gods damn it, let's just say things turn to shite and be done with it, all right? We can call it the First Law of Owen.

Except that ye can clean up the shite if ye have the heart and mind for it—call that the Second Law of Owen—and I'm proud of me apprentices right now for the work they're doing.

We're in Tasmania, saving some marsupial doglike creatures called devils. They got a strange transmissible face cancer back in the nineties and it was wiping them out, but now our job is to wipe out that cancer, finding every devil on the island and curing them, one by one. The apprentices have Atlantisite spheres from Tasmania in the lockets I made them, and the elemental uses that to channel energy through them, which allows them to heal the devils even though they're far from being proper Druids yet.

Tasmania doesn't think we can wait, and I'm on board with the idea. I'm thinking these new Druids will be Gaia's healers above all else, fighting centuries of humans turning everything to shite. I wonder if they have a fancy law or name for the principle that Humans Ruin Everything for Profit. Maybe that's just capitalism. Regardless, it's going to take generations of Druids to undo all this damage.

Greta is with me and so are most of the kids' parents, and we are all feeling pretty good about what we're doing to help. Watching the wee ones heal Tasmanian devils makes me think everything can be healed somehow. Perhaps there's a way to heal the breach between Fand and Brighid so we don't have to have any more war among the Fae. And maybe we can smooth things over between the Fae and Siodhachan—less likely, I figure, since he's still the fecking Iron Druid. But I'd settle for healing the breach between him and Greta.

Siodhachan is here in Tasmania too, on the same mission as we are, and at least Greta didn't try to kill him when we met up. She's got more acid for him than spent coffee grounds have for me garden soil, but maybe in a season or three she will mellow out like a teacher lapping up medicinal bourbon after school. I'm going to give it time.

We've found a den with five afflicted devils in it, one of them as near death as ye can be without stepping over the line. I take care of that one and the apprentices work on the others. We're almost finished when Greta tells me someone's coming; there is a whisper among the ferns underneath the eucalyptus. Since we're away from any settlement, I'm thinking it must be a hiker or hunter, but it's neither. It's Brighid, First Among the Fae, come to find me.

She's all armored up for some reason, red hair spilling over the pauldrons, and it sets me on edge. Where's the fight she's dressed for? I hope it's not with me.

There's a faery with her, the tall, slim sort ye see in underwear advertisements, who always look bored with being so handsome and desirable and minimally dressed. Except he is dressed, all spiffy in his silver-and-green Court livery with high thread count and a powdered wig with curls on the sides of his head. Without even turning on me true vision, I can feel he's covered in magical wards even more powerful than Brighid's.

"Well met, Eoghan Ó Cinnéide," she says, nodding once to me.

"Well met, Brighid."

The First Among the Fae gestures to her right. "This is Coriander, Herald Extraordinary of the Nine Fae Planes." I'm not sure why she puts the adjective after the noun in his title; maybe it's to make him sound as fancy as he looks.

I nod at him. "How are ye, Cory? I'm Owen."

He gives me a bow dripping with excess manners and says in a mild musical lilt, "So pleased to meet ye, sir. I prefer to be called Coriander, if ye please."

If that's his preference then I'm already suspicious we may not be the best of friends. I introduce Greta and me apprentices to Brighid and sort of wave at the parents as a group.

She takes note of the apprentices and says they'll need to undergo the *Baolach Cruatan* soon.

"But I've come here on urgent business," she says. "May we draw aside and speak in private?"

"Of course." I ask Tuya, me youngest apprentice, to finish up healing the devil I'd been working on, and tell them all I'll return soon. Brighid and I step into the undergrowth and the Herald Extraordinary floats about three steps behind.

"It has come to my attention," Brighid says, "that one of the Norse gods intends to begin his pantheon's version of apocalypse. They call it Ragnarok. Are you familiar with it?"

"Aye. Siodhachan caught me up on all that bollocks."

"It poses a serious threat to us. Should they harm a significant portion of our Irish population, we will suffer a similar reduction in our powers, and tethers to Tír na nÓg and the other planes may be severed."

"So it's back to defend the homeland, eh?"

"Yes. But we alone may not be sufficient. We need all the Fae to participate. We need all the Tuatha Dé Danann too."

"Ye mean we need Fand and Manannan Mac Lir."

"Correct. Siodhachan tells me she's in the Morrigan's Fen."

"Aye. I heard the same."

"It is my opinion, Owen, that only you can mend the rift between us."

"I was just thinking something along those lines, but I didn't think I'd have any part in it."

"She will not speak to me or Siodhachan. We are corrupted by iron, both in her eyes and the eyes of all the Fae who follow her. She cannot listen to us or she will lose face among them. But you are of the old ways and have enjoyed their hospitality in the past. You will at least gain an audience."

"Forgive me, Brighid, but I don't think so. All those Fae and the Morrigan's yewmen will cut me down before I can even flash me teeth at Fand."

"That is why I am sending Coriander with you. No one will harm him or dare touch anyone under his protection."

"*His* protection?" I glance back at the bewigged faery and wonder if he can even protect his own sack from a swift kick. Brighid catches this and smiles.

"By all means, Eoghan, feel free to test his defenses if it will ease your doubts."

"What? Ye mean punch him in the nose or something?"

"Whatever you wish." Brighid stops walking and gestures at the herald. "Do go ahead."

"Can I use me knuckles?" I asks her, and she hesitates.

"I would not recommend it. Start with your bare fists or feet."

I squint at the fancy herald. "Are ye all right with this, lad?"

"Of course, good sir. I hope you will not be injured too badly."

Their unworried confidence shakes me own, and I go ahead and check out the herald in the magical spectrum. He shimmers with layers of protective wards, among them a kinetic one of a strength and weave I've never seen before.

"Shrivel me cock, lad, who gave ye such wards?"

"Most of the Tuatha Dé Danann have contributed in one way or another. I represent a group effort. I cannot be harmed nor deliver harm except redirect that aimed at me; I am therefore allowed everywhere in the Nine Planes, since I cannot be used for treacherous purposes."

"I see. And should the yewmen take it into their wee woody noggins that I'm to be skewered sideways, ye can prevent them from doing that?"

"So long as I remain between you."

"Ah, so beware me flanks, then?"

"Precisely."

I turn back to Brighid. "All right, if I go, how do ye suggest I get her to cooperate?"

"You may relay an offer I think she will find attractive, if she be not mad." And once she gives me the details, I asks when I must go.

"Now, Eoghan. I will bind this eucalyptus to Tír na nÓg while you make your farewells."

"But the devils—"

"Will still exist should we prevail. Nothing will remain if we fail."

"Ah. Thank ye for the perspective. And have ye spoken to Siodhachan about this? He's on the island somewhere."

"No longer. He heard from the Morrigan and is pursuing different objectives. We used a tree he bound to shift in and had to travel here at speed over land. You may rest assured that Granuaile will be involved as well."

"Right, then. I'll be back soon. Excuse me."

Greta waits for me, arms crossed and her neck taut with stress as she searches me face. "Damn it," she says. "You're leaving us here, aren't you? I can tell already."

"I have to, love, though I'd rather not."

"You don't have a choice?"

"Not if I want to keep me honor intact."

She growls at me, "To hell with honor! That's the kind of thinking that gets people killed. Gunnar's dead because of his sense of honor, and Hal's dead because of someone else's sense of honor. I don't want you dying for the same reason. I'd rather have *you* intact than your honor."

"Not sure if I can stay physically intact if I don't also protect me honor in this case. I have to go see Fand and convince her to help us fight off Loki. Ragnarok's coming, love. It's not the sort of thing ye sit back and watch and hope someone else takes care of it all."

She snorts in disbelief, then stops breathing. "You're serious? You're talking about the end of the world?"

"Let's hope it won't be, but yes. It's what Loki wants."

"Where are you going?"

"To the Morrigan's Fen. After that, I'm not sure. But I'll come back here to finish this job when I can. Ye can either stay here and watch over the kids—they have the knack for it now—or ye can pack up and fly back to the States. I surely don't know which is safer."

"Okay. We'll decide later."

I bid farewell to the apprentices and their parents, and tell them to keep up their fine work, and spend a little bit of time with each apprentice.

Thandi worries she'll forget everything when I'm gone because she finds something to worry about in every situation. Her father, Sonkwe, is so patient and kind with her that I think this must be a recent behavior caused by her mother leaving them. She will see her strength soon enough.

Ozcar will be fine so long as his parents are all right. He checks on them to see how they're handling my leaving, and since they seem unconcerned, he simply tells me to be safe and they will do the same.

Tuya asks me if she's going to get to learn any more about the plants while I'm gone. Healing devils is fine, but she's really fascinated by flowers and trees and growing things.

"O' course," I says to her. "Remember that ye can talk to Tasmania anytime ye wish through your sphere, there." I point to the locket around her neck. "Ask the elemental about its favorite plants and I'm sure you'll learn all ye ever wanted to know. Did ye know that there are plants here that eat bugs?"

"Really?"

"Sundews for sure, perhaps many more. Ask about them."

"I will!"

Mehdi, a solemn boy from Morocco, assures me that he and his father will pray for my safe return. "We will work hard while you're away," he adds.

Amita hears this and nods. "We will heal as many devils as we can." She's already the sort of person who works tirelessly at a goal once she's been given one. She's going to be a powerful champion of Gaia when she grows up.

Luiz, me animal lover, doesn't care at all that I'm leaving. "What? Oh. Bye," he says, then he whips his head around. "Wait. We don't have to stop healing devils while you're gone, do we?"

"No, lad. Ye can keep at it."

"Good. I love this." He turns his attention back to the devil he's healing, and I'm already forgotten.

Me farewells to the apprentices finished, Greta grabs me by the face, both hands in me beard, and leans her forehead against mine. "You come back to me, Teddy Bear."

"Ye can be sure that's the plan, love." I really don't want to leave her, or any of them. This bollocks sounds like the kind of fool thing Siodhachan keeps getting involved in. Maybe this is what it's going to be like, now, being one of the few Druids left instead of one of the many: Everything's an emergency. I give Greta the sort of kiss that says I want to pick up where we left off and promise a good run through the forest when I'm back.

Brighid is just finishing up when I rejoin them. "All right, Andy," I says to the herald. "Let's go."

"It's Coriander, sir."

I grin at him. "A four-syllable name is impractical in battle, lad, and in most poetry too, if ye care about what the bards say. I'll give ye only two syllables until ye actually save me bones from the Fae. You can pick. Cory, Ian, Andy, Gobshite, I don't care. What'll it be?"

"Coriander, sir." He shoots a pleading glance at Brighid but she looks amused, and I laugh at him.

"How about Fuckstick? Aye, that'll do." He doesn't have a ward against me calling him the wrong name. I know it makes me a fecking arsehole, but he's a far sight more smug than I can stand. And besides, I have to carve off what wee slices of amusement I can from this situation. I'm pretty sure the First Law of Owen is about to enforce itself.

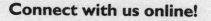